The Last Time We Were Us

The Last Time We Were Us

LEAH KONEN

KATHERINE TEGEN BOOKS
An Imprint of HarperCollins Publishers

Katherine Tegen Books is an imprint of HarperCollins Publishers.

The Last Time We Were Us
Copyright © 2016 by Leah Konen
All rights reserved. Printed in the United States of America.
No part of this book may be used or reproduced in any manner
whatsoever without written permission except in the case of brief quotations
embodied in critical articles and reviews. For information address
HarperCollins Children's Books, a division of HarperCollins Publishers,
195 Broadway, New York, NY 10007.
www.epicreads.com

Library of Congress Control Number: 2015952418
ISBN 978-0-06-240247-9

Typography by Carla Weise
16 17 18 19 20 PC/RRDH 10 9 8 7 6 5 4 3 2 1
❖
First Edition

For my mom,
who always believed in me
and who introduced me to North Carolina

The Last Time We Were Us

Chapter 1

"LIZZIE?"

The name startles me, as I stand in front of the cooler at the Gas Xpress in West Bonneville, where the beer is cheaper and they don't card half as much as other convenience stores, fiddling through my bag for my fake ID.

No one's supposed to know me here. And anyone who does knows I haven't gone by Lizzie for three years now.

Anyone except for him.

I turn around quickly, and there's Jason behind the counter, my fears coming to instant fruition. When I walked in, it was a pimply college kid who didn't look like he'd give me a problem, but now that boy is gone, replaced so suddenly by the last person I ever expected to see. Not here. Not now.

I walk up to the counter nervously. He looks as startled as I am.

"What are you doing here?" I ask.

"I just started my shift."

"I mean, but what are you doing *here*?"

I haven't seen him in almost two years. Besides in the Bonneville paper, of course. And on the special that brought in the news guys from Raleigh, Jason and other delinquents' faces splashed across the evening news (*Westboro County cleans up juvenile hall, sets new example for North Carolina's youth detention centers*).

"I was released on Monday." His voice is deeper, and even though he's my age he could probably pass for twenty-three, his face covered in stubble, his dark hair greasy and thick but neatly cut.

"I thought it wasn't for another six months," I stammer. It was meant to be well into senior year. It's not that I expected his return to cause all that much drama on my end, given that my years as Jason Sullivan's BFF are long gone, but it seems like I should have been given some kind of warning, been allowed to prepare.

"Parole," he says.

"Oh. Well, congrats." I immediately want to whack myself on the head for being so awkward.

He rests his palms on the counter and looks at me with the brown eyes I've known for as long as I've understood the very concept of eyes, and for a fleeting moment, I see us as kids, my finger a toy gun, me playing the bad guy for the afternoon, him ducking for cover behind the great big magnolia tree that split our backyards in two. The nostalgia hits before I can stop it.

I look behind me to see if anyone else is waiting, for the presence of another human to speed this encounter along, but there's no one. Just us.

"So you're working here now?"

"I'm certainly not volunteering."

He must see the discomfort on my face, because he smiles, almost as if he's trying to remind me that we were friends once and that we can joke with each other. Can we?

"I just meant it's kind of far. I didn't expect to see you here."

He fiddles with an errant receipt. "It's only about ten minutes from my dad's condo. And it's part of the whole rehab program. This is one of the few places that happily take excons. My parole officer helped set it up." He grins like that should be funny, but it's not.

I bend my fake ID between my fingers, no clue what to say.

Jason squirms behind the register, his eyes flitting to the case of Natty Light in my hand. "Are you trying to get that?" he asks.

"Oh," I say. "Yeah." I set the unconvincing piece of plastic that says I'm twenty-two on the counter, but Jason hesitates. "I mean, can I?"

Jason's eyes dart around the store, but even though it's still empty, he shakes his head. "I can't really do anything illegal right now."

And just like that, our whole history has culminated in a standoff over a fake ID. "Of course." I grab the plastic as quickly as I can.

"I should really take that, too, but since we're friends, I guess it's okay," he says.

Friends, I think. Present tense and everything. Right. I put it back in my bag.

"Er, thanks then." I grab the beer. "I'll just put this back."

"Leave it." He reaches across the counter, and I hand him the case.

"Well, bye," I say.

"Later," he says.

But as the bell dings and the door swooshes shut behind me, I wonder if there ever will be a later.

INNIS IS WAITING in the car.

He sees my empty hands and his eyebrows scrunch up. "What, did they give you a hard time?" he asks.

I pull the door shut with a slight slam, like I can seal us off from Jason.

"No." I wonder if I should tell him more. "But the cashiers switched shifts, and the new one didn't look like a good idea. We have to go somewhere else."

"Sure. No biggie." He pushes the start button and pulls onto the road, the car purring like only a BMW can as he moves from first to second gear. "They didn't take your fake, did they?"

I shake my head.

We find another gas station, a mile or so down the road. I walk in, and all goes off smoothly. When I get back to the car, beer in hand, Innis smiles, rubs his hand over my knee, gives it a light squeeze that gets my heart beating faster. "Thank you very much, Good Lady of the Fake ID."

He shoots me a teen-model smile, and I focus on how good things are going with Innis. Not whether Jason knows who I came with, or what he thinks of my fake, or the fact that I'm not goodie-goodie Lizzie Grant anymore.

It doesn't work. I wait until we're back on our side of town, until the houses are bigger and older, flanked with columns, wedding-cake white. That's when I spill it. "Jason was in the Gas Xpress."

"What?"

"Jason Sullivan," I say. "That's why I didn't get the beer."

"I know who you meant," Innis says. I can tell he's trying to control his temper but it's not working—his knuckles go white against the steering wheel, and there's a sharp intake of breath—Innis can go from zero to sixty quicker than his car.

Then his voice softens a little: "Why didn't you tell me?"

I start to pick at the skin around my fingernails. "I *am* telling you."

"I mean back there."

"What would you have done?" I ask.

"I don't know." His face reddens.

"That's why. I didn't want you to start something."

He slams his palm against the wheel. "I knew he got out

on Monday, but I was sure it'd be at least a few months before he showed his miserable face."

I stop picking, clasp my hands in my lap. "How did you know? I didn't hear anything about it."

Innis waves my question off with a flick of his wrist. "My dad knows the DA or one of those guys. He was fuming about it last week. Apparently Jason has been nothing but a model prisoner. My dad tried, but there was nothing he could do to stop it." He turns to me. "If you ask me, it's just the broke-ass government letting another monster out. Did he say anything to you?"

I ignore his question. "Why didn't you tell me?"

Innis turns to face me. "You're a good thing, Liz. I don't like mixing good and bad things together. Plus, why would you care? He's my problem, not yours."

I pull out my phone and pretend to be entranced. There are a lot of reasons I would care—I did care—but they're hard to explain to Innis. They're even hard to explain to myself.

His eyes are back on the road. "So what did he say?"

"Nothing. He just made it clear that I should go somewhere else. He could have taken my ID, but he didn't."

Innis laughs, loud but hardly jovial. "What a pal."

We get to my house, and he pulls into the driveway, right behind Lyla's beat-up Honda, the one she's driven since high school.

I catch his gaze before I get out of the car. "Whatever you're thinking about, it's not worth it."

"He shouldn't be here," Innis says. "He really shouldn't be here."

"He's not here." I rub his shoulder to calm him down. "He's living in a condo somewhere and working at a gas station that doesn't card. There are plenty of others. We'll just take it off our list."

Innis stares straight ahead, his hands squeezing the wheel again.

"Promise me you won't do anything stupid," I say.

Dad comes out of the garage then, pruning shears in hand, and Innis plasters on a smile, gives him a polite wave.

"I promise," he says, finally looking over at me. "But only if you agree not to see him."

It's a boyfriend-y thing to say, I know MacKenzie would agree, the kind of words that make me think I could be more than what I am now: his go-to beer buyer, who he's made out with exactly five times. The words are nice.

"Believe me. I honestly have no reason to see him." I step out of the car.

"All right. Then I'll leave him alone."

"Good." And then in a low voice, so Dad won't hear: "See you tonight."

His smile comes back then and my heart takes a little leap as he waves at my dad again and pulls away.

I walk up the driveway, glance quickly at the "For Sale" sign in the next yard—Jason's old yard—the one that to this day sends Mom into a tizzy. "Having a house sit so long on the market drives down the property values for *all of us*," she always says. "It ruins the look of the whole neighborhood!" As secretary of the Alexandria Fields Homeowners' Association, she's even sent letters to Jason's dad, demanding he do something. The sign swings back and forth.

Lucy meets me as soon as I get in with her signature greeting, three soft licks to my leg. I scoop her up and nuzzle her close, her fluffy head resting snugly on my shoulder like a baby's. I give her a scratch. "Did you miss me?"

Her long fur is white and gray like cotton, and her huge brown eyes and floppy ears seem to say yes. I plop her down, and she scuttles into the kitchen, the *tap tap tap* of her paws sounding more like home than anything in the world.

Mom and Lyla are at the kitchen table, stacks of *Southern Bride* between them. They're practically doubles, old and young, Perfect Thing 1 and Perfect Thing 2.

"Liz," Lyla says, looking up from the magazines. "Just the person I wanted to see. I need to talk to you about the bridesmaid dresses."

"Hey, sweetie." Mom looks up at me, a wide smile showing off her straight whitened teeth. "How was your little excursion?"

"Excursion?" Lyla temporarily forgets about the dresses.

"She went out with Innis *Taylor*," Mom says. "What's that, the second date this week?"

"Don't order the engagement announcements just yet," I say. "A trip to Crown Commons doesn't exactly count as a date."

"Crown Commons?" Mom shakes her head, disgusted, like she's found a hair in her glass of scuppernong. "Why would you go there? You never want to be that far down on Irving Road."

"We went to the Target," I lie, sliding onto the chair next to Lyla's. "And for the millionth time, it's not the 'bad part of town.' There're like eight new condo complexes and the Target is brand-new." I take a sip of Lyla's coffee without asking. She makes it extra sweet, just like I like.

"Let's forget about the fact that Liz is hanging out in the hood," Lyla says, even though she knows as well as I do that it's not. "What's this about seeing Innis multiple times a week?"

"Nothing," I say. "Can you guys not get totally ahead of yourselves?"

My mother is already horrified that I'm *seventeen years old* and have never had a boyfriend. Apparently, Carolina girls are not only the best in the world, but they're supposed to have the boyfriend thing down pat. Lyla had been dating Skip for two years by the time she was my age.

"Okay, okay." Mom throws up her hands. "Crucify me for being curious about my *baby's* life."

Lyla's eyes narrow at me like she's got a question on the tip of her tongue, but her smile comes back, and she seems to let it go for now. She tugs on the ends of my hair. "When are you going to grow it long again?"

Mom and Lyla hate my "short" hair almost as much as the fact that I don't go by *Lizzie* anymore.

"It's past my shoulders, geez," I say. "When are you going to shut up about it?"

"Girls," Mom says. "Please."

I sip the last of Lyla's coffee to spite her.

"So anyway." Lyla puts her serious voice on. "I need your opinion on the bridesmaid dresses. Sea foam or baby blue?"

"Neither?" I ask. "You know I hate pale colors."

Lyla holds up two fabric swatches. "Come on. Indulge me."

"How about electric orange with hints of chartreuse?"

"You are going to wear a sea-foam or baby-blue dress." She puts her swatches down and crosses her arms. "I'm giving you, and only you, the option to weigh in, Miss Maid of Honor. Don't waste it."

I let out a sigh. "Blue, then. And please, no ruffles."

Lyla rubs her hands together like she's concocting an evil plot. "I want tiers of them, and sparkles, and tulle, and a big satin bow that goes right on your ass."

"Lyla," Mom scolds. "Your words."

We both laugh, but Mom shakes her head, flipping a page in her magazine. "I should never have let you quit cotillion."

Quit. Mom made the mistake of putting me in Lyla's chapter when I was eleven. After I tossed a dessert fork holding a maraschino cherry at my sister, the rogue fruit splattering all over another girl's formal dress, we were both very politely asked never to return.

"Oh," Lyla says, putting her planner voice on again.

"Before I forget. Can you email me Veronica's address? I know it's late, but I thought it would be nice to send her a proper invitation."

"Veronica?" I ask.

"Yes," Lyla says. "I figured you'd want her at the wedding. She's your best friend."

Mom raises her eyebrows at my sister—I haven't told her the whole Veronica saga, but, like a mom, she's probably figured most of it out—but Lyla doesn't catch on.

"I don't know if she'd want to come," I say.

Lyla, in true big sister form, misinterprets me. "I was trying to be nice," she says. "I thought you'd want someone at the wedding."

I run my finger along the tabs of the huge binder, avoiding Lyla's eyes. "I've just been hanging out more with MacKenzie, I guess."

Lyla knows as well as I do that that's high school code for *we aren't really friends anymore.*

"What happened?" she asks. "I liked Veronica."

Mom clears her throat. "Why don't you just give Liz a plus one and let her decide? We can't invite the whole rising senior class."

Lyla looks from Mom to me, but seems satisfied. "All right." She closes the binder, and I whip my finger away just in time. "Do what you want."

Mom stands up. "That's settled then. You girls want some potato salad or something?"

"None for me," Lyla says. "August sixth is less than two

months away. Bridal potbellies are not the answer."

I roll my eyes because Lyla couldn't gain weight if she tried. "I'm okay."

"Well, if you're not hungry, I'm going to go upstairs and get ready. The Homeowners' meeting is at Suzanne's in half an hour." She looks at Lyla. "Will you be here later?"

She shakes her head, stuffs the binder into her bag. "I'm meeting Benny's parents for dinner."

Mom nods on her way out. "Just make sure you decide on the bridesmaid dresses by tomorrow. Mrs. Barton needs to know."

"Righto." Lyla looks at me. "Extra bows."

Mom is barely up the stairs before Lyla starts in. "So what's this about Innis? You two are dating?"

"I don't know. . . . It's hard to tell."

"What do you mean?" she asks, totally oblivious.

"I mean I'm not you, Lyla. Guys don't ask me to be their girlfriend on day one."

She giggles. "Benny was just eager, is all."

"Everyone's eager with you," I say.

She shrugs. "Well, are you enjoying Crawford Hall at least? That house is crazy."

"I've only ever been in the basement."

"What do you mean?" Lyla asks, scrunching up her nose. "You go straight to the basement?"

Of course Lyla would have had free rein of the main house. She's Lyla. "Yeah," I say. "I told you, I'm not his girlfriend. I haven't properly met his parents or anything."

"Still seems weird," she says, but she sees I'm hurt and tries to lighten the mood. "Well, the house is out of this world. Seriously."

"If I ever make it in, I'll let you know what I think."

"You will," she says. "I'm sure Innis is just different about things like that, that's all."

I lean forward, rest my elbows on the table. "So would it bother you? If we were actually dating?"

Lyla pretends to be fascinated by her hands. When she finally looks up, her lips are pressed together, determined. "He's a good guy," she says. "From a good family. If he's the one you like, then, no, it wouldn't bother me at all."

Guilt hits me first, because she's no good at hiding the pain on her face, but then thankfulness, that in spite of everything, she supports me in this, even though I don't know what "this" is yet.

"Are you going to bring him to the wedding?" She forces a smile.

I am nowhere near asking Innis to any kind of official function, much less my sister's wedding. "Wouldn't that be a little weird?"

She shakes her head quickly. "It's been two years," she says. "All that stuff with Skip is behind me."

For a split second, I wonder if I could tell her about Jason, if it really is behind her.

But I think about Lyla at seventeen, about those first months after that horrible night, and I decide that telling her is not for the best.

Chapter 2

MacKenzie and I get to Innis's just after nine.

Crawford Hall stands in front of us, gorgeous in the evening dusk, a rich, buttercream yellow that only gets more beautiful with age. Shutters flank every window—deep hunter green—and not the kind that are tacked on for show, like the ones on my house. These ones have purpose, clapping together when you want to shut out the world.

We park on the street, just off to the side, because we still aren't sure what we're supposed to do with the circular driveway that leads to the huge garage behind the house.

Kenzie reapplies her lip gloss before hopping out of the car and striking a ridiculous model pose just for me—leave it to the girl to always make me laugh.

We walk past a screened-in wraparound porch full of white wicker and oak rockers. The screens are speckled with thirsty mosquitoes and horseflies. It's the right time of night for lightning bugs; one buzzes by me, and out of habit, I cup my hands together, catch it on the first try.

"You're strangely good at that," Kenzie says.

"I just have a lot of practice. Don't tell me they don't have lightning bugs in Ohio, either." Kenzie moved here from "up North," as Mom calls it, last summer.

"We do," Kenzie says. "And we call them fireflies like normal people."

I peek at the yellow-orange light that fills the cave of my palms. Jason and I used to spend hours filling jelly jars, seeing whose could shine brightest. I let it go, and in seconds, its light goes out.

"So what's so great about the inside of the house anyway?" Kenzie asks. "Why is your sister freaking out about us only going to the basement?"

I put on my best tour guide voice: "Lorne Crawford—that's Innis's great-grandfather a bunch of times over—was an inventive businessman who was able to turn his thriving tobacco business into a successful investment firm after the Civil War. Crawford Hall has been in the family since seventeen-hundred something-or-other."

She looks at me. "What are you, a stalker? Did you study up on his house?"

I laugh. "It's on a plaque in the library, next to something they donated. Although the more informal version is—'The

Crawfords used to grow tobacco. Now they grow money.'"

Kenzie laughs, too. "Toto, I've got a feeling we aren't in Ohio anymore."

We walk a little farther, and the sweeping daylight basement comes into view.

"Did they have slaves and everything?" Kenzie asks, as if the thought's only just dawned on her.

"Probably," I say, and it leaves a bad, bitter taste in the back of my mouth, like the whole place is tainted. Mom says we shouldn't judge the dead, different time and all that, but I can't help but be glad that *my* great-great-great-whatever-grandfather was in Ireland, and not lording over a Southern tobacco plantation, way back when.

"God," Kenzie says. "That's terrible."

"It is," I say.

When we get to the basement, the subject drops, and the mood changes. Through the windows, I see the glow of electric violence on the flat-screen: Innis's latest steal-cars-and-chase-girls video game.

He loads the characters on-screen with bullets and doesn't look up as we let ourselves in.

"Ladies." Payton Daughtry flashes a hundred-dollar grin and raises his beer in a mock toast. His buddy, Alex McGuiness, follows up with a loud, thick burp.

The screen villains are dead now, and Innis pulls his gaze from the TV. He looks me up and down, smiles wide. He doesn't do gushy compliments—at least not in front of other people—but I can tell he thinks I look pretty.

"We can thank Miss Grant for the provisions," he says.

Payton hands us each a beer, and I follow MacKenzie to a couch along the wall. Innis gives my freshly shaved legs another quick look before he goes back to his game.

So far, we're the only girls here. Since the beginning of summer, our bad fake IDs, courtesy of Kenzie's shady second cousin in Ohio, have been our ticket to Innis's weekly hangouts, but we're usually surrounded by at least a few other girls: Alexis Clairemont, Innis's freshman-year girlfriend who still hangs around. Marisa Wong, Alex's on-again, off-again, who loves Goldschläger—"it's like drinking jewelry!"—Jessica Jackson and Nicole Tully, two cheerleaders who practice together, tan together, and even hooked up with Blake Edgeworth together last summer.

Kenzie and I are usually the final stragglers, and the last three times I was here, Innis and I ended the night by making out on the couch while Payton and MacKenzie slipped away to Payton's car or the pool or wherever. Still, it's annoying to have all the other girls around, a little reminder that the boys would be just fine without us.

"You think anyone else is coming?" I whisper.

Kenzie leans in. "Fingers crossed, no."

"Seriously?"

"I told Payton we were tired of providing beer for basically every other girl at East Bonneville. From the looks of it, he got the hint."

If MacKenzie could apply half her acumen for breaking into the popular crowd and "getting us hot boyfriends" to school, she'd be one of those freak geniuses who graduate Harvard at sixteen. To her, there's no love or luck. Just challenges to be solved.

I take a sip of beer and try not to get my hopes up, not too much, at least. If boys are challenges, Innis is Mount Freaking Everest. He's not just high school royalty, he's town royalty. And when he grows up, he'll still be royalty. Just the banker-doctor-lawyer kind. He's got an almost guaranteed admittance to Duke, where both of his parents are big donors. He'll be popular for the rest of his life. Maybe it's the money or the breeding or that he lives in the town's most famous house. Or maybe it's the fact that, in everyone's eyes, he's the ultimate brother. No one will ever forget what happened to Skip, because bad things don't happen to the Crawfords and the Taylors of this world without there being a villain and a hero.

Innis is the hero.

He looks like one, too. His hair is dark and curly, a mop of ringlets set off with cool, gray eyes. His cheeks have a hint of red, and his jaw is strong. He wears a rotation of bright polos and too-tight khakis, like he just stepped out of a preppy photo shoot. And when he's not trying to be a badass, yelling at a guy on the lacrosse team or bragging about a video-game score, when it's just the two of us and he looks at me like I'm his, I have to remind myself to breathe.

"When do I get to play?" MacKenzie asks Payton with a well-designed pout. He gives her a half look, his eyes still glued to the screen. She'll get his attention eventually, though.

Always does. I wish I could convince her that there are better goals than Payton Daughtry, who has the makings of a beer belly at just seventeen and is quite likely to outlive his IQ, but she wants him, and what MacKenzie wants, MacKenzie gets. It only took her five short months at East Bonneville before she moved Veronica and me to a centrally located cafeteria table, buddied up to the popular girls, joined the softball team, and started getting invites to parties.

"Yeah, how about letting someone else have a turn?"

The voice is dark and coarse, like the growl of a dog left in the crate too long.

Skip Taylor leans against the wall behind us, his face partially lit by the flat-screen and low lights. His eyes dart to mine, a mix of recognition and surprise. He's seen me here before, but never when there aren't other girls around, too. I look down at my hands, imagining all the things he could be thinking—about Lyla, the wedding, how she and I have the same nose, how he and I used to be friends kind of, in that weird way you're friendly with your older sister's boyfriend. When I get the nerve to glance up, he's staring at his brother, waiting for an answer.

"I'm almost done," Innis says, before turning back to the screen.

Skip crosses his arms but doesn't move otherwise. From this angle, his nose is strong and sharp, his hair thick and barely waved, his eyes look-at-me blue. Physically speaking, Skip is the ultimate illusion, a cold glass of milk with your cookies before you know it's gone sour. I can't *not* stare at him, wait for him to turn his head, remind me what Jason did.

On the screen, Innis shoots a passerby and hops into a new car. Payton turns the volume up, and a hip-hop song blares.

MacKenzie scoots towards me, her voice a whisper. "Did you hear about Jason?"

I flinch at his name, like it's a bad word in church, something not to be spoken, especially not here. "Hear about him?"

"He's out, like hanging around town."

"How do *you* know?"

"Payton texted me. Said he heard from Innis."

I search her face to see if she knows the whole story, but some of it must have gotten lost in translation. "Can we talk about this later?"

"Whoa," she says, reading me all too well. "You've already seen him."

"For a second," I say quickly.

"Oh my God. Where?"

"When we were buying beer." I lower my voice even further. "For literally three minutes. It's not a big deal."

She stares at me like I've just said two and two is three. "How is it not a big deal? Why didn't you tell me?"

I shrug. "Why are you so worried? You didn't even know him."

"I know enough." She scoffs. "In my book, brutally attacking another person is enough to make me want to steer clear."

She leans in closerand speaks so quietly I have to read her lips. "What if he tries to see you again?"

"Geez, Kenzie, you are so paranoid. He didn't try to see me in the first place, and we weren't even friends before he left." Kenzie already knows that it wasn't Skip or juvie that ended my friendship with Jason. It was so many other things. His instant rise to popularity. My middle-school shyness. The first time he pretended not to know me, right at the end of eighth grade.

"But you were like besties forever before that."

She's right. Mom even used to say we were friends as babies. That she'd invite Mrs. Sullivan for coffee, and Jason and I would rock, side by side, in our carriers. I remember us sitting in front of the TV, Wyle E. Coyote's anvils zipping across the screen, electric orange Cheetos flecks on our fingers, awash in the kind of joy only kids seem to have access to. As soon as the memory comes, I push it back down where it belongs. Bury it deep.

"That was a long time ago," I say.

"Thank God for that." Kenzie takes a sip of beer. "Anyway, you promise you won't do anything stupid? Your capacity for forgiveness is about ten levels too high." She's talking about Veronica, about what she refers to as the "Cafeteria Incident," but I don't pursue it. Not now.

"I promise."

There's a rush of expletives from Innis, then he stomps his foot and throws the controller down. The screen goes black, and we're back at the beginning of the game. Skip comes forward, taking the back way around the couch so the right side of his face is the only one we see, but when he grabs the controller and sits down, there's no hiding it.

I used to think Skip might one day be my brother-in-law. I was young, caught up in how in love Lyla was, sure it was going to work out for them.

But that was the *before* Skip. A different Skip than I know now.

I've seen his face plenty of times since it happened, but it still manages to shock me. His lips are red and puffed. His cheek is too smooth in parts, then wrinkly and raised, almost bubbling along the edges, dark ridges etched across. The side of his chin is achingly white, and his nostril is wide. But it's his eye that is the worst, drooping and sad, the lids mottled like candle wax.

He drives, swerves, speeds up, does everything right. He's clearly better than any of the other boys. Maybe it's because his fake-o job with his dad leaves him plenty of free time. Maybe it's because the games don't know what he looks like.

MacKenzie shakes her head as I take a big gulp of beer.

"I still can't believe Jason had the nerve to come back."

IT'S DARK IN the basement, the glow of the video-game home screen our only light. I can hear MacKenzie and Payton messing around in the pool, shrieks and splashes, and then the quiet as they inevitably come together.

Innis and I have been making out awhile, when he pulls

back midkiss, traces a finger along my jawline. "You're special, you know?"

My heartbeat quickens, but I try to keep my cool. "Why do you say that?"

He runs a hand through my hair. "You're not like other girls."

Does he know this line is straight out of every high school movie ever? Either way, it's too sweet for me to call him on it.

He looks at me, like I really am different. "You don't care about the stupid stuff like makeup and shopping and all that."

"What, are you saying I don't look pulled together?"

He shakes his head. "You know that's not what I meant."

He presses his lips against mine, his tongue darting inside. His hands wander, over my chest, down the curve of my waist, around the back, underneath my bra, onto my bare skin. I feel the chills all the way at the tips of my fingers. I'm one of those coloring book mazes, and he's got the crayon, and he's drawing his way to the prize at the end.

Part of me wants to go there. As he kisses me harder, I imagine him pulling off my shirt, unhooking the button of my jean skirt, us doing more than we have before.

And then I think about what Mom used to say—"Why buy the cow when you can get the milk for free?"—and I worry that, as awful as it is for her to compare girls to cows, our lady bits to dairy milk, is she a little right? What if I'm just something new for him? What if he gets tired of me after this? I always imagined all the sexy times happening *after* I had a boyfriend, not before. I pull back.

"Maybe we should go find Payton and MacKenzie," I say.

He tries to disguise a groan but then leans back in for a light kiss. "They definitely don't want to be found," he says deeply, under his breath. "Neither do we."

He starts kissing me again, his hands pressed into the small of my back, but I push him again, taking a deep gasp of air as our lips part.

"I don't think I want to do anything more tonight," I say.

He groans, louder this time, but he scoots over, gives me space.

I sit up straight, pull down the edges of my skirt, and try to catch my breath.

"What is it?" he asks, his voice kind. "What's wrong?"

"Nothing's wrong," I say.

"Then why?"

"I'm just not *ready*." I hate how much I sound like a PSA.

I wonder, briefly, if he's angry, but then he just shrugs. "All right."

"We're good?" I adjust my top awkwardly.

He nods. "Course we're good."

Innis never asked me to be his girlfriend, and I never asked to be it, but now I wonder how long this whatever-it-is will go on if we don't go any further.

But he leans in again, and his voice is soft and smooth, like it is when he wants to please. "We can wait as long as you want."

And I smile, feel myself blushing, though he won't be able to see it in the dark.

Innis could have anyone.

But lately, it seems like that anyone is me.

Chapter 3

MacKenzie drives us home so we can get back in time for curfew, giving me an extremely detailed play-by-play of her and Payton's night.

"How'd it go with Innis?" she finally asks, when I know a bit more about both of her and Payton's anatomies than I'd like to.

"Good," I say. "Really good."

"*Really* good? Don't tell me you did it on the couch and are only now getting around to telling me."

"Actually, we barely did anything. Just kissed."

"And that's *good* news?" she asks.

"You know, sometimes, I think you have a hard time understanding that I'm not you."

"What can I say?" MacKenzie turns onto our street. "You're my first repressed Southerner friend."

"Ha *ha*," I say as she pulls up to my house.

"Anyway, sleep well. Dream of all the things you didn't do with Innis."

"You're such a jerk." I laugh. "Talk tomorrow."

I hear the shuffle of footsteps above as I close the front door behind me, then the creak of the stairs.

Mom patters down, a smile on her sleepy face. "I wasn't sure if you were going to make it."

"With minutes to spare," I say.

She gives me a hug and a kiss on the cheek. "Good night, dear."

"Good night."

But when I'm in bed and the house is silent, when the sounds of my mother doing her cold cream and serums in the bathroom die off, when the cicadas themselves decide it's time to turn in, when I've slogged through two whole chapters of *Heart of Darkness*, my AP English summer reading, I still can't sleep.

I want to think about Innis, to indulge in his sweet words, but when I close my eyes, all I see is Jason, Jason and his whole family, knock-knock-knocking, just like they used to do when they lived next door.

I flip back the sheets, climb out of bed, and kneel down at the foot of it. I push aside the clothes that didn't make it to the hamper, and navigate the stacks of old art projects and overdue library books and an unused yoga mat until my fingers hit the smooth edge of a shoebox. I pull it out with two hands.

It's my very own Pandora's box. Mom doesn't know about it, just like she doesn't know that I used to go over to Jason's empty house sometimes, something I've promised myself I won't do anymore. If she did, she'd probably burn the contents and seriously reconsider her stance against therapy.

The photos are on the top, which is good because I don't think I can stand to see the news clippings right now. I flip through five or so before I find the one I was thinking of. It's me and Jason and his parents, his gorgeous mom and his always-pulled-together dad on either side of us. It was Jason's eighth birthday, and the two of us have chocolate cake on our faces. Our arms are wrapped around each other's shoulders, and it's so dang cute it makes me angry. My hair is white blond, his long and shaggy, and the birthday hats sit crookedly on our heads.

I stare at the photo, wondering what his condo looks like, how much his dad has aged; if he wishes his mom were closer, more of a mom. She left only a couple weeks after that birthday, went back to Connecticut without warning. Jason used to visit her twice a year. I wonder if she visited him at all when he was in juvie.

I return the photo, shut the box, and push it all under the bed. No matter what Jason went through, no matter how much her leaving messed him up, it doesn't excuse what happened.

Nothing does.

~

I DON'T KNOW when I finally managed to fall asleep, but I wake up feeling groggy. I smell coffee brewing, so I stumble downstairs and into the kitchen, where Mom is stirring a pot of grits, her Sunday morning ritual. She looks up and smiles. "Hey there, sleepyhead."

I rub at my eyes. "I couldn't sleep. What time is it?"

"Almost eleven." She wipes her hands on an old dishtowel. "Sit. I'll pour you a cup of coffee."

I follow her orders and try to get my bearings, as she delivers first a piping hot cup and then a plate of grits and eggs. Then she sits down next to me, opening a magazine.

I can't remember what I dreamed about, but flashes of Jason and Mr. and Mrs. Sullivan are there, hanging around in the back of my mind as if I invited them over for breakfast. I finish my plate and take it up to the sink, but I can't shake it, this burning desire to see him, one more time. I hesitate, Innis filling my mind, the way he wavered from typical boy to sweet boy *(friend?)*—how mad he would be if he knew I was even thinking of going back there. MacKenzie, too.

But it's not about Innis or Kenzie or Mom or even Lyla.

Jason was my friend once. Beyond everything else, he was my friend.

So many years of history, and we can't come down to a fake ID and a case of Natty Light. Dad asks where I'm headed as I pass him on the porch. He's wearing an embarrassing fishing hat and a T-shirt that's hung around from his college days, despite my mother's steady threatening to take it to Goodwill. He's tinkering with the newel post, which seems to wobble no matter what he does. During the week, Dad is as clean and trim as a marketing manager should be, but on the weekends, he lets stubble show, avoids combing his salt-and-pepper hair, and works on the house. Greg Grant, modern-day Jekyll and Hyde.

"I'm going shopping with MacKenzie," I say, instantly feeling bad. Lying about who I'm seeing feels worse than just lying about buying beer. Maybe I'll swing by Kenzie's house, zip up the stairs and tell her I hate everything in my closet and we need to go to the mall, *stat*. She'd do it, I know she would.

"Have fun," he says. "You need any money?"

"No," I say, his generosity only making me feel worse. "Mrs. Ellison just paid me on Thursday."

"I hope you're saving some of it."

"I am." Dad's been lecturing me on the importance of saving money since I kept quarters in a piggy bank. It's one way, at least, I can outdo Lyla, who's terrible with money—not that it matters, now that she's got Benny.

I head to the car. Inside, a hula girl smiles at me, dancing among a shore of receipts and wrappers. I back out and cruise down the street under the oaks and elms dutifully standing guard like tired giants.

I wave to the neighbors and stroller moms, and I slow as I approach MacKenzie's house, pale blue with black shutters. Her car's out front, so I know she's home. I could still spend the day with her at the mall, analyzing what happened between her and Payton, what kind of-maybe-*almost* happened between me and Innis, and then there wouldn't be a lie, not to Dad, not to my friends, not to anyone.

But I don't. I press the gas and keep my eyes from the rearview until I'm on the highway, headed where I know I shouldn't go.

THERE'S TRAFFIC, THE rush of the postchurch crowd, families packed into big gas chuggers and shiny German cars, sitting stiffly in their Sunday best, and it takes me a full fifteen minutes to get out of my end of town.

As I approach West Bonneville, the road widens, new lanes popping up on each side. The buildings are fairly new, and there is, indeed, a Target, but still something's off. The trees that do exist are young, thin, and wiry, like awkward preteens. There are condos everywhere, but many of the windows peek into empty spaces, homes unsold and waiting, a little desperately, to be adopted by a family of their own.

Balloon-speckled car dealerships guide the way, until I see the familiar sign of the Gas Xpress. I take the last spot in the front row, close enough to see through the store's glass but far enough, hopefully, not to be obvious.

I squint to see a man with dark hair at the counter, and I wonder if it's Jason, but then a bigger lady walks through the front door, and my line of vision is blocked. I hear a *knock knock knock* on the passenger window, and I jump, snap my head around. Jason Sullivan stares at me.

He points down several times, a gesture that's impossible to mistake. The full weight of what I'm doing settles in, and my body tenses like a boxer on the big night. In spite of the AC I begin to sweat, and I think about all that fight-or-flight stuff from psychology. Flight sounds pretty good right about now.

But it's too late. My jittery finger finds the button, and I roll down the window.

"You scared me," I say.

"Sorry. I didn't mean to." His voice is familiar and confident, like the two of us chatting in a gas station parking lot is the most natural thing in the world, like the gangly girl he knew is still around, living, breathing, playing with his remote-control helicopter. When he smiles, I notice that a tooth on the right side of his mouth is just the slightest bit chipped. It wasn't like that when we were kids. He leans down. "What are you doing here?"

"I was just driving around I guess." It's so unconvincing, it doesn't even count as a lie.

"You came to see me?" The window frames his lopsided grin. He steps back, takes a last drag of his cigarette, flicks the ash off with his middle finger, pinches it between his thumb and forefinger, and tosses it in the trash. He's still skinny like he was before, but his shoulders are wider, arms more muscly. He wears a dingy white polo that says "Gas Xpress, How can I help you?" and he looks strangely good in it.

He grabs the door handle. "Can I come in?"

"What?"

"I still have ten minutes left on my break. I'd love to sit."

"Okay."

And like that, he's in the seat next to me, two old Frappuccino cups the only things between us.

"When did you start smoking?" It comes out like an accusation.

"Take a wild guess."

I try to imagine his life in there, but it's impossible. I can't see Jason on a stiff cot surrounded by people who do really bad things. I never thought he was that kind of a person, even after he ditched me.

"It's bad for you."

He gasps in mock surprise. "Really? You know, I didn't know that. That changes *everything*."

"I was just saying."

"Hold your judgment, please." He shoves his hand in his pocket and fingers the pack like it's his security blanket. "I didn't exactly have a lot of luxuries."

I shrug. "Your funeral."

He whips his head around. "Did you come here just to criticize me?"

This is the part where I could say no, tell him I'm sorry, explain that I just wanted to see him again.

"I'm not criticizing. I'm just stating a fact."

He pushes his hands against his knees, and he looks truly pissed. I remind myself that he was locked up for being violent. That he's sitting in my car. A surge of anger rushes through me, and it's out before I can stop it. "I saw him last night, you know."

"Who?" he asks, though we both know who I mean.

"His face will never be the same."

Jason's laugh is mirthless. "Yeah, I think I know that."

"So . . ."

"So what?" he snaps. "You came to rub it in? To get some juicy details to take back to *Innis*?" He says his name like it's cough syrup, like the taste of it makes him gag.

"How do you even—?"

"I saw him waiting in the car yesterday," he says. "I'm not stupid."

I shake my head. "Can we please leave Innis out of this?"

"It's a little hard to leave Innis out, when it comes to this." He spits out the words. "*And* he's not good enough for you."

My face is on fire, and I have to stop myself from reaching my hand across the space between us and slapping him.

"You don't know him."

"I'm the one who was friends with him, remember?"

"I remember you're the one who ruined his brother's life." It comes out a yell, and Jason's hand reaches for the door. His mouth opens and hangs there, and then he shuts it tight.

He is not the boy I once knew. He never will be again.

"Then please," he says, "don't let me ruin yours."

And without another word, he's out of my car and out of my life.

Chapter 4

IT'S AFTER EIGHT THIRTY BY THE TIME I DRAG MYSELF out of bed the next morning. Downstairs, Dad's breakfast dishes are in the sink, and Mom is furiously wiping down all of the cabinets.

"When do you get done today?" she asks. I babysit for the Ellisons Monday through Thursday, while Mrs. Ellison either plans charity events, goes to breakfast with other moms, or attends Pilates.

"One," I say. "I'll come straight there." I have an emergency wedding planning lunch with Mom and Lyla. Apparently the band Lyla had chosen had fallen through, and at this stage in the game, that's a *really big deal*. I'm a required attendee.

"Good," Mom says, moving on to the next cabinet.

"Isn't it a little early for Pledge?" I ask.

She doesn't answer, and at first I think it's because of the band fiasco, but then I see the *Bonneville Post-Gazette*, opened to page four.

Local Teen Assault Convict Released Early

He's been out for at least a few days, but I suppose the *Post-Gazette* isn't exactly the Associated Press. Even though it's not news to me, the words feel final, authoritative. Below them sits a photo of Jason, lips shut tight and angry, against a chart that marks his height: seventy-two inches.

Mom's hand stops wiping and follows my gaze. I turn my head guiltily, but she already knows that I know.

"He's not my friend anymore."

"I know."

"So don't worry."

"I'm a mom," she says. "It's my job to worry."

And she goes back to cleaning, her dustrag moving just the tiniest bit faster.

Mrs. Ellison is flustered when I get to the house, Sadie on her hip and Mary Ryan tugging at her cardigan. She steals a glance in the hall mirror, primping her elegantly cut hair with her free hand. I wonder if she read about Jason, too.

What would she do if she knew the just-released convict was her go-to babysitter's former best friend? Or that the dangerous boy was sitting in said babysitter's car not even twenty-four hours ago?

"There's a pizza in the freezer and apples in the crisper." She transfers Sadie from her arms to mine. "Give them lunch at eleven thirty or so. I should be home by one."

"Going somewhere special?" I ask, trying to act normal. "You look lovely."

She shakes her head, a *you-shouldn't-have* smile plastered so wide I know she's not aware of my past associations. "Breakfast with a friend, and then running some errands, but you are just too sweet, Liz." Then she plants a pale pink kiss on both Sadie and Mary Ryan. "Be good for Miss Liz."

The girls and I run through the usual morning activities— story time, dress-up, arts and crafts. I'm fooling with a tiara and adjusting Mary Ryan's favorite princess dress when she turns to me, looks up from beneath her chestnut bangs.

"Miss Liz, do you have a boyfriend?"

My smile falls flat before I can stop it, but I quickly pull it together for her.

"No," I say, voice light and jovial as the tulle on her skirt. She has no clue how much I wish the answer was "yes," how much easier things would be if Innis worked like that.

Only a month or so ago, I thought he did. Innis and I had been flirting in chem for a few weeks at least, and we ran into each other at a graduation party. We were dancing, kissing, right in the room full of everyone. I hadn't even had anything to drink, though I could taste that he had, and I naively assumed that this all meant something—that the next day I'd get a text from him, asking me out properly. Instead, I didn't see him for two weeks. Would he have even invited us over if not for the foolproof fakes?

I know now there's a lot more than a stone's throw between Innis Taylor's girl du jour and Innis Taylor's girlfriend.

Mary Ryan just stares at me, puzzled.

I pinch her nose. "Do *you* have a boyfriend?"

"Gross." She scrunches up her face. "No way."

"Well, there you go," I say. "No boyfriends here. Unless Sadie has one hidden away."

Sadie giggles right on cue, almost as if she knows I'm trying to be funny.

Mary Ryan sighs, looking at me with her big brown eyes. "You're pretty."

Sadie tries to push a square block through a round hole. Finally, she gives up, sticks the block in her mouth, drool running down her chin.

I pull her onto my lap, confiscate the block, and wipe her mouth with the rag I always keep handy. She pops her thumb in her mouth as soon as the block's gone. Mrs. Ellison has told me not to let her do that, along with a whole list of "goals" I'm supposed to focus on during my time with the girls, but I'm a babysitter, not some kind of child behavior specialist.

"Thanks," I say. "You're very pretty, too."

"I thought you'd have a boyfriend. That's how you know if someone's pretty, right, if they have a boyfriend? My dad says pretty girls like my mom always have boyfriends."

My first thought is how much I want to smack Mr. Ellison.

And my second? What if he's right, at least a little bit? Lyla had a total of five boyfriends in the year between breaking up with Skip and meeting Benny. That's a boy band. And not one of them was a boyfriend *prospect*, a casual hangout, or a hookup. They were boyfriends through and through, from the way she introduced them to friends and family to her not-so-subtle updates via social media.

But not me. I'd die of embarrassment if Innis knew I hadn't kissed anyone before him. I didn't even tell MacKenzie.

I run my hands through Sadie's hair. I know that by the standards of the world—or of North Carolina high school, at least—I am pretty. Very. The most popular guy in school does not routinely make out with girls who aren't.

But if I were a little more *something*, would I already be touring the inside of Crawford Hall?

"Your mom is beautiful," I say finally. "But having a boyfriend doesn't make you pretty or special or anything like that."

Mary Ryan nods as she messes with her puffy princess sleeves. Then she looks up again. "Do you think I'm pretty enough to have a boyfriend?"

My heart aches then, because she is so young, and already she's worried about landing a guy. Sometimes it feels like the only requirement of being a girl is to prove to the world that somebody out there is willing to claim you as theirs.

"Miss Liz?" she asks.

I want to teach her that the whole boyfriend thing isn't important, that you can be your fabulous self and that's all you need.

But I worry that if I don't tell her what she wants to hear, I'll hurt her.

I pull Mary Ryan onto my other knee as Sadie leans in closer. "You, my dear, are so beautiful, you'll have so many boyfriends you won't know what to do with them. And when you're old enough, you'll find someone who loves you just as much as your daddy loves your mommy. Okay?"

She nods. "Okay."

But as I squeeze her tight, I wonder who'll be the first person to break her heart.

It's one fifteen by the time I get to lunch. Mom and Lyla are sitting outside, eating hummus and sipping sweet tea. Mom must have dusted away all of her frustrations from this morning, because she looks happy as a clam.

"The great Liz has arrived," Lyla says.

"I was working."

"Yeah, yeah." She ushers me into my seat.

Mom hands me a piece of pita. "How was babysitting?"

Lyla doesn't waste any time. "I ordered you a chicken gyro and a tea. I have to be back at the office by two."

I close the menu in front of me. Lyla's need to control is annoying, but she does it in such a way that it's hard to get mad. In all likelihood, I would have ordered the chicken gyro myself.

Mom's still waiting for an answer. "Babysitting was fine," I say, as a middle-aged woman comes by, refills the teas.

"Anything else for you?" she asks.

"No, thanks. I'm okay."

Mom whacks me on the thigh as soon as the woman's out of earshot. "No, *ma'am*," she says.

"Come on, Mom," I say, fiddling with the straw in my drink. "You know I don't say that."

"You do if I'm paying for your lunch."

I hate forced formality, especially "sir" and "ma'am." Mom is well aware of this.

Lyla lets out a sigh of pure frustration. "Liz, can you please save your grandstanding for a day when my wedding isn't falling apart?"

"Yes, ma'am," I say, slurping my tea so it makes a bubbly sound.

Lyla pulls out her wedding binder and Mom huffs, shaking her head and unfolding and refolding her napkin. The binder is filled to the brim with pages from *Southern Bride*, printouts from DIY blogs, and pamphlets she and Benny have picked up on their many Saturday outings since he proposed. I almost feel sorry for Benny, a lifetime of being dragged around ahead of him, but then I don't, because being in the light of Lyla's affection can actually be pretty fun, as long as you stay in it.

I narrow my eyes at the fat binder. "You really should have been an interior designer or something." She could have been like Mr. Sullivan, our town's unofficial decorator, house filled with binders of fabric and paint chips, before he lost his clients, that is. I wonder if he's got a whole new set now, if he's made up the sharp decline in business, the fallout from Jason's trial.

"I *like* my job," Lyla says, startling me out of my memory. "People are afraid of the dentist. They need a friendly face."

I have to admit that Lyla really sells the whole dental thing, with her huge smile and movie-star teeth, making you feel like you're just one crown, cap, or whitening treatment away from perfection.

"I'm just saying, it would be easy to go back to school with Benny working. You could do pretty much whatever you wanted."

She stares at me like I've slapped her, but Mom actually looks pleased that I've got the guts to say what she won't. It's not that Lyla's not smart, but college, boy, that was not her thing. She tried East Carolina for a semester, just a couple of months after she and Skip broke up. We thought she was doing okay, but when she went to get her teeth cleaned over Christmas break, the woman at the dentist's office told her they were hiring a receptionist and she'd be perfect for it. And that was that. She met Benny six months later. They were engaged six months after that.

"I told you I like my job," she says indignantly.

"I was just making a suggestion."

She flips a page in her binder. "Well, if you're going to say anything, Liz, please make it at least a little helpful."

Lyla pulls out a paper, all business. "Suzanne couldn't come but she emailed me a list of backups." Suzanne is my mom's best friend and Lyla's unofficial wedding planner. "We still have the string quartet for the ceremony, thank God. For the reception, there are a few beach bands that are miraculously not yet booked and might not be that bad. These guys play 'Brown Eyed Girl,' 'Sweet Caroline,' and all the Etta James stuff, of course."

Of course.

The waitress comes out with our food, and I try to win Mom back over by saying thanks in my sweetest and most genuine tone.

I pop a fry into my mouth and lean over her list. "I'm not sure if Billy Boyd and the Drifters are going to do justice to Etta James."

Lyla huffs.

"Why don't you get a DJ? Or let me make a playlist?"

I think Mom actually chokes on her tea.

"What? It's a good idea, if you ask me." I turn to Lyla. "Then you could have whatever music you wanted, not just the usual wedding stuff."

I almost think she's into it, but Mom is absolutely not having it.

"Why stop there?" she asks. "Why don't we just skip the quartet while Lyla walks down the aisle? You can pull up the wedding march on your phone. Why should your dad even pay for a reception hall? Let's just hold it in the community center!"

"Geez, Mom. It was just a thought."

Lyla looks from Mom to me and back again. "Don't worry, we'll have a band." She goes back to the list, ticking through the names, giving us minidescriptions of each.

I sink my teeth into my gyro and let them hash it out. They're all versions of the same boring stuff. And they *all* play "Brown Eyed Girl."

Lyla's on the last name on the list when across the parking lot of the shopping center, I see him. Innis, flanked by Payton and Alex. I don't have time to decide whether to be flirty or coy, wave happily or pretend not to see him, because he immediately catches my eye and starts walking over. I give him a small smile.

"Who are you smiling at?" Mom asks, her Mom-Radar getting very clear reception today. She turns her head. "Well, who do we have here?"

"Mom, *please* try not to be completely embarrassing." I take a gulp of tea and pray there are no bits of cucumber skin in my teeth.

Payton and Alex hang back, but Innis walks right up to us. "Hi, Mrs. Grant," he says, his voice brimming with gentlemanliness and good breeding. "Lyla."

Then he smiles right at me. "Liz."

"Hey." I try to sound cool, calm, and collected as I feel my face go red and hot.

"You enjoying this gorgeous weather?" Mom asks, employing her go-to conversation starter.

"Yes, ma'am," he drawls. "What are you ladies up to this afternoon?"

Mom's practically giggling she looks so happy. "Just going over a few last-minute wedding things."

Innis nods. "I never got a chance to congratulate you, Lyla."

"Oh," she says. It's rare to see Lyla flustered, but her hands fidget in her lap. "Thanks."

There's a flicker in his eyes—in a different world, Lyla would be marrying Skip—but as quick as it comes, it's gone.

He nods to the boys, then looks right at me. "We're just walking around if you want to meet up after lunch."

Mom nods so vigorously it's flat out annoying. Lyla smiles in a way that's at least a little less conspicuous.

"Yeah," I say.

"Text me." Then he looks at my mom. "Nice to see you. Congrats again, Lyla."

He's thankfully out of earshot when Mom turns to me. "Are you going to ask him to the wedding?"

"Mom, he's not my boyfriend."

Lyla's eyes are practically glued to her food, and it's strange, because she was so supportive yesterday. Maybe now she realizes how weird the whole thing is.

Mom either doesn't notice or doesn't care. "Who says you have to be official to take someone to a wedding? What do you think weddings are for?"

"Mom," I say. "Please."

"Plus." She tilts her head towards me, in full girlfriend mode now. "A lot can happen in a few weeks."

Chapter 5

I catch up with the guys in front of Walmart. Alex is smoking a cigarette and Payton's eyes are glued to his phone. I squeeze between them, sidle up to Innis.

"Hey," I say, in the best tone I can muster, a blend of non-chalance and casual interest.

"Hey." He turns to me, leans down and kisses me on the lips, right there in front of Alex and Payton, like this is a totally natural thing for us to do.

I die.

Dirty double doors slide open, and I stumble inside, barely able to handle what just happened. This was not a drunken make-out in his basement. This was in broad daylight. In front of his friends.

We walk past people sifting through bins of DVDs and kids kicking balls in the aisles. Eventually, we find our way to the hunting section. Innis heads for the binoculars, Payton and Alex drift away to look at the knives, and it's just us again.

He meanders down the aisle, without really focusing on any of the pairs.

"You ever been hunting?" he asks.

"No," I say. "It's not really my style. I mean, I know it's supposedly the most humane way to eat meat and all, but I can't imagine killing an animal like that."

Innis holds a pair of binoculars up to his eyes, then sets them back on the shelf. "It's exciting," he says. "You have to wait for the perfect moment, and then, boom, it's there, and if you don't take it, you'll regret it."

He looks at me, holds my gaze and gives me one of those smiles that have made more girls than me lose sleep, and it suddenly doesn't feel like we're talking about hunting anymore.

I want so badly to kiss him again.

I almost think it will happen. He steps a little closer, his eyes still locked on mine, and my heart beats so loud and fast I wonder if he can feel the vibrations, but then a temper-tantrum wail erupts from the next aisle, and he steps back, leaving me hanging there, breathless, and all he says is, "You probably wouldn't like it."

We find the boys in the knife aisle, gawking over about twenty different types of pocketknives that all look the same to me.

Alex grabs one from the top.

"What do you think?" He shows it to Innis.

"Skip it," Innis says. He reaches into his pocket, pulls out a knife. I've seen him use it to shotgun beers in his basement, but I had no idea he carried it on the regular. He flicks it open with his thumb. The gleam of the blade feels bold, dangerous, underneath the fluorescent lights of the store.

"This one's the best," he says. "But they don't sell it here."

I reach out, touch his arm gently. "Shouldn't you put that away? Can't you get in trouble?"

But Innis just laughs, like "trouble" is a foreign concept. When he sees my face is serious though, he flips it down, tosses it to me. Miraculously, I catch it.

He steps closer, points at the knife in my hands. "It's inscribed, see? My dad got it for me when I turned sixteen. Skip has the same one."

I run my hand over the engraved letters: IET.

"What's the *E* for?" I ask.

Payton and Alex burst into snickers. Innis actually goes a little red.

"What?" I ask. "Bad?"

Innis shakes his head. "Trust me, you don't want to know."

"Come on, dude, just tell her," Alex says. "It's too good not to."

I rack my head for embarrassing *E* names. "Elmer?" I ask. "Elwood? Ebenezer?"

The boys laugh. Innis continues to shake his head.

"Come on," I say. "Just tell me."

"Fine," he says, sighing. "It's Erskine."

The laughter comes before I can stop it.

"You take that name to your grave," he says. "Not that many people know that."

"Roger that," I say.

I have to stop myself from skipping as we make our way down the aisle. Because it might not matter, it might be only a middle name, but it still feels like he's letting me in, just a little.

And when it comes to Innis Erskine Taylor, that's a reason to celebrate.

AFTER ANOTHER FIFTEEN minutes or so, we make our way outside. That's when it all starts to go downhill.

I see Alexis, Innis's ever-present ex, who, until the other night, had been in attendance at every one of Innis's hangouts. She's standing there in hot-pink cheerleader shorts and a cute floral cami—the girl makes even gym clothes look good. Her hair is pulled back to show perfect cheekbones, and her bright green eyes practically pop out of her head.

"Liz!" Her voice is high-pitched and full of forced excitement, as she looks from Innis to me and back to Innis again. She crosses her arms, then uncrosses them, letting them hang at her sides. "Shopping with the boys, I see?"

Innis doesn't miss a beat. "We aren't shopping together. I just ran into her in the parking lot."

I feel an instant ache of betrayal in my chest, all the joy from the kiss and the conversation completely sucked away.

Scratch that. It's worse than betrayal. He's not my boyfriend, so there's nothing to betray. This is indifference. It makes me feel empty, hollowed out.

Alexis looks beside herself.

I'd thought he was totally over her, that they were just friends, until now.

The conversation continues without me for a minute, Payton and Alex either completely oblivious to what's going on or just completely uninterested, until Alexis says her mom is waiting and she has to go in.

"Maybe I'll run into you in a parking lot one of these days," she says, her hand grazing Innis's elbow for just a second, before giving me a self-satisfied smirk.

Payton and Alex quickly disperse for the afternoon's activities, but Innis hangs back, the metal din of clanging shopping carts our soundtrack. I think he might apologize, but then all he says is, "Where'd you park?"

I want to rewind everything, to erase the Alexis encounter. I want him to ask me to keep hanging out, to go back to his house, flirt and swim and finally meet his parents.

I try to hide my huge disappointment because, as MacKenzie says, desperation can make even the prettiest girl look busted. "Down by Athenos."

"Come on," he says. "I'll drive you."

We glide through the parking lot, and I guess that I have three to six minutes until I'm back to my car, wondering when he'll text, or *if* he'll text. I nervously finger the book in my bag, trying to keep my cool.

"What are you up to the rest of the day?" I ask, like I have genuine interest in his afternoon plans and am not just angling for an invite.

He's quiet a minute, like he's thinking it over, but then he just shrugs. "Not much. Might play some video games."

He doesn't say anything else, and in a minute, we're in front of my car.

"Thanks for the ride," I say.

"No problem."

My hand reaches for the door.

"See ya around, Liz," he says.

"Okay. See ya."

I get into my car and slam the door, seething with anger. I rev the engine and back out of my spot, so frustrated I almost run into a cart in the parking lot.

I can't decide who I'm more mad at: Innis for being— well, Innis—or me for believing that he could be anyone else.

THE NEXT MORNING, I decide to break my rule about Jason's house.

Maybe it's because I'm disappointed by what happened with Innis and desperately seeking a distraction. Maybe it's because I woke up particularly early, and couldn't even manage more than a page of *Heart of Darkness*. Or maybe it's just that the house has been sitting there, taunting me since I found out Jason was released.

The porch is littered with errant beer cans, a mini-Stonehenge of cigarette butts, a receipt from the liquor store, and specks of what I'd have to guess is vomit. It's so perfectly representative, I almost want to take a photo: the state of affairs, etched in trash.

It used to be filled with cozy chairs and a porch swing. Jason and I would sip Cokes and munch on Utz chips, while my mom and Mrs. Sullivan gossiped about the neighbors.

But that was before Mrs. Sullivan went away. Before Jason went to juvie. Before Mr. Sullivan decided to move. After he did, the place sat untouched for six months or so, but then someone broke a window and the lock on the back door, and people started partying there. That's when Mom began nightly surveillance from the back porch, a glass of wine in her hand and an especially big bee in her bonnet. She called the cops enough that kids stopped coming, at least before midnight, but the door was never fixed. The first time I went over was an early morning just like this. By that point, Jason had been gone a year, and the Sullivans were a taboo topic in my house. Their very mention caused Mom to speak in a hushed voice, Dad to shake his head. I'd convinced myself that I needed to check on the place. I did sop up some spilled beer, but I spent most of the time walking around, remembering. How Mr. Sullivan helped Jason and me with our makeshift card houses. The smell of a Crock-Pot full of chili and the artificial cherry taste of our favorite Popsicles. The first time we were no longer allowed to take baths together, had to go into separate corners to change into pajamas.

I know nostalgia's a trick of the mind, I know it makes things seem better than they were, but I couldn't help feeling that what Jason and I shared was truer than any friendship I'd had in my life. We had this history, one that ran so much deeper than watching cartoons and playing cops and robbers. We were like living journals, all of our good and bad memories locked up in each other's minds. It was such a comforting feeling to have so much understanding reflected back on a face that wasn't yours. A feeling I knew that no event, no matter how terrible, could erase.

The knob turns easily, and I walk inside. It's hot, the room thick with humidity from the day before. I open a window to get the breeze going, running my hands over the gorgeous plantation shutters. Jason and I used to love tilting them up and down, watching the sunbeams dance at our beck and call.

The wood floors are dusty but still nice, and the house feels enormous in the absence of furniture. It used to be packed, a veritable museum of antiques and knickknacks. Mom always said Mr. Sullivan had a gift, and she hired him to do our house before everything happened. Shortly after Jason's trial, she got a decorator to come up from Charlotte to finish the job—this hoity-toity woman in pearls and tall, clanky shoes, with brassy auburn hair and too much eye makeup. Mom said Mr. Sullivan wasn't getting her style. But I knew the real reason. So did he.

In the front, the windows cast an early morning glow, bright and ethereal, the house like a shadow box. I climb up the stairs, remembering so many days playing hide-and-seek. How Mr. Sullivan always yelled at us to get our toys off the stairs. The time that Jason stuck his head through the banisters and Mr. Sullivan had to use a full can of Crisco to get it out.

The fifth step of the staircase creaks, as it always has, and I tread carefully up the rest. I head straight to Jason's room. It's small and sparse. Little-boy blue walls and beige carpet that has slight indents from where bunk beds stood for years. I spent countless nights here, talking with Jason about dinosaurs and astronauts as we looked up at a ceiling of stick-on stars until gravity pulled our eyelids down.

The gurgle of an engine jolts me out of memory lane. It's loud and hardworking, like a whole load of machinery is under the hood. It putters and stops, and then there's a pause followed by the slam of a door.

I creep to the window and look out. There's a truck there, sure enough. One I don't recognize. A pickup, white and tinged with dirt.

And then I see him walking, his gait quick and deliberate.

The nostalgia disappears as quickly as it came. We aren't friends anymore, haven't been for years, since around the time he ditched the bunk beds, tacked up movie posters, blasted hip-hop music, and slowly invited me over less and less, hoping I'd get the hint . . .

I take the stairs two at a time, but in moments he's inside, staring up at me with a look of curiosity and surprise.

"What are you doing here?" Jason asks. I can't tell if he's mad or just confused. He smells like cigarettes.

"I shouldn't be here. I'm sorry."

"I don't care if you're here," he says with a strain. "I just didn't expect you." He looks down. I decided to come over so quick, I didn't even bother to throw on flip-flops. "Without shoes, no less."

"I just kind of ran over. I didn't think you'd be here."

"But it's my house."

"Your dad never comes."

He stares at me a minute, then takes a labored breath. "My dad washed his hands of the place," he says, rolling his eyes. "And I get that he doesn't want to deal with it, but it's not going to sell itself with all the damage and crap outside. And the real estate lady has pretty much given up on it. I'm kind of the last hope." He shuts the front door behind him. "Really, though. What are you doing here?"

I lean against the banister. "I come here sometimes."

"Why today?"

I shake my head. "I don't know."

"Because I pissed you off?"

I shrug. "I thought I was the one who pissed you off."

"You did." He walks to the kitchen, sets his toolbox down on the counter. I follow behind.

He leans down, opens the cabinet doors beneath the sink, starts fishing around in there with his back to me.

"I wasn't trying to piss you off," I say. "I just thought maybe you would defend yourself if I brought up Skip, maybe you could give me a reason or something."

He stops moving, and I think maybe he's about to tell me what I want to hear. He closes the door and turns to me, the corners of his lips turned down. He opens his mouth to speak but then shuts it again.

"What is it?"

He sighs, shakes his head. "I forgot the caulking gun. I came all the way over here without it. I somehow manage to screw up everything."

He stands back up and shifts his weight back and forth. His eyes avoid mine. Maybe there is no explanation to give for what happened that night. Maybe he just snapped—*screwed things up*, if you will—maybe there's no more to it than that.

"I gotta go," I say.

"Stay," he says, taking a step forward and meeting my eyes again. "You don't have to go."

"Yes, I do." I reach for the door, but in seconds, he's right behind me, his hand on my shoulder. His touch feels danger-ous, like an electric shock.

"I'm sorry I got so angry the other day," he says. "You should come over sometime. Say hi to my dad."

I turn to him just long enough to speak the words. "I can't."

And then I'm across the yard and in my house and lying in bed and thinking about Lyla and my mother and MacKenzie and Innis—and what all of them would think if they knew.

For so long I wished that Jason had never ditched me.

But now I just wish that he'd stayed away.

Chapter 6

"THE TRUCK'S STILL AT THAT HOUSE," MRS. ELLISON says shortly after I arrive later that morning. Her eyes are locked on the window and she's holding Sadie almost protectively. "He was your year, right? The boy who did that horrible thing to Skip Taylor? Jack or Jasper or something."

"Jason," I say. "Yeah. We were in the same grade."

"And neighbors, too. Lord help me when these girls become teenagers."

I force a laugh. "You sound like my mom."

She passes Sadie over to me, while Mary Ryan colors at the kiddie table, oblivious to her mom's worries. "Just be careful. And if you guys decide to go out, head towards the pond."

I want to tell her that, dear Lord, Jason would never hurt

a kid, but it seems like the wrong thing to say. "No problem. Don't worry at all."

His truck is there all morning, big and intrusive, while the girls and I cycle through arts and crafts, the allotted thirty minutes of screen time, and pretend play in the backyard.

It's still there when I leave, but I ignore it, heading straight to MacKenzie's.

She gives me a knowing smile as soon as I'm in her room, her dog, Rocky, following behind. She shuts the door. "I know you've got boy news." She runs a hand underneath her golden-brown curls, cultivated after an hour of work. Blow-dry, straighten, curl. It's a bit much, but I've got to hand it to her, she looks great.

"I'm just here to see you."

"Aww, how sweet." She smiles at me, and I reach up and gently fleck a piece of mascara from her bottom eyelid. "Thanks," she says. "But seriously. What's the deal with you and Innis?"

I lean back on the bed and give her a look. "You first. Why are you getting all fixed up?"

She beams. "Payton asked me to come hang out at his pool."

I feel a jealous ache, deep in my stomach. Things are moving fast with Payton, and I should be happy for her, but it only makes me more aware that things are regressing between me and Innis.

MacKenzie narrows her eyes, puts her hair tools down. "Hey, what's wrong?"

I sit up straighter. "I'm sorry I'm not more excited. I just think things with Innis are going to fizzle out."

"What are you talking about?" She sits down next to me. "Payton told me you guys hung out just yesterday."

"Did he say it like it meant something, or did he say it in his monotone Payton way?"

"Hey," MacKenzie says.

"I'm just saying. He was probably just stating a fact, like he does."

Kenzie rolls her eyes. "So what happened then?"

I take a deep breath, my face getting hot, and I feel down-right ridiculous at how upset I am. "I ran into him at lunch. He was all nice to my mom and sister. He asked me to meet up after. We did, and he kissed me, right outside of Walmart, in front of everyone."

MacKenzie's jaw drops. "Okay, the romantic qualities of Wally World aside, he kissed you in the daytime? That's so *boyfriend-y*."

"I know." My body responds to the feel of the kiss with nervous butterfly flutters, as if it hasn't remembered the rest of the story yet. "And so it's all good, and I follow them around the store, and I watch them look at hunting stuff, and he even tells me his embarrassing middle name, and then we run into Alexis in the parking lot. And he basically absolves himself of any connection to me."

"Wait, what's his middle name?"

"Erskine."

"Oh my God, that's hilarious."

"Can you focus?" I ask.

"Okay, okay. So what did he say?"

I do a mock–boy voice. "'Oh, we weren't planning on hanging out. I just ran into her in the parking lot.'"

MacKenzie presses her lips together: puzzled—or even disappointed? Then she forces a smile. "He probably got freaked out by his ex is all."

"But it's been years," I say.

"Yeah, but maybe he *really* likes you, and being seen with a potential girlfriend in front of an ex sent him into some kind of douchey Innis tizzy."

"Or maybe he just wanted us around because we had fakes and now he's over it . . ."

MacKenzie shakes her head vigorously. "Look, Liz. You've got substance. A lot more than me, probably. *And* you're pretty and, with my help, rather popular. Basically, why wouldn't you be the girl to make Innis finally realize that hooking up with randos at parties doesn't even compare to being with someone you're into?"

"You actually think all those things?" I ask. "You're not just saying that because you know he's done a one-eighty and you feel bad for me and it's the kind of thing friends are supposed to say?"

MacKenzie laughs. Then she pats me on the shoulder like she's a cheerleading coach and I only need to practice a few more lifts before I'm beaming from the top of the pyramid. "I'm telling you, don't worry. He likes you."

"Maybe he was disappointed the other night."

"Why?" she asks, genuine concern in her voice for the first time. "You told me it was good."

I take a deep breath. "But I think he wanted to . . . you know."

She raises her eyebrows. "Bake you a cake?"

"Kenzie!"

She folds her hands in her lap, steels herself, and looks up at me with her therapist eyes. "How much have you guys done exactly? Apart from the other night?"

I hesitate, but her eyes say it's okay.

"Just made out."

Her laugh sounds like Styrofoam peanuts rubbing together. "That's it?" I cringe, embarrassed and, for some reason, ashamed. "Really?"

"Geez, Kenzie. Yes, really. Was I supposed to have slept with him on the basement couch by now? He's not even my boyfriend. And I'm supposed to . . ." My voice breaks off, and my eyes fill with tears. MacKenzie's supposed to be the one who understands, even if she is much more chill about sex than I am. She's supposed to be on my side.

"Whoa," she says. "I didn't mean you had to sleep with him. There are other things."

I taste salt on my lips. "Well, thanks," I say. "I didn't *realize.*"

She puts her hand on my shoulder. "I'm not trying to make you upset. I'm just saying that it's okay for things to progress. You might even like it."

"What if I don't want things to progress?" I ask.

She sighs. "Have you been talking to Veronica? Is that where all this prudey guilt is coming from?"

"No," I snap. "I haven't. And could you do me a favor and not bring Veronica into all of this?"

MacKenzie thinks Veronica is all uptight about sex because in a moment of extreme un-Veronica-ness, she essentially called MacKenzie a slut in the middle of the cafeteria. I'd skipped our standing Friday movie date for a party with MacKenzie, and Veronica was fuming at lunch on Monday. "So you're going to start sleeping your way to the top of the East Bonneville food chain, too? You never gave a shit about any of this stuff until the fabulous MacKenzie came along."

It was a seriously crappy thing to say to MacKenzie. But it was also crappy of us to exclude her. I should have followed her out of the cafeteria, told her I was sorry. Instead, I sat stock-still as Veronica grabbed her lunch and stomped away, not looking back once. After that, she went back to the edge of the cafeteria, sat with a bunch of girls from one of our AP classes who she didn't even like that much. And I just let it happen.

MacKenzie scoots closer to me on the bed, and Rocky hops up to join us. She can see she's hurt me, and she softens her voice. "Listen, if you don't want things to progress, they don't have to. I'm just saying, if you wanted to, it's really not that big of a deal."

"He said he would wait for me." I wipe tears from my eyes and take short, quick breaths.

"And he will," MacKenzie says, an upbeat note in her

voice. "I'm only saying that there's nothing to be afraid of. You guys should be enjoying each other. You're young . . . and beautiful . . . and soon to be boyfriend-girlfriend!"

I scratch behind Rocky's ears. "You absolutely do not know that."

MacKenzie ignores my negativity, gives me a hug. "It'll be fine. I promise."

But as I reach for a box of tissues, I'm not quite sure I believe her.

JASON DISAPPEARS SOMEWHERE between four o'clock and dinner, when I'm up in my room, taking a crack at my summer reading, and pretending his truck's not even there. *Heart of Darkness* is confusing enough when your brain isn't constantly flitting to the whereabouts of your old best friend/ sister's mortal enemy/etc. . . .

I can tell something's up with Mom not two minutes into dinner. She cuts her steak with sharp quick movements, hacking at it like it's her nemesis. She's got something on her mind, and she's begging for one of us to ask.

"Easy there, the cow's already dead, Genevieve," Dad says with a signature dad chuckle.

She ignores him.

I butter a roll and decide to put her out of her misery. "Something wrong, Mom?"

She sips her water, I sip mine, and I count to five. Wait for it. Wait for it . . .

Right on cue, she drops her fork on the plate, sits up

straight, and leans forward in her chair. "There was a truck at the Sullivans' today."

I freeze, because she's a mom, and moms don't miss a thing. I wait for her to tell me that she was awake for all of it, that she saw me go over there, that she *knows*.

"Did you see it?" she asks me with genuine, suspicion-free curiosity.

I shake my head just a bit too fast. Bad move. It gives her pause.

"It was probably the realtor," Dad says, shoving more steak in his mouth.

"It was not the realtor," she says. "Realtors do not drive *trucks*."

"Maybe someone's doing work on the house. It needs it."

She ignores him. "Don't you remember Danny was talking about getting a truck right before he moved, to cart furniture around to clients?"

He stares at her. "Yeah. So what?"

"I think it's his."

I eat another bite slowly, watching the volley, thanking my lucky stars that neither of them is hitting the ball over to me.

"It's his house," Dad says. "Doesn't he have a right to be over there?"

"And what if it's his son? Creeping around, fresh out of prison, near *our* daughter?"

She looks straight at me, and I wonder if she's playing a game, seeing if I'll crack. She used to do it when she knew

Lyla was lying to her. When she was out late with Skip or had the slightest tinge of alcohol on her breath, enough for a mom to notice. "He hasn't tried to contact you, has he, Elizabeth?"

I blink once, twice, three times. "No," I say, slow and steady as I can muster.

"I don't even understand how he got out," she says. "*Parole.*" She rolls her eyes like "parole" is meaningless, a trophy they give out on Field Day in elementary school. "And if he did anything; if he tried to contact you at all, you can tell me."

If she knew I'd gone over there, knew I'd seen him this morning, she'd freak.

"If I see him over here, I'm calling the police."

"For what?" I ask.

"I don't know. Loitering."

"At his own house?"

She drops her knife this time. "Are you defending him?"

"Genevieve," Dad says. "You can't very well prevent the boy from visiting his own house."

"You, too?" She shoots death eyes at Dad. "After what he did to Lyla?"

He breathes deep, and I can tell he just wants to eat his steak in peace. "Lyla has Benny now. Things happen for a reason."

If that's not the most effed-up logic I've ever heard, I don't know what is.

"So?" Mom snaps. "Skip was her first love. She could have had . . ." She stops herself, and I wonder if she's thinking

Lyla could have had Skip, or that she could have had Craw-ford Hall. I wonder if that's what she's planning for me now.

"She still could if she wanted him so bad."

Mom gasps, as if the idea of marrying someone maimed is unthinkable.

"Plus," I say. "*She's* not the one with the burned face."

"Elizabeth!"

The phone rings. We don't usually answer during dinner, but Dad leaps for it.

"*Lizzie.*" He smiles. "It's for you."

Dad knows not to call me Lizzie anymore; he wouldn't have said it unless prompted. Mom looks my way, and I curse her for being so perceptive.

I walk slowly towards the phone and carefully take the receiver.

"Hello."

"It's Jason." His voice is heavy, like muddy red clay, the kind that sticks on your shoes for days.

I want to say "I know," but I stop myself.

He clears his throat. "How are you?"

"Okay."

There's a silence as I wait for him to say something else. Meanwhile, Mom's gone back to pushing food around her plate, ears pricked.

"I know you couldn't stay this morning," he says. "But I was serious. You should come over. My dad would love to see you. He asked me to ask you."

"I'm busy."

"I didn't even say when."

"It doesn't matter. I can't."

"Listen, I know that it's weird, but Lizzie—"

"It's Liz." I flip around to see if my mother noticed, but her eyes are still on her plate.

"Okay, Liz."

"I can't talk right now. I'm eating dinner."

"Well, give me your number. I'll text you later. Find a time when you're not busy."

"I don't know."

"Come on, Lizzie—*Liz*—we're friends."

We're not friends, I think. We haven't been for a long long time.

"Please?" he asks. "Come on."

I glance at Mom, whose eyes are now locked on me like a viper's. I rattle off my number just to get off the phone.

"Talk later." I hang up before he can say another word.

"Who was that?" Mom asks immediately.

The lie comes out so cool and easy it scares me. "One of MacKenzie's little brother's friends. He wants to take me to the movies. He probably just needs a chaperone." Dad laughs, always appreciative of a bad joke.

Mom doesn't buy it. "So you said no?"

"Of course I said no. I don't make a habit of going out with thirteen-year-olds." I shove potatoes into my mouth and wait for the third degree to end.

"Then why'd you give him your number?"

I swallow and take a big gulp of water. "To get him off my

back. Joey would've given it to him anyway. I'll just ignore it."

Dad shakes his head vehemently. "Let them down fast, Liz. No need to lead anyone on. Just rip off the Band-Aid."

Mom looks to him and then back to me, and against all odds, she seems to buy it. "Your dad's right," she says. "Nothing wrong with saying no."

WHEN I'M FINALLY back in my room, I go straight to my trusty box.

The other night, I was afraid to look at the news clippings, but after his call, it's like I crave them. My hands tremble as I lift off the lid. Jason's hands, rough and strong, flash before my eyes, but I push the thought of them away. Nip it in the bud, Mom always says. Nip it in the bud.

I skip the photos on top, go straight to the clippings. Some of them are fresher, leaving inky black on my fingertips, but the one I want is almost two years old.

It's folded three times over, neat little squares that unfurl easily, practically asking to be opened.

TEEN PLEADS GUILTY IN BONNEVILLE ASSAULT CASE

Bonneville resident Jason Sullivan pled guilty Monday morning to assault inflicting serious bodily injury in last spring's attack on Sherman (Skip) Taylor at the victim's home.

Sullivan was accused of intentionally acting to

harm and disfigure his former friend. He was charged as a minor and was sentenced to 24 months in a juvenile detention facility, with parole at 18 months.

For the Taylors, who found their son permanently scarred after a teen fight turned brutal, the news was welcome respite after months of pain and rehabilitation. "This was a vicious and intentional attack," the victim's father, Alex Taylor, said over the phone. "We are relieved that justice has been served."

Sullivan, 15, and Taylor, 17, were at the Taylors' home on Myrtle Avenue in East Bonneville on the evening of May 13. When a disagreement erupted between the two boys, Sullivan allegedly punched, pushed, and held Taylor over a bonfire in the backyard.

Innis Taylor, 15, the victim's brother, was at the home and would have acted as the prosecution's primary witness, had the case gone to trial. Innis Taylor alleged that Sullivan forced his brother into the flames and pinned him there long enough for the victim's face to catch fire, before fleeing the scene. The police apprehended Sullivan the next morning.

In a statement, Alex Taylor thanked his family, friends, and the community for their support.

"He's not a bad boy," Danny Sullivan, the assailant's father, said of his son. "I don't know how this could have happened."

I REMEMBER THE police cars that morning, Jason's head bent down as the cops led him away, but I didn't think it was anything that bad. Maybe a little weed or a discovered fake or something. The Bonneville police would jump at anything more exciting than speeding tickets. A few hours later, Lyla called.

"Get Mom now," she said.

"What's wrong?" She was away at the beach with her two best friends. I imagined a tragic accident in the water. A drowning or a shark attack. I still didn't put any of it together.

"Just get Mom," she said again. "I need to come home now."

I rushed up the stairs and knocked twice on my parents' bedroom door before bursting in. Mom was applying eyeliner in front of the mirror, fresh out of a gardenia-scented bath, hair in curlers and a plush robe knotted at her waist.

"What is it?" I could tell from her voice that she already knew something was wrong.

I pushed the phone at her. "Lyla sounds upset."

The eyeliner dropped to the floor and rolled towards me as she took the phone with both hands. "Baby," she said. "What's wrong?"

I stood there, my fists clenching and unclenching, as her eyes got big and she sucked in breath and said, "Oh my goodness," and, "Is he all right?" and, "Where was the fire?"

I didn't move, didn't drop her gaze. I couldn't have even if I'd wanted to.

She gripped the phone tighter. "Wha-*aat?*" Her voice was a half parabola, long and steady at the front and questioning at the end, exponentially shocked.

Someone had done something bad.

"Wait, *Lizzie's* Jason?"

I couldn't hear Lyla's answer, but the look on her face said enough. My stomach lurched. For a few terrifying moments, I was sure something had happened to him.

"No," Mom said. "No. I'll be right there. Don't worry." She hung up.

"What is it?" I asked. "Mom, is Jason okay?"

She looked at me the way she'd looked at me when I was five, when after an hour and a half in the Splash Mountain line at Disney World, I was three-quarters of an inch too short to ride. She knew she was going to break my heart, but there was nothing in the world she could do about it.

She told me what Jason did to Skip, as I sat on her bed and tried not to hyperventilate, hugging me tight, her sharp curlers prickling my cheek. I didn't understand it then. And I still can't understand it now.

I fold the paper, drop it back in the box. Jason got more than his share of newspaper mentions, but this is the one that makes it all real, the one I constantly come back to. The one that reminds me, when my mind gets away from me, just who Jason is.

Because a lifetime of chili dinners and backyard playdates and bittersweet nostalgia can't change what Jason Sullivan has done.

Chapter 7

WEDNESDAY IS DEVOTED ENTIRELY TO WEDDING stuff. As soon as I'm back from babysitting, Mom's all ready to go. She's got a whole list of things for us to do before the bridal shower, next Sunday, and I have to help her with all the details, because she wants everything to be a surprise for Lyla.

Suzanne meets us at the caterers. "Hey, y'all," she says in her chirpy voice. She gives me a big tight hug and says, like she always does: "Honey, you need to eat more."

"Oh, stop," I say, and I gesture under my lip. Suzanne picks up my cue, wipes away the smudge of pesto. She must have started tasting without us.

There are two kinds of Southern belles. There are the

ones like my mother, prim and proper, the ones who always know the right thing to say, who send thank-you notes in a week or less, and who monogram pretty much everything they own.

Then there are ladies like Suzanne. Indulgent and just a little bit wild; they live on dishes like creamed spinach and mac 'n' cheese, swear a little more than they should, cackle when they laugh, and occasionally lace their sweet tea with bourbon.

It's not that they don't have anything in common. Suzanne is also a Protestant, straight-ticket Republican, and fiercely Southern. But unlike my mother, she's just a little bit shameless. They're on the Homeowners' Association together, and they've been inseparable for almost a decade, since around when Mrs. Sullivan left.

A girl brings us minibowls of shrimp and grits, jalapeño cheese straws in heart-shaped tins, and various other pint-sized Southern dishes. Suzanne takes the lead, saying what she likes and doesn't, Mom nodding in agreement because we all know that Suzanne cooks better than almost anyone in Bonneville. Between tastings, the two of them trade "local news," as Suzanne likes to call it, gossiping about everyone from neighborhood women to Lyla's new in-laws. Eventually, the conversation makes its way to me.

Mom lowers her voice like she does when the tidbits get really juicy. "So guess who we ran into at lunch yesterday?"

"Who?" Suzanne asks.

"Innis Taylor." Mom clasps her hands together out of

sheer delight. "He was very polite. Congratulated Lyla and invited Liz for a walk." She says it as if he's Mr. Darcy and I spent the afternoon promenading the grounds of Pemberley as opposed to getting blown off in the Walmart parking lot. "They're going together."

"Mom, we're not going together," I say. "Geez. And no one's said 'going together' in like a million years."

She waves her hand. "Oh, I know, I know. I'm not allowed to talk about anything. Let me have at least a little excitement."

"That *is* exciting," Suzanne says, winking at me as she scrapes the bottom of her bowl of grits.

None of us talk about how it's actually kind of strange, Innis being Skip's little brother and all. That I wonder sometimes whether Innis is trying to live the life that Skip could have had, if he only chose me because I'm Lyla's younger sister. And I neglect to mention that Innis might have feelings for his ex-girlfriend. There are some things you just don't say out loud.

When they're stuffed and talked out, Mom puts in one order for all of Suzanne's favorites, as well as six jugs of sweet tea.

After a stop at the florist for hydrangeas and one more at the stationery store for napkins with Lyla's initials, we head to Belk's department store. I mess around at the jewelry counter, while Mom and Suzanne head to the lingerie section, giggling like schoolgirls, to find something for "Lyla's big night." It takes almost a half hour, but I don't dare go over and try to hurry them up. The idea of Mom scrutinizing nighties for my sister to wear for Benny makes me want to barf.

MacKenzie texts me when Mom and I are back in the car.

> any word?
>> nothing, how was your swim?
> so good, details later, u should txt him
>> i don't know
> do it

I type two words to Innis: *what's up?* My thumb hovers over the Send button as Mom babbles on about the shower, how happy she is that Lyla found Benny, whether I heard Suzanne say that our neighbors five doors down are trying to get a tacky nautical-themed mailbox approved by the Association.

I steady my breaths, tap it before I can stop myself. In seconds, the message is out there, in the ether, floating its way to his phone.

"Liz," Mom is saying. "Liz. Are you listening?"

I look up to see her turn into the shopping center near our house.

"That phone," she says. "I swear you're addicted to that thing."

I bury the phone in the bottom of my bag. Maybe if I can't see it, it'll be like the message wasn't sent.

"Did you even hear me?" she asks.

I turn the radio down, give her my full attention. "I know, I know. The mailbox heard round the world."

"No, I was saying we should treat ourselves."

"Huh?"

She smiles mischievously and drives to a spot right in front of the nail salon. "Let's get mani-pedis."

I raise an eyebrow. "Are you serious?"

She looks like a bobblehead, she nods so vigorously. "It'll be fun. Mother-daughter date."

"All right . . . I mean, if you really want."

"It'll be *fun*." This time it comes off more like a command. I bet she read this in a magazine, a checklist of Mother-of-the-Bride duties. *Don't ignore your younger daughter—take her on a date to show you care!* Either that or she thinks my half-chipped nails will distract from the decor at the bridal shower.

She obviously has an appointment, and two ladies lead us to matching pink chairs. I set my bag on the floor next to mine, slip off my flip-flops, and dip my feet in the bubbling pool of water.

Mom strongly encourages me to stay in the red or pink color family when I try to go for purple, so I pick a coral, and she gets a classic red. I look up at the ceiling and try to calm myself down as the woman starts to scrub my feet. I remind myself that an unsolicited *what's up* isn't grounds for a breakup, or even a non-breakup; plus, if he does still have feelings for Alexis, it's all moot anyway.

"So who were you texting?" I can tell she's trying to sound casual, confiding and friend-like, but she sounds questioning, like a mom.

"MacKenzie."

"Oh." There's a brief note of relief, but then true to form, once one worry is taken care of, she's on to the next. "I thought maybe it was Innis."

The lady switches to my other foot, and I think about telling her *I* texted *him*, made a move, broke the rules, just to rock her world a bit. But before I can, I hear the *ding ding* sound of an incoming text, and I can't help but grin, lift my chin a little higher, because I know it's him. I just know it is.

"Actually, I was texting him, too."

She beams at the lady scrubbing her feet with pride, like everyone must know about the famed Innis Taylor.

"We're friends," I remind her.

"Whatever you say."

We spend the next forty minutes in mani-pedi bliss. They coat our nails, and I feel fresh and clean and like maybe this Lyla-fest isn't a bad thing after all. So far it has yielded yummy lunches and a manicure I'd never pay for myself.

Mom leaves a big tip, and we head to the car. It's only then that I reach for my phone and see that it's not from Innis, that Innis hasn't answered in over an hour.

That Innis will probably never answer.

it's jason, i want to see you again

THERE ARE A fixed number of phone calls you can ignore from a best friend, even a former one. For me, apparently, that number is three.

Because when Jason calls for the fourth time that evening,

I can't help myself. "You are relentless."

I shut my bedroom door tight so my mom won't know what's up, sit back on my bed, and wait for him to tell me whatever it is that's so dire.

"Nice to talk to you, too." For a second, I hear his childhood voice. The essence of it hasn't changed that much, only deepened.

"One word from me about you calling incessantly, and all of Bonneville will be up in arms."

"I'm sure they will be, as they will be no matter what I do. Didn't Shakespeare say, 'Guilty for a minute, guilty for life'?"

"I'm pretty sure Shakespeare didn't say that."

"Oh, must've been someone on the internet."

And—Lord help me—I laugh.

He does, too, but instantly I remember the box under my bed. "I'm sure your probation officer or whoever wouldn't be too happy about it, either." My voice comes out half chiding, half serious.

Jason ignores my tone. "I actually met with her yesterday. Nice woman, if a little quiet. Believe it or not, 'Calling Lizzie Grant' was not on a special list of things I'm not allowed to do."

I suddenly feel ridiculous. Of course he's allowed to call me. What Mom and the neighbors think is appropriate and what's legal are two very different things. "Why did you call?"

"Straight to the point. You always were direct, even when we were kids."

"Please don't talk like you know me. You don't anymore."

There's another pause, and this time I can hear him breathing, and I wonder what his face looks like right now, if he's shaved since the other day, if his lips are pulled to a frown.

"And you don't know everything you think you know about me, either," he says finally.

He sounds almost like a character in a movie, with his vague allusions to innocence: *You don't know the whole story! I was framed, I tell ya, framed!*

Is he telling me the truth, or is it just what he thinks I want to hear?

"I know enough." As it comes out, I realize it's exactly what MacKenzie said.

"Listen, I understand why you don't want to be seen with me. And why you don't really like me calling your house. I know you're not going to invite me over for dinner and pretend it's the good old days."

I lie back on the bed, stretch my feet out. "You're catching on. Good job."

"But if you saw the look on my dad's face when I told him I saw you. And then he just kept asking about you, and . . ." He sighs. "Maybe I gave him the wrong impression. Maybe I made it sound like we're still friends."

"What?" I sit back up.

"You did come to see me."

"That was a mistake. And I don't want you blabbing about it."

"I'm not. And I won't. But I kind of told him you'd come over for dinner."

I pick at the skin around my nails, hunting for an excuse.

"You don't have to stay long," he adds. "But he'd love to see you. You can't possibly know how much he would love to see you."

I do know how much, because I want to see him, too. "I don't know."

"Please. For him. My dad never touched Skip." It's the first time I've heard the name come out of his mouth. "He doesn't deserve what happened. Maybe I do. But he doesn't."

And it's true. It's the only thing he's said about that night that I know, without a doubt, is true.

"Come by tomorrow night," he says. "Please."

I'm supposed to be home for dinner with Benny and Lyla tomorrow, but it'll give me an excuse to leave early. "Okay, okay. But I can't stay for dinner. I have plans."

"That's fine. Just say hi. That's all he wants."

"Okay. I'll be there around five. You happy?"

"Very happy," Jason says. "Very, very happy."

INNIS DOESN'T TEXT.

Sadie and Mary Ryan are in hellion mode the next morning, which distracts me for a little while at least. Still, I spend my post-babysitting hours in a haze of Chunky Monkey ice cream and advice pieces on the internet. Survey says that if he doesn't respond within twenty-four hours, he's *definitely* not that into you. A follow-up quiz on the teenybopper site I'm embarrassed to say I still frequent is annoyingly inconclusive. Needing to throw more search terms at my problem, I ask the internet what age you should be when you first have sex, and I get a mix of creepy posts and sad blogs, so I delete my history in case Mom looks later, and I try to focus on other things.

I have no choice but to lie to Mom as I head to Jason's. I tell her I'm going to MacKenzie's, and I promise to be back in time for the all-important family dinner. She tells me how amazing my nails look as I head out the door.

His apartment is just a few miles from the gas station, in a tall, plain complex that rises out of the parking lot like a bump on a cartoon character's head.

I pull out my phone to confirm the address, and see a text from Jason.

excited to see you

Of course, there's nothing from Innis.

I know it's Jason's apartment before I even see the number. The door sports a wreath of creamy magnolias, and there's a mat I recognize from childhood: WELCOME, Y'ALL.

Nostalgia strikes again.

Jason opens the door before I even knock. "You came."

"Were you just standing there waiting for me?"

"I heard shuffling. I was excited. I thought maybe you wouldn't show up." He waves me in. "I'm glad you did."

The apartment is filled with all the things I remember. There's the tufted sofa. The Oriental rug. The pair of Louis the Something chairs that Mr. Sullivan never let us sit in when we were kids.

"Have a seat. I'll get you some tea."

I sink into the couch, still wary of messing up the fancy chairs. I feel like I've stepped back in time, back to before Jason did what he did, before, even, he ditched me. Like if we both stayed here in this room, it would all be okay.

"Lizzie!" Mr. Sullivan rushes up to me. I stand up, and he wraps me in a big hug. "Gosh," he says as he pulls back. "Haven't you just grown up?"

"And you look the same." I laugh. From his perfectly clipped mustache to his bright clothing to his preppy bow tie, he is just the way I remembered him.

"Come on, dinner's almost ready."

"Oh." I nod to Jason for help. I specifically told him I couldn't stay for dinner. "I wasn't really planning on . . ."

"Nonsense," Mr. Sullivan says. I follow him to the kitchen to protest, but I see the table set for three, the nice cloth napkins all laid out. Jason shrugs, a mischievous smile turning up the corners of his mouth.

Mr. Sullivan lifts the lid on the pot, and the smell rushes around me. His famous chili, just for me.

"Wow," I say. "That smells so good."

"Your favorite, right? Jason remembered."

I look at Jason, give him a hint of a smile. "Yes. My favorite."

I END UP staying for dinner.

I'd like to say it's because my mother told me never to refuse something offered to me while a guest in someone's home. I'd like to say that I don't have any loyalty to the boy who hurt all of us so much.

But I can't, because it's not true. I didn't stay because of my manners or the cheddar-topped chili or even the familiar image of Mr. Sullivan's bow tie. I stayed because of Jason, because when he looked at me with eyes wide open and pleading, like all he wanted in the whole world was this tiny scrap of forgiveness, I found I couldn't say no.

I eat a full bowl, and we drink tea and talk about safe things: what I like about school, where I want to go to college, Mr. Sullivan's job at the flower shop just one shopping center down the road, how he still does some decorating in between shifts. We don't talk about juvie. We don't talk about Skip. We don't talk about whether Mrs. Sullivan is still in Connecticut, if she visited him while he was gone.

Jason does everything—gets the cheese, refills the tea, clears the bowls, starts the dishes—and he doesn't do any of it grudgingly, like I've been known to sometimes. Seeing him like this, it is so hard to remember he's a criminal.

When I finally manage to pull myself away from the table, when I've thanked Mr. Sullivan for dinner, refused multiple offers of dessert and promised to stay in touch, Jason walks me to the front door.

"Thank you so much." His hand lands on my shoulder, squeezes ever so softly.

"Jason—" I start, and I don't even know what I'm going to say, but his name feels so natural, it just slides off my tongue.

He interrupts me. "My dad wasn't just saying that. We shouldn't go years again without seeing each other."

I shrug his hand off my shoulder. "It's not that I want to, but it's not that simple."

"You don't trust me," he offers.

I shift my weight, buying time. In the deepest part of my gut, I do trust him. But it's hard to trust those feelings. They're fueled by nostalgia, not reason, by the way he looks at me in this way that says, I know you better than anyone else besides your family, and maybe even better than them. Finally, "No. How can I?"

I shrink away from him, turn and fiddle with the door. After a moment, Jason helps me with the lock.

"I really think you should give me a chance," he says.

I turn back to him, but I don't know what to say. "Tell your dad thanks again for dinner."

I'm already a half hour late by the time I get in the car.

Chapter 8

I SLIP IN THE FRONT DOOR JUST AFTER SEVEN THIRTY, smell turkey tetrazzini, hear Lucy's pitter-patter as she comes to greet me, poking her furry head into the hallway.

"You think they're mad?" I whisper to her.

There's a lot of talking, and I ignore the weight in my stomach, hoping it won't be a huge deal if I grab a plate and pretend to eat for a half hour. As I get closer to the dining room, I hear my mother's voice, in its highest octave of stressed-out and put out. "That *must* be her."

I meet Mom head-on, pushing through the swinging doors almost with bravado. "Sorry I'm late. I hope you saved some for me."

One glance around the table tells me it's not going to be

that easy. Dad and Benny both stare at their plates, while Lyla and Mom look straight at me like cats ready to pounce.

Mom goes first. "Where have you been?"

Lyla crosses her arms in front of her and juts out her bottom lip, looking like she did as a kid, telling me I couldn't have a square of her bubble gum. I curse myself for staying so long. We have to go to her dress fitting tomorrow, and Lyla never stews for fewer than twenty-four hours. Benny wraps his arm around her, gives her an I'm-here-for-you squeeze. She softens, just a little.

"There was traffic." I plop down in my seat, unfold the napkin, and set it on my lap like nothing's the matter. "Sorry."

"No," Mom says, and the rest of them watch her like it's the beginning of a presidential debate. "Where have you *been?*"

"I told you. I was with MacKenzie."

Mom throws her napkin down on the table. "Damn it, Elizabeth, don't lie to me."

"I'm not."

She looks at Dad, like, somehow, this whole thing is his fault, and if he doesn't *do something* about it, all hell is going to break loose.

I feel Lucy's warm body lying across my feet, like even she knows I need the support.

"Elizabeth." He summons the deepest, most scary dad voice he can manage. "Please tell us where you've been."

"I said—"

Mom's so frantic she knocks over her water glass. Benny

jumps up to stop it, but she doesn't even give him a glance. "I saw MacKenzie walking Rocky an *hour* ago. I asked her where you were, and she just shrugged."

Craaaaap. I should never use MacKenzie as an excuse. She's too close.

My eyes flit around the table. Dad is helping Benny sop up the mess. Lyla's nostrils are flaring.

"Why is everyone so mad? It's just dinner."

Mom drums her fingers against the table, waiting.

"I was with Veronica."

"Stop it, you were not."

She must know, I realize. Or else she wouldn't be half so mad. Is she upset because she's worried about me, or is she worried about what everyone will think?

"Come to the kitchen," Mom says, her voice cold and demanding. Underneath the table, I hear Lucy give a little whimper.

"Why?"

"We need to talk."

"Why can't we talk here?"

Mom nods to the other side of the table at Benny. He's back to comforting Lyla.

"He's supposed to be part of our family," I say.

Mom bursts out of her chair, walks over to mine, and grabs my arm so hard I have no choice but to follow her.

"Genevieve!" Dad says. "Come on."

But she ignores him, and by the time we're in the kitchen, I know that this is not about my safety. It's not even about

Lyla's feelings. It's about her social standing in this town, what Benny might tell the very parents she gossiped about yesterday afternoon. For her, that's something worth fighting for.

"I heard you on the phone," she whispers. "Dad said Lizzie. No one calls you Lizzie anymore."

I take a step away from her, cross my arms.

"I've seen him over here, lurking around," she says.

"It's his *house*. You can't lurk at your own house."

"Keep quiet. Did you go to see him?"

"See who?"

She clears her throat. "Did you?"

"Geez, you can't even say his name."

"Jason!" Her whisper is somehow high-pitched, her neck muscles strained.

"You're crazy." I turn around without saying another word, blow through the kitchen door, and stomp up to my room.

But I know leaving is the only answer she needs.

MOM AND I don't talk the next morning—I dash off to baby-sitting without so much of a glance her way—but after I've made myself lunch, after she's meticulously done her hair, when we're in the car together on the way to the fitting and the silence buzzes between us, she goes first.

"You know before I met your father, I dated other guys."

"Uh, duh," I say. "It wasn't nineteen fifty."

"Attitude, Liz," she says.

"Sorry."

She turns into the parking lot for the bridal shop, driving about three miles an hour as she always does in parking lots. "I just mean I've dated bad boys before. I think half the appeal was just that they weren't right for me, that I knew they'd piss my mother off."

It takes a second for me to realize she's talking about Jason. Do I *want* to date Jason? Of course not. But in her motherly brilliance, does she know me better than I do?

"I'm not *dating* Jason," I say, as much to myself as to her. "And I don't want to. I went over there to see his dad."

"Why?" She asks this with genuine curiosity.

"They used to be a big part of our lives, remember?"

Mom sighs as she pulls into a spot. "I know everything that happened with them has been hard on you, and I'm sorry about that. But Jason is dangerous. Look at Skip."

Sullivan allegedly punched, pushed, and held Taylor over a bonfire in the backyard.

My skin crawls as I think of it. What would it take, what kind of person would you have to be, to do something so sick?

Mom turns the car off, folds her hands in her lap. "I want you to promise me you won't see him anymore."

"*Mom.*"

"Liz." She turns to me, and her voice is calm. "I don't ask a lot, but I'm asking this. Promise me."

Maybe it's the evenness in her voice, a polar shift from her tone last night. Or maybe it's the box under my bed, the words themselves a kind of fire that destroys everything in its path.

But I hold her gaze, and I think I actually mean it when I say it. "Okay. I promise."

THE BRIDAL SHOP is small, a lot of swanky packed into a tiny space. Lyla and Erica are already inside, charming the hell out of the shop lady. Erica's been Lyla's best friend since forever, and I'm pretty sure Lyla really wanted to have her as her maid of honor, but, you know . . . sister code.

Lyla rushes to Mom and gives her a big hug. "I wasn't sure if you guys were going to make it." She glances at me, her eyes icy little darts.

"Don't look at me. I'm not the one who decided to straighten my hair."

Mom bashfully runs her fingers along the edge of her perfectly straight bob. "I hope we're not too late."

Lyla dismisses Mom's words with a flick of her hand. Apparently if it's not my fault, then it's no problem.

"Good," Mom says. She puts a hand on my shoulder. "Jackie, this is Liz. Liz, this is Mrs. Barton."

The woman is old and Southern as can be, with curled hair, pale pink lipstick, and peach foundation caked over every wrinkle.

"Nice to meet you." I reach out my hand, and she takes it, her knobby knuckles and expensive rings digging in ever so slightly. It's the Goldilocks of handshakes, not too strong, not too soft.

"You, as well. Have you seen the bridesmaid dresses yet?"

"I haven't even seen the wedding dress," I say. "I can't wait."

"Can you save your sarcasm?" Lyla snaps.

I turn to her in shock. "I was being serious."

Lyla rolls her eyes. I went to the first three dress shops happily, spent about nine hours of a Saturday bouncing around. But the one day I bow out is the day that Lyla finds "the one." Erica was there, of course, and I swear Lyla's going to hold that against me forever.

Mrs. Barton ushers us towards her, without missing a beat. We follow her down a hallway that leads to the back fitting rooms, Mom's heels clicking against the hardwood floors.

"Are you excited?" I ask Lyla.

"I've seen my own dress before." I'd clock her tone at about thirty-eight degrees, cold but not freezing. She zips through the pale linen curtain before I can say another word.

"It's gorgeous," Erica says to me, trying to ease the tension. "Totally Lyla."

I follow them through the curtain and immediately see the loveliest dress in the world hanging on the door. Strapless, with about a million beads on the bodice, but somehow not too many. A silky wisp of a skirt that goes all the way to the floor and poufs out ever so slightly. Mrs. Barton turns the hanger around, holding it delicately, like the dress is a homemade pie, or a giggling baby, perfect but fragile all the same. A line of silk-covered buttons runs down the back, turning into more wisps of fabric that make the train.

"Wow." I take a step forward.

"Don't touch," Lyla says.

"It's perfect, Lyla," Mom says, even though she's seen it before. "Liz, isn't it perfect?"

"It is." I smile at Lyla, but she looks away. Screw you, Lyla.

I don't notice the dress hanging on the next door until Mrs. Barton takes my arm in hers, leading me over. "This, dear, is yours."

And I gotta hand it to Lyla, the girl has taste. It's a rich navy, deeper than the baby blue she mentioned, with thin straps and a neckline that's low enough to look good but not so low that it will terrify Mom. It's fitted through the waist and flares out in a flurry of soft pleats. It's not floor-length, thank God, and it looks like it was made for dancing.

"What do you think?" Mrs. Barton asks me.

Mom smiles at me, her eyes eager.

I glance to the dress on Erica's door, see the baby blue I feared. Lyla changed the color just for me. "It's beautiful. Thanks, Lyla."

She ignores me.

Mrs. Barton gives me a nudge. "Try it on."

"Try not to mess it up," Lyla calls, as I head into the fitting room.

As soon as I shut the door, I hear a rush of strained whispers that could only be about me. Then the door next to mine opens and I see silk and Lyla's bare feet through the space under the door.

I take off my clothes and pull the dress over my head. It's very loose, but Mom said that's how it's supposed to be, that Mrs. Barton will adjust it to fit me "like a glove." I pull the side zipper, step out into the open.

Mom's eyes light up and get instantly watery. "Oh, Liz."

"Looking good, lady," Erica says. "That color is perfect on you." I feel kind of bad for Erica and the other bridesmaids, stuck in that god-awful baby blue.

"Very nice," Mrs. Barton says. "Come this way."

She leads us to another room with three stools, pedestal-like, in the middle. I take the side one, and Erica takes the other. We both know my sister well enough to leave the spotlight for her.

"Amy," Mrs. Barton calls into the next room. In seconds, a much younger woman with jet-black, asymmetrically cut hair comes out and smiles at me, a few pins stuck between her teeth. She proceeds to pinch every bit of me, pinning her way around my dress.

Lyla comes out then, and God does she look amazing. Mrs. Barton leads her to her pedestal, and Mom begins a rather steady stream of tears, only breaking to take pictures, her camera flashing against clouds of tulle and silk.

It hits me then: my big sister is getting married, and to a nice guy, no less.

I catch Lyla's eyes in the big mirror. "Your dress is really awesome."

"Whatever." She's trying to whisper to keep up appearances, but she's not doing a very good job.

"What's wrong?"

Her words come out as a hiss. "You know what's wrong."

"You're upset about last night?"

"Ya think?" She crosses her arms.

"I'm sorry," I whisper. "It was just dinner."

"It was *not* just dinner."

From inside the dressing room, my phone dings, and Lyla humphs, dropping her arms to her sides, nearly whacking Mrs. Barton in the process.

"Who's that?" she demands, her voice louder now. Mrs. Barton looks up. Erica raises her eyebrows, eager for something juicy. If you're going to be Lyla's BFF, you have to develop an appreciation for drama.

"I don't know, Lyla. I'm standing right here."

"If that's—"

"Girls," Mom says, flitting her eyes from Erica to Mrs. Barton and then back to Lyla and me. "Please."

Amy has stopped now, too, and everyone is looking at us on our pedestals.

My phone dings again, and Lyla hikes her dress up and jumps down. "I can't take this. Is that him?"

"I don't know."

"Lyla." Mom's voice is stern. "Mrs. Barton hasn't finished pinning you."

"Can I have five?" she asks, with all the politeness she can muster. Mrs. Barton nods, giving Mom a look that says she's dealt with her fair share of nightmare brides before. She and Amy head to the next room.

As soon as they're gone, Mom turns to us. "What's gotten into you two?"

"Me?" I ask. "What did I do?"

"What did you do?" Lyla asks. "My wedding is *six weeks away*, and you're running around with Jason Sullivan."

"Lyla," Mom says. "Keep it down."

"God, Mom, it's Erica. She already *knows*."

Erica pretends to be fascinated by one of the straps of her dress, and Mom shakes her head. "Still, just keep your voice down." The last thing she wants the shopgirls to hear is that her younger daughter makes a habit of carousing with *bad boys*.

"I'm not *running around* with him. I went over there once. Can you stop crucifying me already?"

Lyla throws her hands up in the air. She's full on crying now. "He ruined my life. He turned Skip into a different person. And you. You . . ." She looks to Erica for backup.

"Maybe not the best idea, Liz," Erica says weakly.

Mom puts her arm around Lyla and glares at me. And I feel so bad, I really do. "I'm sorry. I didn't realize it would mean that much to you."

"How could you not realize?"

"I don't know. I won't do it again." It's the same promise I made in the car, but it means more now, because she's my sister. I'd do anything for her.

She looks at me, the bottom of her eyes smudged with mascara. "You promise?"

"Yes."

Mom wipes Lyla's eyes with a tissue, leads her back to her spot, heads to the front, and in a few minutes, Mrs. Barton and Amy are back, and we're dolls again, being fitted for our dresses.

Lyla smiles at me, like we're perfect sisters.

Like she's totally forgotten about the one who ruined her life.

But I haven't, even if I never see him again. I don't think I ever will.

Chapter 9

I WAIT UNTIL I'M HOME AND SAFE FROM LYLA'S PRY-
ing eyes to check my phone.

There are two texts, one of them from Innis.

My room seems to spin and I let myself fall back onto my
bed, grinning wide and toothy. I read the words over and over
again, drunk on the notion I was wrong.

hey, was on a fishing trip, how are you?

Just a few short words, and Innis Taylor isn't over me.

My hands shake, and I decide not to text him right away.
He left me hanging for four days. I should wait at least a few
minutes. MacKenzie picks up on the second ring.

"Girl, I was just about to call you."

"I have news," I say.

"Me, too. You first, though."

"Okay," I say. "I don't think Innis hates me."

"Duh."

"I mean, he finally texted me back."

"I told you he would."

I sigh, immediately steeling myself, preparing. "It doesn't mean anything for sure, of course. It still took him a long time. And he could still be into Alexis."

"Trust in your fabulousness," she says.

I laugh. "I'll try . . . it's good though, right? He wouldn't have texted if he wasn't interested at all?" I grip the phone, waiting for her answer, for judgment from on high.

"Relax," she says. "All you have to do is relax."

"Okay." I breathe deeply. Good things can happen, I tell myself. Innis Taylor, the boy I've had my eyes on for months, might just like me back. Why is it so hard to believe?

"So what's your news?" I ask.

There's a patter of steps and then the shutting of a door.

"Okay," she says. "We went to the movies last night, and afterwards, we were driving, and we went over to that spot near the woods, the one I told you about? With the good views?"

"Uh-huh."

Her voice is a river, rushing fast and full of promise. "And, well, we stopped, and we were messing around as usual, and then, I don't know, it just felt different, I guess, and, well—I better just spit it out . . ." She pauses for effect. "We had sex."

"Wow." I stifle a gasp and calm the heavy weight in

my stomach. I knew they'd been fooling around a lot, and MacKenzie's so easygoing about the idea of sex, but it's still big news. "What was it like?"

"It was fun!" she says.

"Really?"

"Yeah. I mean, it did hurt. Kind of a lot. I don't know, maybe Payton is specially endowed or something . . ."

"Okay, okay," I say. "No measurements, please."

She giggles. "It definitely wasn't as life-altering as you seem to think it's going to be. It wasn't any different than hooking up, only a little more *involved*, I guess. And everyone says it gets *way better* the second time."

"And you don't feel . . . different?" I ask. I imagine the bottom half of her lighting up, fluorescent arrows pointing to the zipper on her skinny jeans. A sign above reading: "Payton Was Here."

"It's not major surgery," she laughs. "I mean, I guess I feel a little different. Like now I understand what everyone's going on about, but not that different than anything else you do for the first time."

I hold the phone closer. "Really?"

"I'm telling you, it's not that big of a deal. Basically, I really want to do it again."

I laugh. "So you're happy you did it, then?"

"*Am* I?" she says. "He's been texting me nonstop. *Pro move* on my part. And like I said, it can only go up from here." She pauses to let the joke sink in. "Literally."

I feel strangely prudish, because when it happens for me,

I want it to be more than a "pro move." With my proper boyfriend and my proper first love. I want it to *mean something*. Is that ridiculous and old-fashioned, or is it just me?

"Oh," she says. "I forgot why I was going to call you."

"That wasn't enough?"

"The other reason. Say you're around tonight. It's all part of the plan." There's a palpable glee in her voice. She's probably already orchestrating the loss of my virginity in Innis's basement, after which we can all live happily ever after, smiling and sexually knowledgeable, ready for the Perfect Senior Year.

"I'm around."

"Perfect," she says. "Perfect, perfect, perfect. Innis is going to be at a party tonight with Payton and Alex and everyone. And we're going."

I hesitate. "If he wanted me there, wouldn't he have asked me? I am *not* being your and Payton's third wheel."

"First of all, it's a party. You're allowed to go even if Innis doesn't ask you. And second of all, you won't be. We'll go together. Innis won't even be expecting you, and then you'll be there, and it will be *magic*." She says the last word with a sigh. She can be surprisingly romantic for a girl who calls her first time a "pro move."

"Or he'll be all, who is this crazy girl, stalking me at parties?"

"You're insane. I'm going to forgive you for that one."

"Fine," I say. "But what do I text Innis?"

"Say you're good and leave it at that. Play it cool. Trust me."

"Okay," I say, because Kenzie really does know best, at least when it comes to this.

"Come over at eight thirty," she says. "We'll tell my parents we're going to see a movie. It's going to be a good night for you."

It's only after I hang up that I remember I had another text.

i had a great time last night.

But I think of Lyla, our agreement, and Innis and the promise of tonight, and I know I'm doing the right thing when I hit Delete.

I GET THE okay to sleep over at MacKenzie's house, so I pack an overnight bag and head there around eight. Her parents accept our plan without question—a late movie followed by milk shakes at the twenty-four-hour diner near the theater, home by one thirty.

We wear baggy zip-up hoodies borrowed from her brother, who we've bribed to keep silent with ten bucks towards a new video game, and we wait until we're several blocks away before we roll down the windows, crank up the music, and de-sweatshirt.

My dress is royal blue and just a little sparkly. Kenzie's is a slim black halter that accents all the right places. We both leave our flip-flops on. Kenzie and I are united in our dislike of heels. Plus, she's so tall that if she wears them, she'd have a good two inches on Payton.

Kenzie has the address plugged into her phone, the GPS

lady raising her voice over the pop music Kenzie listens to nonstop.

We're almost there when I hear a direction I wasn't expecting.

"Turn right in point two miles."

As Kenzie makes the turn, I feel myself tense up. "What street are we going to?"

"I don't know," MacKenzie says. "Fontaine-something."

"Fontainebleu Court?"

"Sounds right."

I pick at the skin on my thumb.

"What is it?" she asks. "Why all the doom and gloom? Are you freaking out about Innis again? *Relax*."

I shake my head. "It's not Innis. It's just that Fontainebleu Court is Veronica's street."

My words hang in the air. We have a rule—don't bring up Veronica—but MacKenzie hasn't exactly been respecting that lately.

"You know she didn't actually call you a slut," I say.

"Oh, thanks, Liz. I feel so much better."

"In point one miles, turn left onto Fontainebleu Court."

MacKenzie makes the turn, but I don't let it drop.

"And she did have a right to be mad," I say. "I mean, you kind of stole me from her."

"What are you, one of her possessions? I didn't steal you. I started hanging out with you. So I didn't invite her to every single little thing? So what? Are you guys, like, a package deal?"

MacKenzie drives past a line of parked cars and I see a light on in Veronica's room, the one above the garage with dormer windows that were particularly good for spying on her cute, popular, and wholly unattainable neighbor, Pip McKibben.

"The party's at Pip's?" I ask.

"Yeah, I thought I told you that."

"I don't know. Maybe I wasn't listening."

MacKenzie pulls the car over about three houses down, where there's room to park. She turns the engine off. "What, you wouldn't have come if you'd known it's in Veronica territory? You need to chill out about this whole issue," she says.

I cross my arms. "Veronica's not an issue. She's my friend."

"So hang out with her," MacKenzie says, her voice raised. "I'm not stopping you. Go over there right now, for all I care. I tried to give you the chance to spend time with Innis. Sorry that it happens to be next to the house of one of your friends who also happens to hate me. And I'm the one in the wrong here, right?"

"MacKenzie," I say, but before I can do anything, she hops out of the car, slamming the door behind her.

I follow, but she's moving as fast as she can on her über-long legs.

Loud, bass-y music pumps as I approach the lawn. I'm close enough to see Payton come out of the house, plant a juicy kiss on MacKenzie's mouth. The two disappear inside.

When I get to the lawn, I feel more out of place than I ever have in my life. I look again at Veronica's house. On a

Friday night in another world, we'd have gone to the movies—anything would do: bad action, romcom, whatever—and we'd be in her room now flipping through magazines and talking about our crushes.

Two junior cheerleaders breeze past me without a glance, a lacrosse player trailing behind.

I pull out my phone and try to look appropriately occupied. The last text I sent was to Innis Taylor: *good*. And now I'm here, ready to throw myself at him, sparkly dress and all. My only real friend left is mad at me, probably already having sex with her soon-to-be boyfriend.

No one ever asks you if you want to be popular. There's no door one, two, or three. No ask the audience for help. If you see your chance, you take it. When MacKenzie moved here at the beginning of junior year, she spent a good few months pretending to be content to eat lunch with just me and Veronica, but after Christmas break, she insisted we move to a more centralized cafeteria table, despite Veronica's protests. And because she's her fabulous self ("MacKenzie with a capital *K*"), the popular kids actually took notice. A couple months later, I was trading my ritual Friday night movies for lacrosse parties.

It's not that I didn't feel bad about what happened, but I guess I never felt bad enough to fix it. Is that how Jason felt when he ditched me?

Veronica's info is still in my phone. I pull up the contact, start a new message.

i'm weirdly right next to your house, want to hang out?

I delete it, letter by letter. It's too much, too presumptuous. Instead, my fingers tap out the only words that could possibly be worth anything.

i'm so sorry

My thumb hovers over the Send button, and I think I'm almost about to do it, when I feel a tap on my shoulder.

I turn to see Marisa behind me, a small bottle of Goldschläger in one hand, Alex right behind her. "I didn't know you were going to be here!" She gives me a big hug, something I don't think she's ever done before.

"Hey, Liz," Alex says, wrapping his arm back around Marisa as soon as she's free from our hug.

"Well, here I am," I say awkwardly. "Surprise!"

They both laugh, and Alex squeezes Marisa's shoulder. Apparently the two of them are on-again.

"You want to go inside?" she asks. "I need something to wash this down."

I follow them to a slightly less crowded corner of the living room. She sends Alex off to the kitchen, in search of beer and mixers.

"Let's not wait for him." Marisa pops the cap off and takes a swig, then hands it to me.

"I've actually never had this before." I run my fingers along the bottle's shimmery seal.

"Really?" she asks. "It's like drinking jewelry!"

I laugh to myself, but I take a sip. It burns all the way down.

She grabs the bottle back from me, takes another swig,

then screws the cap on, and holds it to her chest like it's something precious.

"So Alex told me that Alexis was a total bitch to you at Walmart."

"He did?" I ask, shocked. Not only am I surprised that Alex cares enough to pass that info along, but I would have expected Marisa to take Alexis's side. I always thought the other girls at Innis's hangouts were in cahoots together, that I was the odd one out. But now it's like Marisa is buddying up to me.

"She's just mad because she knows she's not going to have a spot at homecoming."

"Huh?"

Marisa looks around, doesn't see Alex, uncaps again. She takes a sip and passes it to me. I follow her lead. "Are you telling me you don't know about homecoming?"

I hand the bottle back to her. "What, do you guys all get a limo together or something?"

Marisa smiles at me like I'm a fresh-faced young pupil. "Wow, you must really like him," she says.

I feel myself blush. Either that or the Goldschläger's catching up.

"All right, so yes, for everyone else, homecoming and prom are just dances. But for Innis, it's this huge production. We all go over to his house, and there's a whole formal luncheon, like something you'd see in a movie, and then Mrs. Taylor literally has the head stylist from Tresses over to do all the girls' hair and makeup. And everyone's parents come over, and we take loads of pictures, and then we all go out somewhere awesome, and there's a stretch Hummer or Escalade or whatever, and the Taylors pay for the whole thing."

She pauses for breath—and another sip of Goldschläger.

"But what does that have to do with Alexis and me?" I ask.

"So here's the thing. Alexis and Innis haven't been officially together since freshman year, but they've never seriously dated anyone else. So he always takes her to dances as a friend, even if he's hooking up with someone else at the time. It's kind of sweet, in a weird way."

I steady myself on the wall. The booze is catching up. "But it's not like he's made any kind of homecoming promise to me. It's months away."

Marisa smiles. "Sure it is. And maybe he won't take you," she says. "Who knows? Maybe Alex will start driving me nuts again, and I won't get to go, either. But the point is, she sees you with Innis, and she knows you guys have been hanging out, and she kind of feels replaced."

"So you don't actually think he'll take me?" I ask.

She beams. "The thing is, we kind of do think that Innis will take you. I mean, he never hangs out with girls this long. We're happy he's with you."

I'm slightly weirded out by the fact that a committee of girls is sizing me up, that Marisa's using the royal "we" like Queen freaking Elizabeth. And yet I suddenly feel so accepted, like I never have before. There's a chance I could boot out Alexis Clairemont, probably the most popular girl in the whole school, from her coveted spot in the stretch Hummer. If that doesn't make me feel validated, I don't know what would.

Ever since the week after our first kiss, I've thought of Innis as this huge challenge, but I never really thought about the other side, about everything that could come with him. How instantly my status would change.

Alex walks back then, a jug of orange juice in one hand, two open beers in the other.

And behind him is the person I want to see more than anyone right now.

Innis.

Chapter 10

Innis is wearing a white T-shirt, coral shorts, and leather boat shoes. His eyes are friendly, and he says, "Hey, Liz," like he didn't just avoid me for days. Like he's been standing here waiting for me the whole time.

Alex hands me my beer, and I take it gratefully. "Hi."

Innis steps closer, so close, in fact, that I can feel heat emanating from his body, smell the hint of cigarette on his breath. Unlike Jason, Innis only smokes when he's drinking. It's still not my cup of tea, but it's more acceptable to me, somehow.

"I didn't know you were coming," he says.

I tip my beer back, take a sip. "You didn't ask me." It comes out so bold it surprises me.

But he just smiles and says: "I know. I should have."

Out of the corner of my eye, I see Marisa step aside, pulling Alex with her, leaving us alone. "How was fishing?" I ask.

His eyes light up like shiny river rocks, but he doesn't answer.

"I like your dress."

Before I can stop myself, I yank the hem down. If I were really bold, as smooth as I imagine myself when I replay conversations in my head, I'd wave my hand and say, *I wore it for you*, or, *And what are you gonna do about it?* I'd reach into his pocket and grab his pack of cigarettes and balance one on my lips and ask for a light. Not for the smoke—*gross*—but to look like Lauren Bacall in *To Have and Have Not*, Mom's all-time favorite movie. *You know how to whistle, don't you, Steve? You just put your lips together and . . . blow.*

But I don't do anything that cool. I just say thanks.

"Come with me," he says. "I need another beer."

It's even more crowded as we push our way to the kitchen. The Lords and Ladies of East Bonneville High fist pump and nod at us as we walk by: Mary Burke, head cheerleader. Luke Brown, basketball giant. Ainsley Landry, senior student body president who's on the softball team with MacKenzie. Erich Moon, a fellow one time plebeian who realized he's funny enough to make it in the cool crowd, standing on an ottoman and regaling the others with an especially weird face—their dedicated court jester.

Innis ignores everyone, dragging me into the kitchen, where it's only us and a few empty coolers.

"Looks pretty beerless," I say, immediately cursing myself for my corniness. It's a dadism if I ever heard one. *Ten-four. We've got a beer shortage. The kitchen is beerless. I repeat, the kitchen is beerless.*

"Don't worry," Innis says. He whips open the fridge. Inside is another case of cheap stuff. He grabs two and hands one to me.

I finish the one I'm holding quickly, the cold fizziness rushing to my head. Innis leans on the counter, and I sink back against the fridge.

"I really didn't expect to see you here," he says again.

I mess with the strap of my dress. "Why not?"

"I didn't know you'd even know about it."

"MacKenzie asked me," I say, wondering, briefly, if she's still mad.

He nods. "She and Payton are getting pretty serious, I guess." His tone is flat and unreadable. Either subtle approval or bro-y protectiveness. Or he's just too cool to care.

Maybe it's the adrenaline from my fight with MacKenzie, or maybe it's all the nice things Marisa said, how hopeful she made me feel. Or maybe it's just the cocktail of Goldschläger and beer, winding its way through my bloodstream. Whatever it is, I channel all the moxie I've got and look him straight in the eyes, finally ready to speak my mind. "You know, you're not exactly making me feel welcome." I take another sip—okay, a gulp this time—and relish my boldness.

"That's not it," he says.

"And I'm not about to sit around waiting on invites from

you. They don't ever seem to come."

Innis sets his beer down and steps closer. "I deserve that." His voice is so soft and kind and intimate, I find myself holding my breath, waiting to wake up.

But I force myself to focus, to say what I want to say. "Uh, yeah, you do. You basically tell your ex you only saw me accidentally. Then you don't text me for days. You leave me thinking that . . ."

"That I'm a dick."

"Well, I wasn't going to say that exactly—"

"That I don't care, then?" He's so close now I can feel his breath on my lips. Mine begin to tremble.

"Yeah." I look down for relief. "That's what I thought."

He cups my face in his hands and tilts it up to his. "I like you."

If my stomach were a gymnast, it would medal in the Olympics. Because these are not the words I expect from Innis. They're contrary to every fiber of his being.

He lets his hands fall but he doesn't step back, doesn't give me the room I both crave and despise. "With Alexis," he says, but then he stops himself. "Sorry, I'm sure you don't want to hear about Alexis."

"No, I don't."

"The thing is, I haven't liked anyone in a really long time. And I already had the fishing thing planned with my grandpa, and I thought maybe if we didn't talk for a few days, it would go back to normal."

"What is normal?" I ask. "Buying beer and watching you play video games?"

He shrugs. "Sure."

"Sorry to ruin your plans."

"Hey." He reaches his palms to my cheeks again. "You didn't ruin anything."

Then he leans in and touches his lips to mine, and it's soft and sweet, with a question mark at the end. My blood pumps quicker, and I'm kissing him back, fast and furious, like our lives depend on it. My hands are all over him, and I want him, just as much as he wants me.

And whatever the question is, the answer is yes.

EVENTUALLY, WE MAKE our way out of the kitchen, moving hand in hand through the crowd. I pass MacKenzie and Payton in the living room, and she looks so happy to see me with Innis, and I'm so happy to be with Innis, that all we do is smile at each other, like the argument never even happened. "Good luck," she mouths, and I just smile wider in return.

We're almost to the stairs that lead up to who knows what, when we pass Skip, standing on the hall table, leaning one hand on the wall and singing into a beer-can mike with the other, belting out lyrics in a drunken stupor.

In a parallel universe, he'd be poring over reception menus with my sister, getting fitted for a tux, not standing here, humiliating himself at a party he's way too old for.

Innis stops, standing there, lips pressed tight, taking it in. I'm about to ask him if Skip's okay when one of the rising juniors, a lanky guy whose name I can't remember, turns to his friend. "What a loser."

My hand instinctively reaches for Innis's arm, but I can't stop him. Before Skip can get to the next line, he's got the guy by the collar, up against the wall.

"What the hell did you say?"

The guy shoots off a string of apologies I know won't do a thing.

Innis hits him once, quick to the gut, and the breath goes out of him as he melts against the wall like a Popsicle in summer.

The crowd rushes around, but I grab Innis, pull him to me, and catch the slightest mist of tears in his eyes. I wrap my arms around him and hug him tight, but he wiggles away, looks at me with a face so sad I want to do anything I can to make him feel better.

"Come on," I say. "Let's go upstairs."

He nods, and our fingers entwine, and we step through the crowd and head up. I turn back to see the lanky boy and his friend stumble away.

We walk down the hallway, covered with floral wallpaper and looking more wholesome than it should. We stop at a door that's slightly ajar, and he squeezes my hand, pushes the door open.

Inside, there's a half circle of people passing around a bottle of rum. Blake Edgeworth, Innis and Payton's friend from lacrosse, is there, and the two of them exchange a look. Then he stands up, says they should all go smoke, and stumbles out the door, his cronies in tow.

Innis shuts it behind him, and in seconds, we're kissing again. He smells like Downy and cologne and faint cigarettes. His lips are salty with summer sweat.

My hands rake through his hair, tugging at his soft curls, pulling his lips even closer to mine, as his hands move up and down the length of my body, searching and finding.

He is so good, I realize. He cares so much, enough to stop anyone who dares to say a word against his brother. He is so much more than his looks and his money and all the things that everyone else sees.

He pushes against me, and we fall onto the bed, the sheets rumpled from Lord knows what's happened in here already. Our kisses are hard and hungry; his hands mess with my skirt before reaching up underneath.

His fingers brush against my lace underwear, one half of the set I hid from my mother because I felt weird buying it, the one I only bought because MacKenzie told me I should.

I think about stopping, but then MacKenzie's words are with me—"you might even like it"—and there is beer on my tongue, and he is good, so good, and I kiss him harder, because I'm not 100 percent sure now, but I'm not sure I'll ever be.

"Is this okay?" he whispers.

This time, I don't push him away.

THE NEXT MORNING I'm already awake and thinking about last night when MacKenzie's eyes flutter slowly open.

"Hey there, lady. I think someone's got a story to tell." She smiles groggily. Sunbeams peak through the blinds, and she looks like my guardian angel, sent to teach me the ways of boys and parties.

I bite my lip. "How do you know?"

"I saw you guys walk upstairs. I was sober, remember? I had to drive your booty-getting booty home."

I gulp down the glass of water MacKenzie benevolently left on the nightstand. Even though she force-fed me water last night, I still have a headache.

"So . . . ?" she asks.

"You want details?"

MacKenzie shakes her head. "Just a basic understanding."

My skin gets all hot and tingly as I think about what we did. "It wasn't anything huge, okay? But a little more than before."

"Did he finger you?"

"Shh," I snap. "Your parents are going to hear!"

"Oh, stop worrying. You need to relax. Amirite?"

The look on my face must say yes, because MacKenzie claps.

"And? Was it as awful as you feared?"

I shake my head. It was exciting, heart-pounding, and completely unlike anything else. I wasn't really sure how long it was supposed to take, and eventually, I just pulled his hand away and we made out for a little bit more. I rejiggered my dress, and we went back downstairs.

"It was good," I say. "But we didn't have sex."

She laughs. "You implied that much."

As excited as I am, it feels like Innis has a part of me, a tiny part that no one else has.

And I don't quite know what he's going to do with it.

Chapter 11

My phone buzzes as I walk back from MacKen-
zie's. My heart beats against my rib cage, because I want so
badly for it to be Innis. *I still like you as much as before. I have
not spent the morning carving a half notch into my bedpost.*

It's not.

> you ignoring me?

I type back furiously.

> what do you want?

I can see Jason typing. Whatever he wants, I can't give it.
He stops, then starts again.

> to be your friend

Part of me wants to be all that we were to each other. But

I can't. Not after the promises I made to Mom and Lyla. Not after last night with Innis.

I type the words quickly.

sorry i can't

It's not until I'm back in my house, in my room, lying on my bed and replaying the night before, worrying that Innis won't text, that my phone buzzes again. I pick it up, ready to tell Jason no.

As soon as I see the message, I feel warm all over and alive as hell. Because it's not Jason, it's Innis.

dinner tonight? on me?

I look at the clock, my fingers already antsy, because in five minutes, I know I'm going to text Innis back and say yes.

INNIS SAID HE'D pick me up at seven, and Lyla gets off work at four on Saturdays, so that gives me just enough time to go over there and make peace with her. She looks surprised when she answers the door.

"Liz." Her eyes flit to a deep lilac potted orchid in my hands, an expensive little olive branch. "You shouldn't have."

Except I should have. If I want Lyla to forget about everything, I *really* should have. Lyla loves grand gestures and hates cheap flowers. Luckily Mom floated me some money to help heal our sisterly rift, otherwise it would have equaled two hours of babysitting.

"Sit down." She gestures to an off-white overstuffed sofa. "I'll make some tea."

"Is Benny here?" I plop down. Everything matches, from the pillows to the walls to the ribbon holding up the engagement photo she's already gotten framed.

"He's playing racquetball," she calls from the kitchen.

My hope deflates a little. Lyla's on her best behavior when Benny's around, which isn't really that good, but I'll take what I can get.

She returns with two steaming cups, and I jump right in. "I want to talk about yesterday."

Lyla's pasted-on smile instantly goes flat. "It's over," she says. "Let's just not."

I take a sip, and it scalds the roof of my mouth. Lyla slips a coaster beneath it before I can put it down.

"I want to explain."

"What's there to explain? You said you weren't going to see him anymore."

"And I'm not."

"So what, then?"

I know her tricks. Lyla *says* she doesn't want to talk about it, but all that means is she doesn't want to talk about it with me. Without a doubt, she spent two hours talking about everything with Erica yesterday.

"I just want you to know, what he did to Skip was horrible, and I get why you're mad. But you know he was my best friend. And maybe they weren't to you, but the Sullivans were like second parents to me. I wanted to see his dad again—that's it."

Lyla huffs. "I hope it was worth it."

"Lyla," I snap, "I didn't screw your fiancé or spill red wine on your wedding dress. I went to see an old friend. It doesn't make me a horrible person."

She shakes her head and crosses her arms. "You know I thought I was going to marry Skip?"

"Every girl thinks she's going to marry her high school sweetheart."

"This was different." Her voice cracks, and her eyes get glossy. "We loved each other. It wasn't just about high school. We had plans. We were going to go to D.C. or Atlanta and really do something with our lives. He was going to be a model."

"Well, then why didn't you?" I ask. "It's not like he was freaking paralyzed. People get past way worse than that. Not everyone can be a model, anyway."

"God, Liz, is that what you think of me?" Her eyes properly tear up now, and her hands reach to dry her face. "That I broke it off because he didn't look perfect anymore? I wanted to be with him. I tried. It wasn't just his face, it was everything. He was so angry, and he didn't want to see me, he didn't want to touch me or kiss me, and he sure didn't want me to touch him. He broke up with *me*."

"What?" I ask, before I can stop myself. "Really?"

"Yes, really," she yells. "Don't you remember? I could barely get out of bed and go to school. I should have been thinking about college and spending every weekend with Skip. I was a mess."

I do remember. I remember her tears, her fights with my

mother. I remember terse phone calls and the visits to the hospital. And then I remember one night when Lyla wouldn't come down for dinner, and Mom, who's strict about things like that, telling me to leave her. That she and Skip had broken up. After that, we didn't say his name in the house.

And in my idiocy or naivety or jealousy of Lyla's utter perfectness, I assumed she'd been the one to make the choice. Because, Lord, it's hard to imagine someone making it for her.

"I thought you were upset." I run my finger around the rim of the teacup, avoiding Lyla's eyes. "I didn't think—"

"You thought I was shallow enough to end it with the love of my life because he got hurt?"

"I'm sorry," I say. "I didn't know."

She stands up and gets a tissue and wipes her tears. It leaves mascara trails underneath her eyes. "Well, now you do. Now do you understand why I'd be upset?"

I nod. "I'm sorry, Lyla. I really am so sorry."

That's when Benny walks in, with a chipper hello. He's dripping with sweat and wearing a cheesy exercise headband. He looks ridiculous in that way that makes everyone warm up to him instantly.

Lyla quickly rearranges her face. "Hey, baby." Her voice is as sweet and smooth as whipped butter. I think of the song that always comes on Dad's oldies station, "Love the One You're With." Suddenly, I wonder if Benny is just her fallback, if even after everything, Skip's the one she'd be with if she had the choice.

"I should probably go." I stand up.

She looks at Benny, then looks at me. "Yeah. You probably should."

DAD'S IN FULL Dad Mode that evening, his face stern as he opens the door for Innis.

Innis wears a button-down lavender shirt over jeans. His face is freshly shaven and his curly hair is rocking the slightest bit of gel.

"Hello, Mr. Grant." He shakes my dad's hand.

"Nice to see you, Innis," Dad says, and I can tell by his tone of voice that Innis used just the right amount of firmness. Dad cares about things like that: Not firm enough is weak and ambivalent. Too firm is like you're angry, got something to prove.

Dad ushers him in, and Innis's face breaks into a smile as he looks at me.

"Hi, Liz." His eyes lock on mine. "You look beautiful." I don't even care if it's fake and solely for acquiring the Dad Seal of Approval. Innis has never called me beautiful before.

Mom grins and tucks a bit of hair behind her ears, while Dad proceeds through the list of questions he always used with Lyla's dates: *Where are you going? How long have you been driving? What does punctual mean to you?*

Innis passes with flying colors, and after a kiss on my mother's cheek and a hug from Dad, I'm walking down the front sidewalk and past the elm that Jason and I would use as home base for our more involved games of hide-and-seek.

The summer air kisses my bare legs and shoulders, and my sundress flutters around me just the way I want it to.

I feel pretty and lucky, and I know that things are changing, that this is new.

Innis makes a point of opening the car door for me before he goes to the other side, pulling away slowly while I wave at my parents, but once we're a few blocks down the road, out of sight, out of earshot, he revs it, and we're flying with the windows down, my hair blowing around me, every strand I fussed over getting completely messed up, but I feel so alive it doesn't matter.

"So how'd I do?" His voice is a little bit gruffer, a whole lot more Innis.

"I think you totally charmed them," I say.

He laughs. "Parents tend to like me."

"Where are we going?" I ask.

"You'll see."

WE PARK IN one of the spots downtown, among the rows of perfectly spaced trees and brick sidewalks. Along the street, I recognize a couple of cars.

We get out and walk towards the pizza place on the corner. I spot Marisa and Alex—apparently, they're still on today—standing at the edge of a circle of kids from school.

"Liz!" Marisa says, handing her greasy slice to Alex and rushing up to me, giving me a big hug. Apparently, we're besties now? I scan the crowd for Alexis, but I don't see her anywhere—all for the better.

"Did you guys come to nurse your hangovers, too?" she asks.

"I don't know," I say. I nudge Innis with my elbow. "He's keeping it secret."

Marisa's eyes light up in admiration, but she doesn't have a chance to say anything, because that's when Innis grabs my hand. "We're actually going to Cafe Rouge," he says.

"Seriously?" I ask. My parents only go on special occasions. I didn't even think they let high school kids in.

We say our good-byes and he pushes me towards the door, his hand flat on the small of my back. I feel shivers, cool and jolting, down my spine. I turn my head to see Marisa raising her eyebrows and smiling. Even Alex looks impressed.

"You sure?" I catch his eyes, as he opens the door.

He plays it off like no other guy can, like he took dating lessons from one of those swanky old movie stars. "For you? Nothing less."

People are crowded into the vestibule, waiting for their name to be called. Innis walks right up to the hostess, a tall, skinny girl with gorgeous dark hair and tasteful cleavage. She smiles right at him, ignores another guy trying to catch her attention. I wonder if he thinks she's hot—MacKenzie says guys think about sex a million times a day—but the girl doesn't seem to faze him.

"Innis." She sets down the marker she uses to assign tables. "Good to see you."

"Any way we can get a table for two tonight?" He nods to me.

"Of course." She waves a young guy in a crisp white shirt over. "Enjoy your dinner."

We follow the guy through linen-covered tables to a spot in the back. As soon as we're alone, he's back to regular old Innis. "I don't know crap about French food, but it's the nicest place in Bonneville, and my family knows the owner."

We order safe things: roast chicken and carrots, steak and fries. We pronounce it all wrong, and we laugh at the number of forks, almost as many as in cotillion. There's no way we'd get away with ordering wine, but I feel drunk anyway, on French food and Innis's smiles and how delicious it is to be admired.

"I'm glad we've been hanging out," Innis says, in between bites of steak.

"I'm glad we have, too."

He takes a sip of water. "So you haven't seen Jason again, have you?"

I shake my head instantaneously, even though it's a lie. It's a necessary one, the kind that makes everything a little bit easier for all the right reasons. It's hardly even wrong.

"Good," he says. "And you don't have to worry. I'm not going to go beat him up or anything, even though he deserves it."

"Good," I say. "It's not worth it anyway."

But Innis has this smile on his face, mischievous, like a little kid caught with an empty package of Oreos.

"What?"

He smiles, grabs a fry from my plate, pops it into his mouth.

"What?" I ask again.

He shrugs. "I have my ways."

"What do you mean?"

He casually takes a sip of water. "Nothing huge. Only Payton went to that gas station and keyed his truck."

"Are you serious?" Just like that, the good feeling, the lightness I've had the whole meal is gone.

Innis laughs. "You sure didn't think I wasn't going to do anything, did you?"

"You said you wouldn't go there."

He shrugs. "And I didn't. Payton did."

I set my fork down. "He shouldn't have done that."

Innis's tiny fork drops to his plate with a clang. "Why are *you* defending him?"

"I'm not."

"You are."

I unfold the napkin in my lap, refold it. Take a sip of water.

"Well?" he asks.

My bladder feels full.

"Are you trying to be friends with that prick? I thought you'd be happy, after everything with your sister."

"I'm not friends with him." I scramble for the right words. "I just think you should be careful."

"*He's* the one who should be careful."

I think of Innis just last night, how he punched that junior right in the gut.

"What's your deal with him, anyway? You still carrying a torch from middle school?"

I swallow, but my throat feels suddenly parched, like I can barely speak. "Middle school?"

"Jason always said you had a thing for him. That's why he had to stop hanging out with you."

It still hits like a blow, after all these years. Did I have a thing for him? He was the only boy I knew. When I imagined kissing someone, it was always Jason. I'm not sure if it's because I really liked him, or if he was just there, but I liked him being around.

I remember it so vividly, the moment I realized we were no longer us. It was right at the end of eighth grade. He'd gotten taller by then, sprouted a few hairs on his chin—he was in a leather jacket he'd dug up from his dad's old things and jeans that fit just right, that made him look good, cool. I'd grown, too, but I was still a kid, wholly unaware that best friends were things that could be lost. I was still Lizzie.

He was standing with Innis at the edge of a circle of guys and girls, leaning on a locker.

"Hey," I said, walking up to him.

He barely looked at me. He almost pretended not to notice me.

"Jason," I said.

And then he looked down at me—scratch that—he looked *through* me. "What?" he said, and the others turned then, saw me standing there, slack-jawed, picking at my thumbs, uncomfortable. I bet Innis doesn't even remember that was me.

"What do you want?" Jason's voice was caustic, annoyed.

What did I want then? I wanted us to still be us.

Innis stares at me, waiting for an answer.

"It wasn't like that."

"Then what was it like?"

But I don't have a chance to answer, because the chef comes over then, sidles right up to Innis. "In-*ise*," he says in a thick French accent. "I didn't know you were 'ere."

For a moment, I completely forget about Jason, because it's like watching a congressman at a meet-and-greet, or an ad man from the nineteen sixties. There is a total and complete transformation. It's not like Innis isn't usually sure of himself—he is—but now he seems like a proper adult, making things happen with his drawly voice and ease of conversation. He introduces me to Jacques, and they look at each other like equals. The chef tells him to make sure to tell his father that everything is set for the gala.

It is so clear to me all the things that Innis could be, all the promise he has in him.

It takes a minute after Jacques goes back to the kitchen for me to come back to reality. "So do you just talk to French chefs about upcoming galas on the regular?"

Innis becomes normal Innis again. "*He* calls it a gala," he says. "Because French people are weird. It's just the library fund-raiser."

"I see."

Lyla was dating Skip for two full years before my parents finally went to the Taylors' famous library fund-raiser. Dad complained about the expense for weeks in advance, and Mom said it was shameful that they hadn't gone earlier.

"Everyone who's anyone in Bonneville goes," Mom said about once a day. Dad's probably thanking his lucky stars that Innis and I started hanging out after the tables sold out, sometime back in April.

"So do you actually get to go?" I ask.

Innis rolls his eyes. "My parents insist that me and Skip make an appearance. We usually stuff our faces and go back to the kitchen and drink beers with the caterers—they're the only people who aren't completely uptight."

"Sounds pretty fun to me," I say, grabbing one last fry. It's the kind of thing my mom pines after, and to him, it's nothing.

"You can come if you want," he says.

I nearly choke on my fry. Here I am, hoping he'll even text me back, and now he's taking me to proper dinners and *inviting me to galas.*

"Seriously?" I ask.

He shrugs. "It's on Saturday. I warned you that it's a bore, but if you want to."

"Do I need a dress?" I ask.

Innis nods.

"Wow," I say.

He raises his eyebrows. "Sounds like that's a yes?"

I smile, beside myself. "Sounds like it is."

I HAVE NO beer or liquor to loosen me up tonight, but I don't need it. It's just me and him in the dark of the car, only a few feet down from my house, where the streetlights don't shine.

Our hands wander, and we kiss each other hard, the minutes going by way too fast. Eventually, the clock shines 10:59, and we have no choice but to stop.

"Get yourself home, Liz Grant," Innis says.

"Thanks for dinner," I say.

It's only as I walk up to my house, past Jason's empty driveway, that I remember about his truck. In all the talk of the party, it's like I completely forgot to care.

I feel instantly defensive, like I let something bad happen without doing anything to stop it. If I weren't so worried about Innis liking me, would I have had the guts to tell him that deep down, this is wrong?

I shake my head, pushing it away. It's a small thing. The side of a truck, not the side of someone's face. I focus on the library fund-raiser, all that stretches out before us.

Because the way things are going with Innis, I can't afford those other kind of thoughts anymore.

Chapter 12

On Monday, it's miraculously cool enough for the girls and me to actually enjoy the outdoors. I push Sadie while Mary Ryan pumps, her face bright and full of pride at not having to be pushed. Mild days are rare here, and we're making the most of it. Swing set, big slide, tricycle—repeat.

I'm pulling Sadie out of the baby swing when Mary Ryan hops off, walks up, and taps me on the leg. "Miss Liz," she says.

"Yes?" Sadie grabs onto me tightly. The girl is deathly afraid of falling. I prop her on my hip and hold her close.

"Guess what?"

"What?"

"We saw you on Saturday," she says. And by the look on her face I can tell she's excited.

"You did?" I turn to Sadie, grab a tissue from my pocket. "Did you see me?" I wipe the snot from underneath her nose. She nods. "Well, why didn't you say hi?"

The words spill out of her mouth like a big bucket of LEGOs, clunky and jumbled around. "It was right after dinner, see, you were in the car and Mom said, 'Look at Miss Liz,' and then I said I wanted to stop and say hi, but she said we can't because you were with someone special and then Sadie started giggling for no reason because she's such a baby."

I feel an unexpected sense of pride that Mrs. Ellison has seen me with Innis. "Come on." I hoist Sadie higher on my hip and grab her sippy cup. "Let's go inside."

"But Miss Liz," Mary Ryan says. "Who was the boy?"

Who was the boy? He's the boy whose smile can make me tingly in a matter of seconds. The boy who sticks up for his brother, no matter what. The boy who wants to take me to the biggest Bonneville event of the year. The boy who texted me to tell me he had a great time yesterday—and three more times after that.

The screen door clangs behind us, and Sadie starts screaming. She wants more juice.

"He's a friend." I quickly pour some apple juice into the cup, trying to pacify her.

"A *boy*friend?"

"Maybe." I beam. "Maybe not."

Mary Ryan bursts into giggles, and Sadie finally stops wailing. "Don't you *know*?"

Oh sweetie, I think. No, I do not know. Not for sure. Not yet, at least.

My phone buzzes. I pull it out, and there he is. Innis.

happy monday, pretty lady

My heartbeat quickens, and I don't wait to text him back. Since Saturday, I haven't felt the need to.

;) happy monday to you, too

Mary Ryan is looking at me like I'm the Queen of Sheba. "Is that your boyfriend?" she asks.

"Maybe," I say again.

Maybe, *indeed*.

MOM'S GOT LUNCH set out in the kitchen when I get back. Potato salad, cold cuts, and cucumbers and tomatoes with lots of dill.

"What's the spread for?"

She fiddles with the strings of her half apron. "I thought it would be nice if we had lunch out on the porch. It's only eighty-two out, and there's a breeze."

She looks at me like a lost puppy, waiting for an answer. This funny thing happens to moms, right about when you turn fifteen. They start trying to be your friend.

"Sure."

"Great. Grab a plate. I'll pour the tea."

"Half-and-half, please." During the summer, our house always has two pitchers of tea in the fridge. One sweet and syrupy for Mom—the kind that's led many a Southerner into the throes of obesity—one unsweet for Dad. I like a little of both.

I fill my plate with a slice of ham, lots of cucumbers, and a dollop of Mom's neighborhood-famous potato salad, and head out front, taking a seat on a wicker bench covered with floral pillows. It took Mom four solid months to find pillows in a pattern she liked that you could keep outside. I kick up my feet on the ottoman and pop a cucumber into my mouth, watching as the bugs collect on the wraparound screen, looking for food or a long drink.

Mom pops out, a plate on her arm, a glass of tea in each hand, and forks and napkins tucked into her apron.

"Thanks." I stand up to help her with the tea and grab a fork and napkin out of her pocket.

She takes a seat opposite me and smiles. "Isn't it nice out?"

I glance at the thermometer tacked to the post. "Only here is eighty-two in the shade considered a good thing."

"Only here, only here." She takes a sip. "What do you know about other places? You've only ever lived here." There's this crazy little thing called the internet, I want to say, but I let it drop.

"It does feel nice." I flip the switch of the fan behind me. "Thanks for lunch."

She takes a small bite of potato salad, yellow and thick with eggs and mustard and Duke's mayonnaise, *only* Duke's mayonnaise. "So I want to hear all about your date."

"Mom." I lift a hand to block the sun so I can see her better. "I told you yesterday. It was great."

I have yet to tell her about the library thing. I didn't want to mention it when Dad was around yesterday. The very thought of it still annoys him, and I know he's not going to want to pay for a dress. Mom says that Dad spends money like he's still a broke college student.

Plus, it's the day before Lyla's bridal shower.

Plus, plus, and maybe this is the biggest plus, if I tell Mom, she'll totally freak about it. She'll assume Innis and I are officially dating, that he's coming to the wedding, that he's my proper Boyfriend, capital B. I don't want to jinx it.

"So you're going to be secretive?" She pouts. "Okay, okay."

"I'm not being secretive." I take a sip. "But what else do you want to know? We went out to dinner."

"Only at the nicest spot in town. Was the food good?"

I nod, shoving potato salad into my mouth, and she starts talking about the first time she went to Cafe Rouge with my dad, more than a decade ago. She pauses every now and then to get a juicy detail. Did he open the door for me, what did we talk about, do I think he goes there often?

She's deep into a story about her postcollege trip to Europe, a jaunt through Paris on bikes that she and her girlfriend rented, a restaurant in Montmartre that had roast chicken that practically fell off the bone, when I see Jason Sullivan pull the truck into his driveway, get out, and walk towards the front door. I'm far enough into the shade of the porch that I don't think he can see me, at least not enough to catch my eye, but if Mom turns around, she'll definitely see him. It'll mean a rehashing of all those earlier fights, stern warnings, more questions.

"Liz," Mom says. "Liz?"

"Sorry," I say. "What?"

She adjusts herself like she's ready to turn, follow my gaze.

"Innis invited me to the library fund-raiser," I say.

As I expected, her jaw drops. Then it hangs there for a moment, before she shuts her mouth, pulls herself together. "He *did*?"

I nod, watching as Jason fiddles with the key. Could he go any slower?

"Why didn't you tell me yesterday?"

I shift in my seat. "It's the day before Lyla's bridal shower."

"So?"

"You don't care?"

"Do I care?" she laughs. "Do I care? I certainly would care if you *didn't* go! Oh my goodness, what are we going to do about a dress?"

"We'll figure it out," I say. Jason finally gets the key right and opens the door.

She ticks off her fingers. "Library fund-raiser, Lyla's bridal shower, and the Fourth of July block party . . . you've got yourself a busy weekend ahead!"

"I know, it's all at once." I glance at the house, see that Jason is safely inside, breathe a little easier.

"Oh, I'm so pleased!" She sighs in excited exhaustion, puts her clean plate down, leans back in her chair, and runs her fingers across her bangs. "I'm glad he took you there. And the fund-raiser—the fund-raiser!—it's so wonderful."

My phone dings, and Mom looks at me and smiles. "Is that Innis?"

I pull it out, expecting it to be him.

everything is not what you think

I thank the good Lord that I never saved the number into my phone.

"Is it?" she asks.

"Uh-huh." I nod.

She rocks back in the chair and rests her hands over her stomach, content. "When I was your age, we actually called each other. But I guess I'll have to forgive him for that."

I put the phone back in my pocket, force the words out of my head. I take another bite of potato salad, relish the good things, the not-Jason things.

New dresses. Fancy galas. Innis's sweet words. The excited look on my mother's face. Easy, open, screw-your-vague-secrets things.

The kind of things you're supposed to ponder when you're young and it's summer and you're sipping sweet tea.

MAYBE THE TRUCK was just far enough out of her range of vision, or maybe she was too caught up in gala news to notice, but we manage to get back inside without a word about Jason. Thankfully, she heads straight for the laundry room, where her chances of seeing Jason are low.

As soon as I clean up the dishes, I lock myself in my

room, look at the text message again. Why is he saying this now? What good can it do?

I delete it before I can change my mind. I pull out the article, run my fingers across each line, and read the words again and again, reminding myself that these are facts. *Jason Sullivan pled guilty Monday night to assault inflicting serious bodily injury . . .* They're printed words. Black and white. Etched in town history. As unchangeable as the scars on Skip Taylor's face.

I put the article away, close the box, slide it back under the bed.

But it's no good, because with all my heart I *want* to believe that Jason isn't lying. That there's more to the story than I know.

It would make the world make sense again.

From downstairs, I hear the dryer kick into full gear and Mom's feet on the stairs. She religiously spends the hour the clothes are drying curled up in bed with an embarrassing paperback novel.

I meet her in the hall.

"Going somewhere?" she asks.

"I was thinking about taking Lucy for a walk."

I squeeze past her, but she stops me, holds me tight for a quick second. "Love you."

"Love you, too."

Lucy knows the deal as soon as I get downstairs. She hops off the couch and runs to meet me, panting and pacing until I hook the leash to her harness.

We walk on our usual loop, up past Luke Brown's house, his ultramanicured front yard, with a brick fence, lush azalea bushes, and neatly pruned crape myrtles. At Bradford Court, we turn, Lucy does her business, and we head down the treelined street, past houses with white siding and dark shutters and all the things that are almost too beautiful, that don't allow for any mistakes, don't forgive.

Lucy trots along like she's the queen of the world, and soon, we're at the end of our loop, coming down the sidewalk, almost to Jason's house. She tugs at me to go faster, but I slow down as we walk past the truck, anxious to see what Payton has done. There's a spiderweb of scratches from the driver's door all the way to the tailgate, and in the clear daylight, it seems cruel and unnecessary. This is just a car, I remind myself. Skip is disfigured forever. And yet it doesn't change the queasy feeling in my stomach. I think about Innis last night, how he announced this development so casually, as cool as if he were ordering off the menu: *I'll take auto vandalism to start, please. Heavy on the scratches.*

everything is not what you think

I walk quickly back to my house, open the front door, let Lucy off the leash, and give her a treat. I glance at the clock. Mom will be reading for at least another forty minutes. I slip out the back door, traipse across the grass, around the magnolia tree, and up to his door.

It feels awfully strange, but I reach up, knock.

"Who is it?" Jason says brusquely.

The windows are open, but the blinds are tilted so I can't

see through them. I wait in front of the door like a guest would. "It's Liz."

There's an immediate turn of the doorknob, and then there he is.

"Lizzie."

The weirdest thing happens. Seeing him standing there, smiling at me, it's like his energy is contagious, like all the good things in our past are, for a second, our present.

"Hey."

"Come in." He makes way, and I step onto a sheet of plastic as the smell of paint hits me. It reminds me so much of us being kids. Both the Sullivans loved color—they were always trying out one shade or another.

"I'm sorry," I say. "I didn't know—"

"Don't worry. I need a break anyway."

The cabinets are covered in tape and plastic, and a soulless beige is already on half the kitchen wall. A fan blows the fumes into the next room and through the open windows.

"You decided to paint?" The red kitchen was always my favorite room. Mrs. Sullivan used to say she picked the color so if she got crazy with the pasta sauce or wine, no one would know the difference.

"The realtor says it's hard to sell colorful houses."

"That's a shame."

"Yeah, it is." Then he just stands there, gazing at me, his eyes so wide I think I must have spinach in my teeth or a huge zit on my nose.

"What?"

He shakes his head. "I really didn't think I was going to see you again. Not if you had anything to do with it."

I run my hand along the counter. "So why are you sending me cryptic texts?"

"I have to try, don't I?"

"Why do you have to try?" I look up at him, but he ignores my question.

"It's hot in here." He runs his hand across his brow. "Do you want some water?"

I shrug. "Sure."

I follow him over layers of plastic into the nook behind the counter. He grabs the only two cups in the cabinet and fills them from the tap.

He downs his in a few gulps, but I hardly touch mine. He leans back against the counter, cool and relaxed. His arms are strong, and his eyes are kind. His hair is mussed, half matted down with sweat, the other half flecked with tiny droplets of paint, almost like he's been out in the snow.

I place my hands back on the counter, propping myself up, and all of a sudden I'm telling him about the awful bridal fitting and how I can't see him, even if I wanted to, and I don't even know if I want to, because I've made this promise.

He nods, waits for me to stop. "I know," he says. "But I'm still glad you came over."

"Why?" I ask again.

He lowers his gaze. "You're my best friend."

"No, I'm not. We didn't even hang out before you left. Remember? You wanted nothing to do with me."

"Is that what this is about? Middle school drama?" He steps closer, practically pinning me against the counter. There's no AC in here, and the two of us only seem to make it hotter. "I was thirteen. I wanted to be popular. You do stupid shit when you're thirteen."

I can't tell if I want to laugh more or cry more because "stupid shit" you do when you're young is what got him in this mess in the first place.

"Why did you text me?" I ask again. "What did you mean by it?"

He stands up straighter. "I meant what I said. It's not what you think. The story is not that simple."

"So tell me." I cross my arms. "If there's anything you could say to explain, then tell me. Don't you think I want to hear it?"

He shrugs. "Can't you just believe me? You've known me forever. You know me better than anyone. Can't you trust me now?"

"People change," I say unconvincingly.

"I haven't changed. I'm still me." He steps closer then, just inches from my face, so close that I can almost taste his breath, and his eyes catch mine and my heart beats faster and the bad stuff fades to the background and he is the Jason he always was. And I am Lizzie.

His lips are on mine before I can think to stop them, his mouth open, his tongue soft and velvety. His hands are on my cheeks, and I can feel cool sticky paint on his fingers. Our arms are around each other, and we know each other like we never have before, and all I feel is *want want want*.

And then I realize it, a delayed reaction, like a hand placed on a burner, you don't even feel the pain until you've already been burned, and I pull back, shake my head.

"No." I push him away with both hands. "We can't . . ."

I squeeze away from him, my feet crunching against the plastic, rush out the door before he has a chance to stop me.

Back home, in front of the mirror, I see beige fingerprints all over my cheeks.

And I scrub as hard as I can until my face is clean again.

Chapter 13

MacKenzie clears her throat. "To achieve sex-goddess status, you have to truly master his man bits."

We're stretched out on her lawn in our swimsuits the next afternoon, reading cheesy sex tips from a magazine. MacKenzie's been out here all morning, but I got here a half hour ago, as soon as I finished babysitting and grabbed a snack. I haven't told her about Jason yet. I crafted three texts last night, but I didn't have the guts to send them. In this weird way, the kiss felt inevitable, like a Tetris piece fitting into place. But that doesn't change the fact that it was wrong.

"What does that even mean?" I try to sound humorously critical and not overly naive. It's the first time we've read sex tips together when one of us has actually had sex.

"They give a detailed explanation right here." She pushes the magazine to me. It's detailed, indeed, and very graphic. "Have you actually done stuff like this with Payton?" I can't imagine doing any of the things listed on that page with a straight face. Not with anyone.

"Not exactly," she says. "But anyway we did have sex four more times."

"You're counting?" I adjust the back strap of my swimsuit.

"It's a fun thing to keep track of! It's really awesome once you get the hang of it."

"I'm sure it is." I push the magazine back at her.

Her eyes dart down the page, and I prepare for another ridiculous tidbit, but suddenly she shuts the magazine, tosses it aside. "Is something going on with you? You're acting strange."

I try to assume a normal, innocent face. "I am?"

"Yeah." She rolls her eyes. "You haven't said a single word about your date with Innis. I didn't want to ask, in case it went badly, but I figured you'd volunteer even that, eventually. And you don't even seem to care that Payton and I are having wonderful sexytimes together."

"Sorry. I'm excited for you. I really am. And I texted you yesterday about Innis."

"Yeah, but now we're in person. I want *details*."

I shrug. The excitement of everything, including Mac-Kenzie's boy developments, is muted by the weight of the guilt I have around the kiss. If Jason had just kissed me, it would have been one thing, and all day I've been trying to tell myself that that's how it was. But I know I kissed him back. Just for a second or two, for a *thrilling* second or two, but still.

"It was great. He took me to Cafe Rouge, and we hooked up in the car afterward." I pause for effect. "He even asked me to go to his family's big fund-raiser with him. My mom's giddy with anticipation."

MacKenzie sits up straight and kicks the sprinkler away. "So why are you acting like you totally don't want to talk about it?"

I sit up, too. "How do you know if someone is right for you?"

She laughs. "Innis Taylor is right for anyone."

"I'm serious. How did you know with Payton?"

She shrugs. "I don't know. Why are you getting so philosophical about it? You've never questioned anything before."

I turn to catch her eyes. MacKenzie is my best friend. Lately, MacKenzie is my only friend. If I can't be honest with her, who can I be honest with?

"You promise you won't be judgy?" I ask. "And you'll keep a secret?"

"Uh, duh," MacKenzie says, all smiley now. "Who do you think I am?"

"Okay." I lick my lips, taste salty summer sweat. I go fast, ripping off the Band-Aid. "I've seen Jason a few times."

She cocks her head, stares at me. Her smile is gone, her lips a thin line, her eyebrows knit in the way my mother told me would give me wrinkles if I didn't stop.

"Jason? Jason *Sullivan*?" Her voice goes quiet on the last

word. Jason Sullivan, the boy who can't be named.

"Yeah," I say.

"You're seeing Jason *Sullivan?*"

"I'm not *seeing* him," I say. "Geez. You said you wouldn't be judgy."

"That's 'cause I thought you were going to say something else!" She kneels on her towel, puts her hands on her thighs, looks at me like I'm a child who's misbehaved.

"What did you think I was going to say?"

"That you slept with Innis." She says it like it's the most obvious thing in the world.

"What? What gave you that—"

"You were acting all strange about the sex tips, and I thought you probably felt bad about it, and I was going to remind you that it's *no big deal*, but God, Liz, this *is* a big deal."

"He's my friend. Is it crazy to see him occasionally?"

"It is if you want anything to happen with Innis. He's like his archnemesis."

"I know."

"And what about your sister?"

"It's not a regular thing. I just went over to his condo to see his dad, and then he was over fixing up his old place, and—"

"And you, like, had to go over?" she snaps. "He was a dick to you. Remember? Even before everything went down. He ditched you a *long* time ago."

"You know, I really don't appreciate this. You don't even know him or what happened."

"Whatever," MacKenzie says, grabbing her towel. "You want to ruin everything? Go ahead."

She stomps into her house without looking back, the sprinkler still running, her magazines spread out in the yard.

I have no choice but to let myself out her back gate.

MacKenzie and I have had two fights before, both about Veronica.

And now fight number three, this time about Jason. I know she was wrong about Veronica, and I want her to be wrong about him. But I'm scared, so scared, that she's not. That if I go back to hanging out with him, I'll lose everything that I have now.

When he calls this time, I don't ignore him.

"Hey."

His voice is gentle. "You answered."

"You called."

The line stretches quiet between us, and I open my bedroom window, flop back on my bed, wait for the summer breeze to hit me. I want to fill the space with everything that's unsaid. *Why did you do what you did? What did the kiss mean to you? Why did you ditch me in middle school?*

How did you and I become a secret?

"I'm sorry about yesterday," he says.

"Me, too." I force a calm, even tone into my voice.

"Good." And then he clears his throat. "Lizzie—" He interrupts himself. "I'll never be able to call you Liz. Sorry."

"It's okay."

"You're the only friend I have here. Before the accident, I spent all my time with Innis and Skip and Alex and Payton— and they aren't exactly eager to bring me back into the fold, not that I want to be around them anyway. There are guys at the gas station, and next year I'm going to go to a different school, but you're the only one I have from . . . before."

I ignore the desire to tell him that his lack of friends is 100 percent his fault. It fades behind the other desire, to hear what he feels about me. "And?"

"And if we, I mean . . ."

"I don't want that anyway," I rush to the words, hoping to save face, beat him to the punch, because I don't. It's not even a lie—I want Innis. Through and through. I don't want to want that, at least. What happened yesterday was a dalliance, as all the old-timey books would call it.

"Okay," he says. "Good."

"Okay, then."

"So can I see you tomorrow? I have the day off, and we could hang out."

"Why?"

"Like I said, you're my friend."

"You know, it's not very flattering, being someone's last resort."

"That's not what I meant."

"I have to babysit in the morning."

"Good. I have a meeting with my parole officer. We'll hang after."

I try not to reveal how much the words "parole officer"

have thrown me. Of course I know he has one, he's mentioned her before, but the way he says it naturally is so weird. "I have to be back by dinner, or my mom will be asking . . ."

"No problem."

I know I should say no. I promised Lyla, after all. But I think of MacKenzie, of how wrong she was about Veronica, of how supremely I effed that up, how quickly I let go of a friend. Could she be wrong about Jason, too? Could everyone?

"Please, Lizzie," he says.

"We need to talk about your text, all 'everything is not what you think it is.'"

A few seconds of silence, but then he says, "All right."

"Okay, then," I say, almost relieved. I need the truth from him. All of it. "Two. I'll come over."

"Awesome," he says. "See you then."

When I hang up, I'm surprised to see in the mirror my face is red. I touch my cheeks—they're hot. Jason Sullivan, I scold myself. Jason freaking Sullivan.

It's not ten minutes before my phone rings again. I jump to it, strangely eager to hear Jason's voice. Maybe he'll tell me he wasn't sorry about the kiss. Maybe he won't even wait until tomorrow. Maybe he'll just come out and tell me whatever it is he's been holding back.

But as I pick it up off my bed, I hold my breath. Innis.

MacKenzie's words shake through me. *If you want to ruin everything, go ahead.*

I let it ring one more time before answering.

We exchange the usual openers while I practice lies about what I'm doing tomorrow afternoon in my head. He tells me he has to drive Skip to Raleigh, for a check-in with his burn specialist at the research hospital there. The words make bile rise in the back of my throat. The boy I've liked for so long is taking his brother to the hospital, and it's all Jason's fault.

He asks if I'm free on Friday. His dad is taking everyone out on the boat. I say yes. Of course I say yes. Friday's my day off. There's absolutely no reason not to go.

Then he asks if I still want to come to the library fundraiser.

Another obvious yes.

I hang up feeling all kinds of bad. Innis is upping the ante, with family-meeting events, daylong outings, and here I am, spending time with the person who hurt his family more than anyone else.

I stare at the phone, wondering if I should call Jason and cancel. Tell him that even if he tells me the whole sordid truth it won't be enough—that whatever he did is too much, far too much, to forgive.

But I don't.

Chapter 14

As I pull up to the apartment complex, I can almost taste the kiss on my lips. It feels warm and good but desperate, like a second piece of chocolate cake.

This friendship is going to be tricky.

I honk twice, and Jason comes down in a few minutes. He opens the car door and hops inside. He's clean-shaven, and I wonder if that's for me.

"How's it going?" He smiles nervously. His cheeks sport a hint of red, like he's blushing.

For a brief, infinitesimal moment, I have the urge to run my hand through his hair, pull him close, kiss him again. But I can't. And I can't have thoughts like that, either. It's not fair to Innis. "Where should we go?"

He shrugs. "What were you thinking?"

"I don't know. I hadn't really thought about it."

He smiles awkwardly. "Me either."

I let out a sigh. "You know, I'm risking a lot to be your friend. You're going to have to come through on the planning, okay? We can't very well go where anyone can see us."

"All right, all right. I just hadn't thought past this point."

"Of course you haven't." I say it under my breath, but loud enough for him to hear. Just like he didn't think what would happen if he attacked Skip. Or if he kissed me.

"Whoa." He swallows hard. "Why did you come if you don't want to be here?"

I grasp the wheel, then let go again. "I do want to be here. I just need you to take charge. I don't know a thing about secret friendships."

"Me either." He laughs a relieved laugh, then cranks his seat back almost all the way. His hands rest on his knees as he thinks. It's the same thing he used to do when he was a kid.

"You know where I haven't been in years?" he asks.

"Where?"

"Wellesley's Grove."

It was our spot for a year or two. It makes as much sense as any.

"That's fine," I say.

He looks out the window, and I head back to the main road, towards a small highway that doesn't go much of anywhere. Tobacco fields stretch out on either side of us, speckled by the occasional diner or gas station.

Fiveish minutes of silence pass before I speak.

"So are you going to tell me your side?" I ask.

The trees disappear, and the cars thin out, and it's just me and him on the open road.

He flinches. "Do we really have to talk about this right now?"

Trees pop up ahead, and I turn onto a small windy drive.

"Why did you say you would then?" I ask. The drive leads to a parking lot, and I pray there aren't any cars here. Luckily, there aren't.

"I didn't say within the first five minutes. Give me a break."

"What's the difference?" I turn off the car and pull the emergency brake with a jolt. "Why even bring it up if you don't want to tell me?"

His head snaps towards me. "Because I knew you wouldn't talk to me if I didn't say it."

It hits like a load of bricks, right on my chest. "Are you just screwing with me? Just making everything up?"

"No, I'm not." He rubs his hand across his eyes. "But can we have this afternoon?"

He looks, suddenly, so very sad, and my anger fades as quickly as it comes, because all I see is him as a little kid, eyes red-rimmed and bleary in the days after his mom left. And I feel deep shame for making him focus on what he did, on the darkest part of himself.

"Please?" he asks.

"You keep saying that," I say.

"Saying what?"

"Please."

His breath is deep and slow, like he's counting in his head. Finally: "I never used to ask for help. Even when I needed it. That's one of the things I learned, these last couple of years."

"So now you want it from me?"

He shrugs. "I want you to be my friend, and for us to not talk about all the bad things—not even think about them—for an afternoon. I need it, Lizzie. I wouldn't ask you if I didn't need it."

I pause, adjust my bag in my lap. He looks so helpless, but it's different from when we were kids. Because when you're a kid, you're supposed to be helpless. You don't have to put on the tough face. You're allowed to cry, whether it's because you skinned your knee or you missed your favorite TV show or that mouthwatering scoop of strawberry ice cream just plopped on your sandal. But he's not a kid anymore. He's a teenage boy, six feet tall with stubble and a chipped tooth and all the clues that say, *I'm supposed to hold it together for 99 percent of the world.* But I'm not that 99 percent. Not for him.

"Okay," I say, finally. "But none of this is going to go away, not if we keep seeing each other. I'm not going to just forget about what you said."

"I know."

"You have to explain it all eventually."

"I know." His smile is a mix of relief and gratefulness, like I've offered him a big fat umbrella, the kind that takes up the whole sidewalk, in a downpour.

"Well, what are we waiting for?" I open the door and head towards the grove. When we get to the small path, Jason takes the lead. Trees taller than you'd believe rise up in front of us, green and lush.

Dirt and rocks slip beneath my feet, making a dusty trickling sound as I lose purchase. Jason turns around, but not quick enough to help me. I fall back, catching myself with my hands.

"Christ, are you okay?"

"I'm fine." I check myself for scrapes and brush the dirt off. "Chill." He leans down and takes my hands, pulling me up. My skin burns hot where he's touched it, and my whole body thrums.

I steady my feet, let go of his hands. "Thanks."

I sidestep the rest of the way down, between dogwood bushes and wildflowers and weeds that are too pretty to even be called weeds, and then finally we reach the clearing, a grassy circle surrounded by trees and climbing ivy. There's a mass of crumbling bricks on one end that used to be one of those huge barbecues no one makes or uses anymore. I look up, and all I see is sky, a blue, clear ceiling. I look back down, and there's Jason, looking at me.

I see him, no more than eleven, the first time we came here on our bikes. The night before, I'd peeked out my window to see Lyla and one of the boys she dated before Skip, one of the ones who didn't ever matter, leaning in close beneath the back porch light, lips locked together. I remember standing in this same spot, wondering what it would be like to kiss Jason like that.

Now I know.

"Come on." Jason grabs my hand.

When he gets to the old barbecue, he lets me go, starts to hoist himself up.

"What are you doing?" I ask.

"Climbing."

"Why?"

He's at the top now, and he turns back to me. "Do I need a reason to climb?"

I shrug, but I follow him anyway.

"It's been years since I climbed something," he says.

"Me, too."

"Come on." He jumps down a level and reaches his hand out to me. "We used to climb lots of things together."

I wonder if Innis would ever reach out to me like that, ask me to join him on a mini-adventure.

Jason's hand clasps mine, and I pull myself up. The air is cooler, breezier, as I follow the steps to the top. We're standing together, right where we used to. I stare down at my tan feet and toenails with chipped paint.

"You have no idea how good it feels," he says.

"What?"

"Being free to do whatever you want in the world."

I'm about to ask him what it was like, being in there for a year and a half, when my phone dings. It's Innis. Instinctively, I cover the screen so Jason can't see.

He's sent me a photo of a street, must be in downtown Raleigh, focused on a page torn out of a book. I zoom in on the photo, look at the top line.

"'I am in love,' he said, not to her however, but to some one raised up in the dark so that you could not touch her but must lay your garland down on the grass."

My hands tingle as I look closer at the picture, see what it's from. *Mrs. Dalloway*, one of my favorites.

I scan Innis's words at the bottom.

something for your collection

Veronica and I started the game a couple of years ago. We'd seen all these pages torn out of a book on the street in front of school, and we thought it was such a waste. So now, whenever we see a page somewhere, we take a picture and add the first line to a running story. It's amazing how many you find once you start looking. Last summer, we were up to a full page. Usually, the lines are from random books, cheesy mystery novels, bodice-rippers. But *Mrs. Dalloway*, that's a gem.

And, Innis remembered. I'd embarrassingly mentioned it one of the times he'd walked me to my car after chemistry, after I saw a page in the parking lot. It was the first time I'd said anything nerdy to him. And from the look on his face, I decided I wouldn't say anything nerdy ever again.

But he remembered.

My heart beats at the words *I am in love*, and right now I'm not even sure what or who it beats for, it just beats.

"You okay?"

I look up quickly, slip the phone back into my pocket.

Jason's face is stern and tight, and I wonder if he saw the text. He suddenly looks a lot less like the Jason I knew as a kid and a lot more like the other Jason, the one who hurt Skip, Innis, the whole family. The one who hurt me.

All the compassion I felt moments ago in the car, it disappears, just like that. "We can't just keep doing this," I say, surprising myself.

"Doing what?" He sits down, dangles his feet over the ledge, leans back on his palms. I stoop down to join him. My hands are scratched and raw from my earlier fall.

"Not talking about what we're both thinking about."

His voice is questioning, betrayed. "But you just said—"

"I don't care." I spit the words out before I lose my nerve. "We need to talk about what you did to Skip."

He hops down, walks away from me.

"What?" I rush to keep up with his long, lanky legs. "What?"

I grab his arm, and he whips around, glaring at me.

"What about what you *just* promised me in the car? Did you completely forget about that?"

"What about all the promises you broke to me?" My voice wavers with anger. It's not just what he did to Skip, even though that's plenty. It's what he did to me, before.

He wiggles out of my grasp. "I thought you were the one person who believed in me."

"How can I believe in you when you don't tell me anything?" The shakiness leaves my voice, because now only anger is left. "Go ahead. Enlighten me."

"You said we didn't have to talk about it."

"Well, I changed my mind. Did you attack him or not?"

He opens his mouth to speak, then shuts it again. "Lizzie, you have to trust me. I'm not a bad person. I'm the same person I always was."

"You can't even say no, can you?"

He turns his palms up like he's searched for words and come up empty.

"I think I should go home." I head for the car.

"Lizzie."

I turn back, waiting for him to tell me the truth.

But his shoulders are slumped. All he says is, "I need you."

"No, you don't." I'm so sure of the words about to come out of my mouth that it hurts. "You just need someone."

MacKenzie calls me that night after dinner. I hesitate before answering, hardly eager for another lecture about ruining things with Innis, especially when I feel so stupid about believing Jason, but I want to hear her voice so bad, I take my chance. "Hey."

"Hi," she says. Relief floods over me—she doesn't sound pissed.

"You're not still mad, are you?" I ask.

"No. You?"

"No."

She laughs. "Hung out with any criminals lately?"

I force a laugh myself. "Not lately," I lie.

"Excited about the lake?"

"Yes." And that's not a lie, because Innis was so sweet to send me that picture, and when I texted him back, he said he couldn't wait to see me tomorrow. "Wait. Did I tell you about the lake?"

"No sirree," MacKenzie says. "Innis asked Payton, and Payton asked me. Alex is coming too, with Marisa. Isn't it perfect? It'll be like a triple date. Assuming you *are* still interested in dating Innis."

"I am." It comes out a bit too quickly.

"Good. Because this is huge for us, Liz. Huge!"

"Totally." I know I sound distracted. Now that she's not mad, all I want to do is tell her everything about Jason—the kiss, our conversation today—everything.

It's like we're telepathically connected or something. MacKenzie clears her throat, and I can hear her wheels turning. "You're not still thinking about Jason, are you? I mean about actually like . . ."

I stall. Should I tell her? I know she doesn't want to hear it, but she's still my best friend.

"Because it's crazy if you are," she says.

Her words shake me out of my fantasy. "No, Kenzie, I'm not."

"You just sound a little out in right field, is all."

"I'm pretty sure it's *left* field."

"Whatever," she says. "You Braves fans take your baseball metaphors way too seriously."

"You play softball," I say. "You should definitely know that."

She laughs, but then she's silent, waiting for a real answer.

I offer the first excuse that comes to mind. "Lyla's driving me crazy with wedding stuff. She's a total control freak about it."

"Ahh." From her tone, I think she believes me. "Well, even more reason why you need a break."

"Right," I say. "Yeah."

"So Marisa and I are going to the mall tomorrow to get new swimsuits. Everything's on sale now. And I was thinking you could maybe even get a dress for your big fundraising shindig . . . as long as you're still going?"

"Of course I'm still going."

"Perfect. Well, I have to go 'cause Payton's texting, but I'll text you with the deets. When do you get done babysitting?"

"One."

"Awesome. *Layta.*"

"See ya tomorrow."

And when I hang up the phone, I suddenly feel more clearheaded.

Because I may have countless yesterdays with Jason, but I have a whole world of tomorrows with Innis.

And there's no point in effing up tomorrow in the hope of getting a yesterday back.

It probably wasn't as good as I remember it, anyway.

Chapter 15

"NEXT ORDER OF BUSINESS," MACKENZIE ANNOUNCES, as we shuffle through the food court the following day. "Finding Liz a fancy-schmancy but still supersexy dress."

"Can we stop for a pretzel first?" Marisa asks. Nicole Tully, a cheerleader who I'd met at Innis's a couple of times before, nods eagerly.

We make a beeline to Auntie Anne's and get two pretzels for the four of us, extra napkins.

Standing here, licking our buttery fingers, I can't help but think of Veronica. She always had a special ire for girls who roamed the mall in packs. One afternoon, we were sitting in the food court when five or six senior girls walked past us, giggling loudly. "I've never understood," Veronica said, between sips of her Frap, "why you need five opinions to buy a pair of jeans." I didn't have the guts to say then what I was really feeling—that they looked like they were having a lot of fun.

Just as I suspected, being part of a crew isn't bad at all. In the last couple of hours, I've laughed so hard my stomach hurt as Marisa tried desperately to park and Nicole chanted, "Reel 'er in Nelly, reel 'er in!"; I've helped Kenzie pick out a swimsuit that seems way too scandalous for family boat time; and I've completely changed my opinion of Nicole, who I'd always thought was ditzy but is actually supersmart and nice.

Once we've gotten most of the butter off our fingers, we head to Belk's juniors department and start picking through the rows of sparkles and beads and flashy colors. Mom generously lent me her credit card with a warning not to tell Dad, and I have eighty dollars to spend. The girls all pull their favorites in my size, and we head to the dressing room, ignoring the "6 Items Only" in our tiny, gala-focused rebellion.

The first one is baby pink and has MacKenzie written all over it.

"Love it!" Kenzie says as I walk out.

I look back in the mirror, see nothing but ruffles. "I'm moving on to the next one."

There are a few boring black things and one with way too much lace. Finally, I slip on one of the ones I grabbed. Sweetheart neckline. Flared just enough at the bottom to make it perfect for twirling. Beads all over. Dark purple, and totally me.

When I walk out, I can see that they all love it.

"That's it," Nicole says.

"Say yes to the dress!" Marisa yells.

"Lady, you are going to blow his mind," MacKenzie says, before nodding down to the bag in her hand. "I mean, not as much as I'm going to blow Payton's at the lake tomorrow, but still definitely up there." She smiles mischievously.

"It is a pretty great dress, isn't it?" I glance back in the mirror and take it all in. I'm here, with MacKenzie and two potential new friends, and I'm about to spend nearly the whole weekend with Innis and his family.

Things are good, I remind myself. So good.

All I have to do is not mess them up.

Mom can hardly contain her excitement when Innis's dad pulls up in his Escalade the next morning. She insists on following me down to the car—she's not going to let an opportunity to rub elbows with Mr. Taylor pass her by.

Innis smiles at me as I open the door and grab the only empty seat next to Skip. MacKenzie and Payton are cuddled up in the back; Marisa and Alex are idling in Marisa's Mercedes, behind us.

"Liz, this is my dad," Innis says. He sounds happy to introduce me, like I'm something to be proud of.

I've seen Mr. Taylor in pictures in the paper and around town before, but never really this close. His dark brown hair is smooth, combed back and still full, even though he must be in his forties. He's in good shape, his skin tan and taut, and he wears expensive sunglasses, a crisp visor, and a shirt that looks freshly pressed. "It's great to finally meet you," he says, but it sounds a little forced. Then he looks to Mom, and I swear I see a flash of annoyance in his eyes. She's hovering outside the car, beaming like it's some superhuge occasion. "Genevieve," he says automatically. "It's been way too long."

"It has, hasn't it?" She's oblivious to the fact that he was just saying it, that he didn't really mean it at all. Am I nothing but a reminder of Lyla, of the moment his son lost his place as golden boy? "Thank you *so much* for inviting Liz along." Mom raises her eyebrows at me. "It's so kind of you."

"Yes, thank you so much." I shoot her a look. I was totally going to say it, as soon as she stopped awkwardly hovering.

"Of course," Mr. Taylor says, perfectly polite and yet cold all the same. "Anytime. We'll be back before dark."

Skip spends most of the drive staring out the window, watching little North Carolina towns pass us by, his bad side facing me the entire time. When I'm not making eyes at Innis in the side-view mirror, I allow myself to take him in: His strong features stand out against his damaged skin, and I realize that his hair is even darker than Innis's, more like his father's. Beyond all the scars, there is a grotesque sort of beauty about him, a closed-off, say-nothing Quasimodo sort of grace.

I wonder what the burn specialist did yesterday, if he's in any pain. I wonder if Jason wonders these things, too, or if he even cares.

Eventually, we turn onto a road that looks just as new and kept up as the Escalade. We pull up to a house, almost gluttonous in its grandness. Mr. Taylor turns off the car, and we all get out.

MacKenzie and Payton steal maybe the seventeenth kiss of the morning, as Innis looks my way and pretends to hold back vomit, and Marisa and Alex get out of her car, obvious annoyance on both of their faces. I chuckle to myself. They'll probably be off-again soon.

Innis grabs his duffel, takes my bag and swings it over his shoulder, and shoots me that big Taylor smile. "Not a bad drive, huh?"

I shake my head. "Not at all."

"Come on, I'll give you the tour." He grabs my hand and pulls me with him, and a subtle fluttering descends into my stomach.

"I'm just going to show her around," he calls to his dad.

MacKenzie manages to pull back from Payton long enough to give me an excited look. Behind her, Marisa beams. The two are like my own personal cheerleaders.

Innis pulls a key out of his pocket and opens the door. I follow him in. Black-and-white tiles set off the entryway. The inside is huge, open and airy with high ceilings and wooden rafters. It looks like a house from one of Mom's magazines.

Innis slips his loafers off, and I follow suit with my flip-flops. Barefoot, my head doesn't even come up to his shoulder. He looks down and gives me another smile, the kind that says he's happy I'm here. His gray eyes glisten, and his skin is tan and glowing from the light streaming in from the windows.

We walk across a lush striped rug, past a dining room on the left, formal as all get out and just waiting to host a fabulous dinner party, and a sitting area on the right, each sofa so full and fat, it looks like you could sit down and be swallowed whole.

But it's not just the furniture that's luxurious. It's an air about him and his dad, even Skip. Innis is in his element. He's confident, proud of what he has. And beyond that, he's not scared. The future is bright, very much so, and you can see it in all of their faces. Maybe that's why Jason is so hated; he messed up the order of things. In one night, he broke what should have been unbreakable.

He grabs my hand and squeezes, giving me another tug. "Wait 'til you see the view." His voice is a whisper, his lips just barely brush my ear as he says it, and chills rush through me, a soft, tingling sensation I can feel all the way down to my toes. He laces his fingers through mine, and I follow.

The back wall is covered in windows, floor to ceiling, side to side, so we're staring out at a living landscape, an oversized oil painting set off with glass. The house sits right on the lake, which is a deep blue, set apart by verdant trees and a sweeping sky with only the slightest wisps of clouds.

He turns to me and smiles, our fingers still interlocked, and my heart beats quick and light, wings flapping like it's going to fly right out of my chest.

MacKenzie and Marisa and I lie on the dock while the boys do boat stuff, getting the shiny beast of a machine ready for the water. Things are easier here. There are no beach bags and coolers, no carting towels around or planning lunch. Right off the dock, there's a fridge with ice-cold bottled waters, thinly sliced salami, and cheese with a name I don't know. A cabinet holds thick towels, extra flip-flops, visors, sunglasses, and sunscreen.

I take a sip of water and pop a piece of salami into my mouth. "This is the life." I smile at MacKenzie. "Isn't it?"

She leans closer. "Innis is gaga for you. He looks your way like every five seconds." I glance towards the boat and start counting. At eight-one-thousand, he looks over at me, smiles and goes back to work.

She lowers her voice even more. "Payton says that he's thinking about asking you to be his girlfriend."

My heart starts beating fast again. "Seriously?"

Marisa laughs. "Don't act so surprised! He's taking you to the ball like Prince Charming or something."

"It's not the ball." I laugh.

"It's Bonneville," Marisa says. "Take what you can get."

The two of them snicker, but I wonder what I would say if Innis did ask me to be his girlfriend, officially and all. I would have to stop seeing Jason, no doubt about it. But it doesn't matter—the answer *has* to be yes. It's Innis Taylor. As the sun beats on me and a bit of water laps onto my feet, the choice seems crystal clear.

After a while—I don't know how long because I feel so delightfully lazy—the boat is ready, and we all pack on, Mr. Taylor at the helm, Innis at the front, me next to him. Skip takes the seat to my right, his face even harder to look at in the blanket of sun. He doesn't say a word.

We motor out to the middle, towards a bridge far-off

with beach-bum dandruff, little specks of people flaking off into the water every few seconds, the sounds of screams and splashing in the distance. As we get closer, I see that the kids are our age, cars blaring music, a slight smell of weed surrounding them.

Mr. Taylor plays Lynyrd Skynyrd as he leads us under the bridge and into a glistening cove, far from the sounds of the partyers. After a few minutes, he stops the boat, Innis drops the anchor, and we strip down to our suits.

Payton doesn't lose time. He pushes MacKenzie in and watches her bob up before jumping in after her. Alex follows, pushing Marisa and jumping in himself, but from the look on her face when she pops up, I really don't think she likes it. Innis hops in next, and then they all stare at me, waiting.

I turn to Skip. "You coming?"

He shakes his head. "Nah."

I jump. The water is cool and refreshing, and it sends my stringy swimsuit everywhere. I pop up, adjusting, and Innis looks at me with waterlogged lashes. "How's it feel?"

"Great."

"Good to hear." He says it mischievously, and I only have a second to grab a breath before his hands are on my shoulders, dunking me under.

I kick to the surface, gasp for air. "You know you're going to pay for that."

I swim towards him as he makes his way to the other side of the boat. Innis doesn't know what a good swimmer I am. In the summers, Mr. Sullivan would drop us off at the

YMCA pool while he worked out at the gym. We made it a contest to see who could do the most laps, while all the other kids messed around in the shallow end. Jason was built for it, his body thin and lanky, and he always won. But I got pretty close.

I whip my body through the water, scooping handfuls away from me, kicking quickly, and in seconds I'm behind him. I launch myself forward, throwing my whole weight onto his shoulders, pushing him down under and giving him a little tap with my feet.

From underneath, I feel him grab my ankles, pulling me down, too. And then we're under together, and he wraps his arms around me, and we meet the sunshine and the surface at the same time.

"Very sneaky." I gasp for breath.

But he doesn't say anything. Just plants the lightest of feather kisses right on my lips.

TWO GAMES OF chicken later, I'm cold and exhausted. I climb back into the boat, but Innis and the others stay, swimming around and playing a silly game that Kenzie has just invented.

Mr. Taylor still sits at the helm, drinking a beer, turning up Lynyrd, and announcing his various complaints to Skip and me, by proxy—the riffraff who've practically taken over the lake, the new congressman who wants to increase property taxes, Mrs. Taylor, who keeps texting him about details for the fund-raiser tomorrow.

I grab a water from the cooler and a towel from the stack and sit there, quietly, watching my friends in the lake, thinking how lucky I am to be here, when Skip turns to me. "How's your sister?"

The question shocks me. Mr. Taylor digs through the cooler for another beer and turns the music louder. Skip scoots closer to me, waiting for an answer.

"She's good," I manage. My eyes flit to Mr. Taylor. His face is red, and I doubt it's from the Coors Lights. I bet he thinks exactly the way I used to, that Lyla left his son when he needed her most.

"Her wedding's coming up, isn't it?"

I nod, fast and furious. He takes a long sip of his beer. "Is Benny good to her?"

This is what I want to say: *Better than you! You broke her heart! She would have stayed with you! You could have been something together!*

With all my heart, I want Mr. Holier-Than-Thou Taylor to know that Lyla's not the villain here. That it wasn't even her choice. I want to remind Skip that even if it all hits the fan, you're still in charge of your fate. You're still responsible for what you do.

I want to scream at Jason for putting us all here to begin with.

But I catch his eyes, and in that moment I see the Skip I used to know, the guy who always gave me sticks of cinnamon gum when he came over to pick up Lyla, the guy who drove to Walmart the day I started my period, because my parents were gone and we only had Tampons in the house, which I was afraid to use. He is not a tragic character, not a player in a Victor Hugo classic. He's the boy who dated my sister, pinned a corsage on the edge of her pale pink gown while Dad videoed the whole thing. He's a person, just like anyone else, a person I used to look up to, even.

A person who maybe didn't realize that Lyla would have kept on loving him, if only he'd let her.

I hold his gaze when I answer. "Yeah. He's very good to her."

He nods, looks down, and I think I see a glistening in his one perfect eye, but I can't be sure.

Chapter 16

THE NEXT NIGHT, WE ARRIVE AT CRAWFORD HALL AT seven o'clock, sharp.

Dad pulls around the long driveway, the one Kenzie and I were always afraid to approach, and a college-aged guy in a crisp white shirt and black tie, who looks like he'd rather be anywhere but here, walks up to the car and opens the door. "Welcome to Crawford Hall, ma'am."

"Oh," Mom says, flustered. "We're just dropping our daughter off."

The guy looks confused. "So you don't want the complimentary valet service?"

Mom gives him a nervous smile. "I think we're okay."

"Could you pull up there, then?" He points to a dirt drive off the roundabout.

"Sure thing," Mom says.

"Innis couldn't have picked you up and avoided all this awkwardness?" Dad asks. "Then we wouldn't have to pull over in a dirt road watching the Beamers pass us by."

"Greg," Mom says. "His family is running the whole thing. She's lucky to even get an invite. Maybe if we were going ourselves, it wouldn't have been so *awkward*."

Here we go. "Guys, I'm gonna get out now."

Mom stops bickering and rolls down her window. "Wait a sec, wait a sec, honey," she says. "Let me just get one picture. Move over a little. I want the whole house in the shot."

"*Mom.*"

"Just a little to the right. Perfect. Okay, smile."

"Don't put this on the internet."

She doesn't answer.

"I mean it."

"Fine, fine." She holds up the phone, and I give her my best get-on-with-it smile.

"Oh, don't you look just gorgeous?" She pushes the phone at Dad. "Greg, look at her."

His mood softens. "You look wonderful, Liz. Have a blast."

I don't look back as my parents pull away. I take in the scene before me instead: the front of the huge mansion, which I've never even been this close to; the men and women in gowns and tuxes filing elegantly through the arched front door; the glow of real gas lamps; the bustle of more valets moving Mercedes and Audis to the back.

I follow the crowd of people up the steps, and one of the guys holds the door open for me. Saying thanks, I quickly step inside.

I don't know the perfect word for the inside of Crawford Hall. Exquisite comes to mind, of course, but everyone says exquisite about places like this. Or breathtaking, but I am still breathing. Mom would call it stunning. Dad would call it ostentatious. But for me, it isn't really any of these things.

For me, it is simply a different world than I have ever known.

And it's not just in the silk drapes pooling on the floor, the perfect golden yellow of the walls, the intricate snow-white molding, the ceiling medallions and shimmering crystal chandeliers, or the elegant symmetry of the scrolling central staircase—I've been to the Biltmore, after all, seen houses far fancier than this.

Instead, it's the soft smell of baby powder on an older woman in a floor-skimming gown. It's the din of orchestra music coming from down the hall. It's the way people are talking: confidently, yet not too loudly; and the way they are walking: heads lifted high, feet gliding effortlessly, one in front of the other, as if the whole world is an invisible balance beam. It's the glance of myself in the oversized gilded mirror that leans against one of the walls of one of the sitting rooms. I look older somehow, my hair done up in Mom's signature chignon, the beads of my purple dress catching the light, the swath of dark red lipstick that makes my lips look all pouty and, dare I say, chic. It's the way I look like I almost belong.

I text Innis to say I'm here and wait for him at the bottom of the staircase, like he told me to. I scan the crowd of people coming in, looking for anyone I recognize, and see a middle-aged woman in a simple black dress. She's one of our librarians, and though she doesn't recognize me, I certainly remember her. She's the person who encouraged me to read classics, before I was ever assigned them in high school. Gave me a list of the greats, which I ticked through religiously the summer after eighth grade, the summer after Jason ditched me and before I met Veronica, the summer I didn't really have a friend.

"Hi," I hear behind me, and I flip around to see Innis, towering over me on the second step of the staircase.

Innis in a tux is wild and I'm completely caught off guard because the tux doesn't call to mind dreams of homecoming or prom; instead, I have this flash of him and me, walking down our own aisle, of how lovely a wedding would be at Crawford Hall, the curve of his lips as he says the words *I do*, as he leans in to kiss his bride . . .

"You okay?" He steps down to meet me, kisses me softly on the lips. I feel the blush rise to my cheeks.

"Yeah," I say, embarrassed at how easily I let Lyla's wedding prep get to my head. "You just look nice is all."

He places his hands on my shoulders, pushes me back a touch, looks me up and down. He shakes his head. "*Nice* doesn't even begin to describe the way you look."

I link my arm in his, and we follow the people around the staircase, down the hall, and through the double doors in the back. Innis walks with purpose, as usual, and I barely even have time to soak in the seemingly endless rooms on either side of me.

He leads me onto a panoramic back porch, and I smile to myself as I realize that the basement where I've watched him play so many video games is just a few feet below us. The juxtaposition is hilarious.

A handful of tables are set up on the porch, the rest on the huge lawn below. What must be a hundred strings of twinkle lights glow in the ever-darkening dusk, a pink sun just setting over a horizon of woods behind the property. There's a gazebo for the occasion, and the Charlotte Symphony plays Beethoven or Tchaikovsky or one of the old dead guys with hard-to-pronounce names.

Innis squeezes my hand. "Fancy, huh?"

"Uh-huh," I stammer, and all I can think of is the scene in *Pride and Prejudice*, where Elizabeth Bennet looks out on the grounds of Pemberley, after she's refused Mr. Darcy's proposal, thinking how all of it could have been hers. And I've always judged her for that scene, because, come on, Elizabeth, you're not *that* materialistic. But I was wrong, totally wrong. Because the feeling is completely natural, when someone holds your new life out on a silver platter, offering crème brûlèe when all you've ever had—all you've ever even thought to want—was chocolate chip cookies.

"We're right over here." He leads me to a round table in

the corner—white tablecloth, calligraphy place cards, the works. Skip is already there, eating shrimp cocktail and messing around on his phone. Behind him, a tall, elegant woman I recognize as Mrs. Taylor hugs and cheek-kisses another woman, before turning to us.

"Mom, this is Liz," Innis says. "Liz, this is my mom."

She takes my hand immediately, then pulls me into a hug.

"I'm so glad to meet you," she says. "God, don't you look just like Lyla?"

Skip lifts his head at the mention of Lyla, looks at me, and says, "Hey, Liz," but then goes back to his shrimp.

Mrs. Taylor looks the part, of course, in a black silk evening dress that falls just above her toes, several strings of pearls, and diamond earrings. Her eyes are hazel and her hair is the same shade as Innis's, curly and cropped close to her head. They look strikingly alike, only she is graceful and feminine where he is not.

"She looks like herself, Mom," Innis says proudly.

"Of course," Mrs. Taylor says. "Oh, you know what I meant. Now how is your family?"

"My parents are good," I say. "They wish they could have come but the tickets sold out so quickly." Mom has always said that there are lies and there are polite untruths. This one, of course, is in the latter category, and she absolutely insisted I say it tonight.

Mrs. Taylor clasps her hands together. "Next time, next time. I'm just so glad we're able to raise so much for the library.

I think this will be our best year yet, between the tickets and the silent auction. Speaking of, I have to arrange a few things. Cocktail hour is for another thirty minutes before we all sit down, so enjoy yourselves!"

She leans in conspiratorially. "And have some bubbles if you want. One glass of champagne won't kill you, and Mr. Taylor agrees." And then she floats off, silk swooshing as she walks.

I stare as she goes, impressed. She is warm and welcoming where Mr. Taylor is cold and distant. She is everything my mother wanted me and Lyla to be if only we hadn't gotten kicked out of cotillion—mannered but not snobbish, poised but not uptight. And whatever anger Mr. Taylor seems to harbor about me and my family, she has none of it, or she's a very good actor.

"She'll be running around the rest of the night, has to say hi to everyone," Innis says.

"Well, she's the star of the show," I say.

But Innis shakes his head, looks down at me. "That title's already taken."

WE HAVE MORE than one glass of champagne, though no one seems to notice, and Innis eats every ounce of the four-course dinner and part of mine. Mr. Taylor does mainly what he did on the boat, complain loudly about various news and events—except in a tux this time—and when Mrs. Taylor isn't making announcements and receiving oversized checks and generally running the whole thing, she sits next to me, talks about how nice it is to have another woman around, and looks at me with "help me!" eyes when the boys talk about boy things—or at least what people like Mrs. Taylor would consider boy things—like boats and the Braves.

At one point, Innis tells me a story about when he and Skip were kids, when his brother made him laugh so hard milk came out of his nose, only it didn't fall to his plate, it landed right on Sally, the family cat, and she meowed and hissed and never forgave him. And we all laugh then, and even Mr. Taylor smiles at me, and it's like they're just a regular family and I'm just regular me, and we all go together.

Eventually, the dinner dishes are cleared and the crowd mingles again and people move down to the lawn, where a shiny wooden dance floor has been laid out in front of the gazebo. There are a lot of people I recognize now—a few from our neighborhood, others from the one or two times a year we go to church, some men and women on the school board, and it's funny to see them all dolled up, like we've been cast in a movie about rich people.

I almost wish Innis would ask me to dance, but it's for the best, I guess. The only dance moves I know are booty shaking and this fake tango Lyla and I used to do when we were kids with silk flowers clenched in our teeth. There's certainly no bumping and grinding going on here, and I'm guessing most people know how to do the actual tango.

Instead, Skip and Innis and I walk past the dance floor and around to the side of the house, through a door that goes to the kitchen, where people scuttle around, refilling champagne glasses and swearing loudly.

Skip and I hover on the edge of the kitchen, while Innis heads inside, on the hunt for a six-pack.

Skip turns to me. "You having fun?"

"Yeah." I lean against the side of the house, look up at the stars, feel the humidity that hangs in the air. "This is awesome."

He smiles genuinely. "Your sister loved this. It was her favorite night of the year."

I turn to him, but he looks away. "She did," I say. "I remember her getting ready. One year, she had this black dress with actual pieces of mirror on it that I thought was pretty much the coolest thing ever."

Skip still doesn't look at me. "I remember that dress."

Innis comes back out then, two six-packs in his hands. "Bingo!" he says. "Who's a pro?"

Skip instantly changes his tone, rolls his eyes at his brother. "Don't act like such a hotshot. You didn't even get an opener."

Innis pulls the monogrammed knife out of his pocket. "This'll do."

We sit along the side of the house, away from the crowd, just a hint of the music wafting our way, surrounding us like the humidity. Innis snakes his arm around my back, and Skip sits on his other side.

"Dad'll be drunk within the hour, guaranteed," Skip says, as he takes a gulp of beer.

"So will you," Innis laughs.

Skip tips the beer back, empties it, opens another. "Yeah," he says. "But people expect it of me."

We sit there for a while, the two of them talking a lot about their mom and all the people they know at the party and all the parties that came before. It's kind of like I'm not there, which is okay. Skip talks more than I've heard him talk since Jason attacked him, like he can actually be himself when it's just him and his brother.

After Skip finishes his second beer and opens a third, he gets up, says he's going to start watering down Mr. Taylor's whiskey drinks.

Innis nods at him like it's not a joke anymore, like this is something they actually do to keep up appearances. I can't help but feel a tug at my heart as Skip walks away. He's a good guy, I think. He could have been a good husband to Lyla. He could have been a lot of things if Jason would have let him.

I wait until Skip is out of earshot before I ask Innis what I've wanted to ask him for a long time. "Do you think it's weird, you know, you and I hanging out together?"

Innis's eyes scrunch up, and in that second, I can see that he cares about me, that my words have thrown him, even scared him a little. "What do you mean?"

"That your brother was with my sister, and then it didn't work out. And now . . ."

"Oh," he says. "That." His voice shows his relief. He shrugs. "Some things just work out that way."

"Okay," I say. And then before I can stop myself: "So you're not only into me because I'm Lyla's little sister, right?"

Innis actually laughs out loud. He nudges me with his elbow. "I'm into you because of you, got it?"

I nod. "Got it."

"*And* because of that dress, if you really want me to be honest."

"You really like it?"

He turns to face me. "I more than like it. *Believe me.*"

I look down, run my fingers over the back of my chignon. "All of this is new to me. I'm not used to dressing up and going to galas and eating fancy French food."

Innis just smiles. "You might want to get used to it."

And I smile back, lean in to kiss him.

Because I *could* get used to this. Lord knows I could.

Chapter 17

IT TAKES MOM, SUZANNE, AND ME TWO FULL HOURS to get the house ready for the "best bridal shower ever," as Mom has taken to calling it.

I'm a bit groggy as we run through all our tasks: covering a foldout table with a big white cloth, hanging feathery paper lanterns and tissue paper flowers, tying pink ribbons to the back of every chair and tacking up signs with witticisms like "The Future Mrs." and "He Popped the Question!," setting up the pinboard full of photos beneath the "Lyla + Benny" print Mom got made special at the stationery shop.

Even though my parents picked me up at ten o'clock sharp last night, even though I made myself stop texting Innis at midnight and get into bed, it still took me forever to actually get to sleep. There was too much to think about, classical music and expensive champagne and Innis's sweet words, dancing around in my head like glitter in a snow globe.

At eleven thirty on the dot, Mom sends me up to get dressed, with a reminder to go easy on the eye makeup. I'm in the middle of adding extra eyeliner, just to piss her off, when Innis calls.

My hands throb with excitement as I pick up the phone. It's the second time this week that Innis has called me, and it feels so old-fashioned, so chivalrous somehow. I don't even think Payton calls MacKenzie, and they've had sex. Before Innis, Jason was the only boy who ever called me.

"Hey." I sink back into bed and stare at the ceiling.

"I didn't wake you, did I?" His voice sounds warm and polished, like the rich mahogany desk in my dad's office.

"No." It comes out breathless. I try again, stronger, more pulled together. "No, you didn't. I had to get up early. It's my sister's bridal shower today."

"I remember," he says. "But I wanted to ask you to hang out tomorrow."

I sigh. "We have this big neighborhood Fourth of July thing. I'm a required attendee. Unless you wanted to come over here?"

He laughs. "I'm a required attendee on my end as well. The day after?"

"Totally."

"We can go to the movies. Like a real date."

It doesn't get much more real than our dinner at the

French place, but I love that he's calling it out now, treating me like a girlfriend.

"I'd love that."

"Text me from the bridal shower—I want to know how drunk everyone gets."

"Will do."

A COUPLE HOURS in, and the bridal shower is a total success, possibly because, as Innis predicted, everyone's drunk. Everyone but me, that is.

"Ooh, me, me," Erica says, as I make another round with a bottle of champagne, her mouth half-full of shrimp and grits, of which I may have had three bowls while avoiding the painfully awkward lingerie exchange.

I fill her glass extra high until her eyes light up, pleased, but when I try to move on, she grabs my arm, pulls me close to her.

"How's Jason?" she asks.

"Excuse me?"

"Your sister thinks you're still talking to him."

I pull away, aghast at the nerve of her. "I'm not." I don't care that it's a lie. It's none of her freaking business.

"Don't hurt your sister," she says.

Not that long ago, Erica was my ally. Lyla's snapped at her on more than one occasion, stormed out of the room, and left me to patch things up. And now I'm suddenly the enemy?

"I won't."

"I'm only *saying*." Her words are slurred.

"I know what you're saying," I say quickly, before moving on with my champagne, carefully filling Benny's mom's glass, face hot with anger, not like anyone is sober enough to notice.

Whatever Erica's intention was, it didn't work. Her words just make me furious. I've been practically running the Lyla Show for the last two hours, and all she can think about is this one thing that has nothing to do with her.

When I'm done topping off drinks, I let myself sit down, flit my eyes to Erica, who's face-deep in her glass and doesn't seem to realize how much she's pissed me off. I glance to Lyla, instead. Christina, a girl she's known since high school and one of the other bridesmaids, is leaning in close, talking drunkenly about marriage: "There is no one better to build a life with than Benny," she says adamantly as Benny's mom sits there and beams between sips of champagne. "He's got his *shit* together. Everyone thinks it's all about passion, but it's about finding a good man who's *got his shit together.*"

I feel a hand on my shoulder and turn to see Mom, holding a mimosa. "I'm glad to see you've finally sat down," she says.

"You should take a break, too," I say.

"I'm about to." She pushes the mimosa at me. "One won't hurt. It is your only sister's bridal shower, after all."

"Seriously?"

"I made it OJ heavy. So don't get too excited."

I take the glass, and she rubs my shoulder. "You know, one of these days it will be your turn to be the bride. It's going to sneak up on me, I just know it."

"Don't, Mom."

"Okay, okay. I'm just saying." And she walks away to refill her own glass, wiping the moisture from her eyes when she thinks I'm not looking.

It doesn't take me long to finish my first mimosa. I manage to top off my drink several times when Mom isn't looking, and the party kind of blends together after that. Mom gets properly tipsy—she even starts hiccupping at one point—Lyla turns one of the gift bows into a hat, Benny's mom keeps going on about how *thrilled* she is to have Lyla as a daughter-in-law, Suzanne breaks into the Peach Schnapps in one of the upper cabinets, and everyone takes a million pictures. We play a stupid game where we cover Lyla in toilet paper like it's her wedding dress, Erica and Christina running around my sister like she's a Maypole. At one point, Lyla corners me in the kitchen, her eyes wet and mascara drippy, and hugs me tight as she says I'm the best sister ever, and she means it and she's sorry if she's been a little crazy lately, but it's her only wedding, and she loves Benny so much, and she wants it to be perfect, and she couldn't do anything without me by her side. I'm her everything, she says, and then she repeats it. My *everything*.

My spelling gets progressively worse as I text Innis throughout the afternoon. I tell him I'm a little tipsy and that Lyla is crying. He says that he'd expect nothing less and can't wait for our date. I don't tell him that a member of the bridal party has practically staged a champagne-fueled intervention with me.

The girls begin to peter out around six, many of them abandoning their cars, their husbands and fiancés and boyfriends playing designated driver for the night. Mom goes upstairs to lie down, leaving a huge mess, which is completely unlike her, and I take a little too much delight in the fact that she's so drunk.

Dad, who spent the day with his Fantasy NASCAR buddies, comes home shortly after, just in time to see Lyla climb the stairs to her old room with errant pieces of toilet paper still hanging from her clothes and the bow secured haphazardly to her head.

Back in my room, I stumble out of my dress and into normal clothes. I stare at myself in the mirror, and I try to remember if my one mimosa had three or four top-offs.

I count backwards from ten until I think I'm at least somewhat presentable for Dad, and then I head back downstairs to help him clean up.

"You guys had quite the rager, eh?" He tosses two bottles of champagne into the recycling bin, and the clanking makes my head ache. "Looks like you had a little something, too."

"Mom made me a mimosa. Just one."

He gives me a questioning look, then shrugs. "I guess it is a special occasion."

"Can I help?"

"I don't know, can you?"

I'm not too drunk to know the answer he wants. "I'd like to help. May I?"

He smiles, having succeeded in the great Dad battle.

"Want to start taking some of the decorations down?" He gestures to the pinboard. "I'm not sure where all these photos go."

"No problem."

I pull down the signs Mom made, careful not to bend or rip them, and I take the pinboard back to the photo album shelf in the living room. I file Lyla's baby pictures, the only time she was ever chubby, and the ones of her as a toddler, blond ringlets framing her face. I see her at five, arm around little Erica, both of them holding up shakily cut paper hearts.

The photo on the last page surprises me. It's Jason and me, posed on our bikes, ready to cause mischief. I removed all the photos of Jason a couple of years ago, tucked them in my box just in case Mom decided to delete him from our family history, but I must have missed this one.

Mom still doesn't know what we did that day. That we rode fifteen miles to the next town, blew almost all of Jason's birthday money at this big arcade that had just opened. We drank so much soda and ate so much funnel cake that Jason actually puked, and a soccer mom asked us if we wanted her to call our parents. Thinking back, Mom probably would have driven us to the arcade if we'd only asked, but we knew we weren't allowed to bike on the highway. It was the danger of it that made it so fun.

I wonder what clandestine trips Lyla and Erica went on—they must have their secrets, everyone does. I wonder if they ever reminisce about the stuff they did when they were kids.

Lyla still has Erica. Going to her bridal fittings, wrapping her up in toilet paper, watching her live her Lyla life, butting in where she doesn't belong.

Does Erica even realize that the same dedication she feels to Lyla, the kind that allows her to drunkenly confront me, is the kind I feel to Jason, even now? That when you've known someone so long, it's hard not to stick up for them?

When I'm done putting all the photos back, I head into the kitchen, my head still buzzing with champagne. Dad's popping the last of the bottles into the bin. I set the pinboard on the table.

"I've got the rest of this," he says. "Relax."

But I stand in front of the table, tugging on the hem of my shirt.

"What is it?" he asks.

"I just wondered . . ." My voice drops off.

He sets the recycling bin down, gives me his full attention. "Wondered what?"

I spit the words out before I lose my nerve. "Do you think that Jason really did what they say he did? Like exactly how they said it?"

It catches Dad off guard, and I see a hint of fear slice across his face.

"It's not because I want to hang out with him," I say. "I just want to know. And I can't talk to Mom or Lyla."

The fear leaves his face, replaced with relief. He sits down. "I don't know," he says. "Honestly, it shocked me, too. And sometimes people do take pleas who aren't guilty. But a lot of people take them when they are . . ."

"But you think there's a chance?" I ask.

Dad shrugs. "Do I wish that Danny hadn't moved away and that Jason hadn't gone to juvie? Do I wish we were all hanging out at the cookout tomorrow? Of course. But good kids do bad things all the time. The *what ifs* and *maybes* only get you so far."

"But there is a maybe for you?" I ask hopefully.

"I didn't say that," he says.

"I know." I give him my most innocent smile. "Thanks, Dad."

The truth is he didn't have to. I know that, deep down, he feels the way I do. That there has to be more to the night than what we know, that Jason would never do something so awful.

I wait until I'm back up in my room to text him.

Six little words.

i want to be your friend

I WAKE UP feeling all kinds of crappy.

I'm not sure if it's from the hangover or the text I sent to Jason, the one that seemed like such a good idea after a few glasses of champagne.

Mrs. Ellison told me she didn't need me for the Fourth of July, and I thank my lucky stars I don't have to babysit in this condition. I brush my teeth, splash water on my face, and throw on my most comfortable pair of shorts and a tank top. In the hallway, I pass Lyla's old room, hear her snoring lightly through the door.

Downstairs, the kitchen is relatively spotless, but there's a plate of half-eaten grits in the sink and a bottle of Advil on the counter, and Mom is splayed out on the couch—looks like she's hungover, too. Dad sits at the table, flipping through the *New York Times*, completely amused that we're all in such a sorry state.

"Happy Fourth," Mom says. There's a forced cheer in her voice, and her face is, thankfully, lacking in judgment. "You have fun yesterday?"

"Uh-huh."

"As much fun as Mom?" Dad asks, bursting into laughter before eating another piece of bacon.

"Greg," Mom says. "Please."

"Oh, come on. It's rare to see you out of form."

I have to agree with him.

The pot is still warm on the stove, and I scoop some grits onto a plate, grab two Advil. I park on the couch next to her. She's watching a black-and-white movie with lots of tap dancing.

After the credits roll and the old guy on the TV introduces the next classic movie, Lucy paws at my mother, eager for her morning walk.

"I can take her," I say.

"It's all right." Mom slowly hoists herself up and grabs the leash, Lucy hot on her heels. "Some fresh air will do me good."

Dad folds the paper, takes his dish to the sink. "I guess I should start setting the grill up. We don't want any of the neighbors to take the best sidewalk spot. Gen, have you seen the mesquite chips? They weren't out back."

"They're in the garage somewhere," Mom says. "I put them in last time it rained."

"On it," Dad says with a wink and a laugh. He's enjoying this way too much.

They aren't gone five minutes when I hear a knock on the back door. I'm willing to bet Mom forgot the dog bags, and I pull myself away from the impeccably dressed woman on-screen.

My pulse quickens as I see the face through the back door.

I whip it open as fast as I can. "What are you doing here?"

"I was cleaning up the rest of the paint stuff, and I saw your mom go out and your dad head to the garage," he says. "And you're pretty much hit or miss with texts."

"My dad's like, right there." I press my hand to Jason's chest, pushing him back. "And Lyla's upstairs. It's the Fourth of July. Everyone's out."

He backs up, and I follow him, not bothering to put shoes on, from my yard to his and through the back door and into his house before anyone can see.

He's got this big grin, and I swear he's about to laugh.

"What's so funny?"

"You always were afraid of getting in trouble," he says. "Always averse to risk."

The kitchen smells like paint, but it looks finished, beige and boring just like he wanted. I cross my arms in front of me. "With good reason. If anyone sees you, I will seriously be hearing about it from my family for the next week, at least."

"Relax. No one will know." He used to say that same stupid thing when we were kids, when we pawed through my father's off-limits desk, stealing binder clips and manila folders so we could play office.

"Whatever," I say. "Like it matters to you."

He looks at me and reaches a hand to my cheek, pinching it at the fleshiest part. "When you're mad, you look like you did when you were a kid. Chipmunk cheeks and all."

I push his hand away. "Stop it. I've always hated my chubby cheeks."

"What?" he asks. "They're a good thing. Youthful effervescence."

"They make me look like a little girl with pigtails and bubblegum."

He changes the subject. "If I can't come to your house, then you're going to have to come to mine."

I stare at him.

"You said you wanted to be friends."

"I know. But I was tipsy. It was during my sister's bridal shower. I didn't really think it through."

He shifts his weight, tilts his head towards me. "I wanted to tell you, I'm happy for her."

I want to tell him that he shouldn't talk about my sister, that he broke her in a way that is unfixable, but I can tell by the look in his eyes that he means it, that what he did to Lyla is something he lives with to this day.

That's the thing about old friends—you learn to read their looks, trust your own judgment.

When I don't say anything, he shoves his hands in his pockets, shrugs. "Come by for a bit. You wouldn't have texted me if you didn't want to see me."

He's right. In spite of everything, I like being around him, having him back in my life. When we're together, I'm totally me. All the things that divide us—how much people hate him, how he hurt me in middle school—seem so superficial. Maybe it's because I was there when his mom left, or because Lyla and I were so different as kids. Maybe it's the marathon nature of our friendship, the countless seconds we've spent together, all of those seconds adding up to something that's impossible to break. All I know is that when I'm with him, I feel comfortable, safe. Is that actually so wrong?

I would never ask Innis or Skip or even Lyla to forgive him, but does that mean that I can't?

"Okay," I say. "I'll come over. When?"

His face brightens. "How about now?"

"There's the block party," I say. "And I thought you were working on the house."

"If I remember correctly, it doesn't start until two at the earliest. And that's if you want to be one of the awkward first ones there. Plus, I need a break."

"I don't know."

"Come on," he says. "We used to spend every Fourth together. What's one more?"

Chapter 18

BACK AT THE HOUSE, I PULL NEW CLOTHES OUT AND hop in the shower.

When I'm out and dressed again, I leave a note for my mother—*running to Target for sparklers, be back later*—and head to Jason's. It doesn't take long to get to his complex, and I park next to his truck, head slowly up the three flights of stairs.

"You didn't change your mind," Jason says as he opens the door.

I raise my eyebrows. "Should I have?"

He shakes his head, and I follow him inside.

"Is your dad here?" I ask.

"He's working. The flower shop pays time and a half on holidays."

"Oh," I say. "Good." Not that many years ago, Mr. Sullivan would have been perfecting his famous vinegar barbecue sauce, a must-have accompaniment to Dad's ribs.

"I'll give you the proper tour," Jason says, leading the way. "Here's the kitchen." He gestures to the right. "And here's the *great* room"—he gestures to the left—"we like to think of it as the living room, family room, and dining room all rolled into one." He walks down the hall.

"And here." He heads through an open door. "Is my room."

I follow him in slowly, cautiously, because being alone with him in his room feels somehow dangerous, illicit.

The room itself doesn't look like much more than a prison cell, especially compared to the rest of the apartment, which got an ample dose of Mr. Sullivan's good taste. There's a dresser and a bookcase, a small desk in the corner, a box of photos sitting on top. Worn jeans spill out of a hamper mixed with T-shirts and checkered boxers. It feels way too intimate to see his laundry, even though when I was little, I must have seen him naked a hundred times.

The walls are lined with the same movie posters he used to have, but they remind me of a time before, when he didn't want to be my friend anymore, so I scan the bookshelf instead. What I see is a veritable library of impressive books—*A Clockwork Orange, To the Lighthouse*, even *Crime and Punishment*.

"You've got a lot of books." I try not to sound too surprised.

"They let people send as many books as they want," he says. "The library was a little limited, so my dad started shopping all the bargain bins."

"Dostoevsky?" I ask. "Don't tell me you actually got through *Crime and Punishment*?" Because I didn't. Neither did Veronica. I don't think either of us made it more than one hundred pages in.

He pulls it out, weighs it in his hands, puts it back. "It's actually fairly easy to get through when you have a lot of time. Plus, the subject matter made it pretty apt."

"Wait. You still *have* this?" I whip the book off the shelf: *Seamus Sheridan and the Case of the Missing Moped*, a chapter book with illustrations and enough clues to figure out the mystery on your own. Once we had it all worked out, we spent many afternoons going through the book, reenacting our favorite scenes.

"Hold on." He moves for the closet. "You'll love this."

He reaches to the top, pulls down an old shoebox. He opens the lid and starts flipping through. "I was looking at my old papers and stuff and I found these."

He hands me a roll of stickers. *Seamus Sheridan's Private Eye Club*.

"Oh man, I can't believe you kept these." We'd completed an online mystery game and given out way too much of our personal information to earn these puppies.

"Pretty funny, huh? They were a big deal back then."

"They were." I hand the stickers back to him and he drops them in the box.

"Remember when we biked to the arcade in Greendale?"

"I remember puking my guts out," he says with a laugh. "Why?"

"I found a photo from that day. We took all these pictures out for Lyla's bridal shower, and I was putting them back in the albums, and there we were, on our bikes."

"Man, I loved that bike," he says.

"I still have mine. It's in the garage. My mom can't bear to get rid of stuff like that."

"My dad's the opposite." He sits down on the bed. "Got rid of almost everything when he moved here, except for nineteenth-century furniture, of course."

"Of course."

"Why did your dad move anyway?" I sit down next to him. "He never said anything to me, you know. The sign was just up and the moving truck was out front all of a sudden."

Jason leans back on his hands. "Let's just say there wasn't anything left for him on Dogwood Street."

"You mean because everyone instantly shunned him?" I feel shame and guilt, even though it's only mine by proxy. "My mom wouldn't even let him finish decorating our house."

Jason's laugh sounds forced. "You don't feel bad about that, do you? I didn't even know about that."

I stare at the opposite wall. "I don't know. I don't think it was her greatest moment."

Jason rests his hands on his knees. "He did lose a lot of clients, I know that from repeated asking. But it was more that he couldn't handle the notoriety. He'd always been the star of the town, and then it was like either they saw him as some kind of archnemesis of the people who fund the library and the high school and everything, or they wanted some kind of tabloid-y insight on how someone could lose it all."

"That sounds pretty awful," I say.

"It was," he says. "And I have to live with the fact that it was all my fault."

I want, so very badly, to scoot closer to Jason, wrap an arm around him, tell him all the things you're supposed to say when everything goes to hell—that it's not his fault, that these kinds of things just happen, that there was no way he could have prevented it—but it wouldn't be true, would it?

Jason picks up the roll, fingers a Seamus Sheridan sticker, peeling it back and resticking it. "You know my dad gave me a lot of crap when I stopped hanging out with you." He leans closer to me. "He said that friends are really important, and you can't take them for granted, and I said that I was tired of spending all my time with a girl I'd known forever."

I wince, because even though I've wanted us to talk about this, even though the fact that it was *never* talked about drove me crazy for a while, the thought of it all still hurts, right in my gut. "Is this the start of an apology?"

"I'm trying to explain. He said that you wouldn't just stick around if I didn't make some effort."

Veronica comes instantly to mind, how I needed to hear that advice, too.

"But you're here," he continues. "After everything that happened, you're here, giving me another chance. And that makes me the luckiest guy on earth."

I look down at my hands, embarrassed. As sweet as Innis is, this is the kind of thing he'd never say, because everyone knows that in that pairing, I'm the lucky one, not him.

"You mean that?" I ask, without looking up.

"I do."

So many times I wanted Jason to apologize to me, in those months and years after we grew apart. But when Jason left, I stopped thinking that way. I had to. I built a new world for myself. And now he's here, saying it so much better than I could have imagined, and everything I used to feel is rushing back. It's not butterflies, or the thrumming of my heart, but an all-over ache, a wash of appreciation, of deep understanding so strong I can feel it making my cheeks red.

I want Jason to be honest about everything. When you know someone so well, there are some things you just can't stand not to know.

I scoot closer then, force myself to look up. "What is it that you won't tell me?" I ask. "I know there's something."

He doesn't speak for a moment, and I think he's going to spill it. But then: "Some things aren't worth telling," he says finally. "You don't tell everything to me."

I move back, give him some space. "What am I keeping from you?"

"You and Innis."

"What about me and Innis?" I make even more room.

"Whatever you guys are."

"Maybe because I don't know exactly."

"But you want it to be something serious with Innis?" he asks.

I nod. "Jason," I say, and he scoots closer this time. "You're the one who said you didn't want anything to happen . . ."

"I know."

"And so, what's between me and Innis, it has nothing to do with you."

His eyes flash with anger, but as quick as it comes, it's gone. "It's not that simple," he says.

"What do you mean?"

"There are things you don't know about Innis."

I roll my eyes, because he's starting to sound like a broken record. "Have you ever thought that maybe you don't know everything about him?"

Jason doesn't answer my question. "Does he know you're spending time with me?"

My lips press together. It's the only answer he needs.

Jason stares down at his hands. "It was an accident," he says after a moment. I hold my breath, because it's the first time he's given me anything besides the vague excuses, but he doesn't elaborate.

"You mean it wasn't your fault?" I ask.

He scoffs, jerks his head away, and I can see—in a flash—how he could have done what they say. There is a deep pool of anger in Jason, and who knows how deep it runs?

Skip knows. Skip Taylor knows.

"I didn't say it wasn't my fault," he snaps. "I only said it was an accident."

"Then why didn't you tell anyone? Why did you plead guilty?"

Jason rushes his words. "Everyone pleads guilty. That's

what you do. Unless you're willing to bet a whole lot more."

It reminds me of what Dad said, that sometimes innocent people take pleas. I narrow my eyes at him. "What exactly are you trying to say?"

"I'm saying everyone takes Innis's word at face value because he's Innis Taylor."

"So you mean he made a mistake?"

Jason laughs. "Lizzie," he says, with a deep sigh. "You are so naive."

"And you're so vague and secretive," I snap. But as soon as it's out I regret it. "I want us to be friends again," I say. "But you have to give me a reason to believe you."

He stares at his feet. "You're going to believe what you want to. So is everyone else. I only wish you wanted to believe better things about me."

THAT AFTERNOON MARKS my first Alexandria Fields Fourth of July block party with MacKenzie.

It is my third without Jason.

"This is insane," MacKenzie says as she reaches for a deviled egg.

I bat at her hand. "Wait until we get to Suzanne's to get the deviled eggs."

Around us, grills are rolled out to the street, forming a massive communal cookout, while card tables hold slaw, potato salad, corn on the cob, and everything else delicious. As to be expected, there is sweet tea *everywhere*, and there are at least four or five cakes made to look like flags.

"Does it really matter?" MacKenzie asks. "Isn't an egg just an egg?"

"I've been doing this for years. I know the tricks. Suzanne has the best deviled eggs. My mom has the best potato salad. And Mrs. Packton has the best creamed spinach in the world."

MacKenzie eyes the spinach already on her plate. "Yes, so I've heard."

We grab corn bread instead and make our way to Suzanne's. She's standing at her table with my mother, drinking white wine from a clear plastic cup, laughing loudly. The tray of deviled eggs looks disappointingly picked over.

"Are you out?" I ask.

Suzanne leans over, pulls a fresh tray from underneath the table. "You know I'll always save some for you, dear."

We take two each and find seats on the curb in the middle of the cul-de-sac. I spot Lyla down the street with Benny and his whole family. She looks happy, if a little hungover. Dad hasn't moved all day from his spot at the grill, but it doesn't look like he wants to. He used to have company in Mr. Sullivan, but a lot of things used to be different.

I take a bite of the first egg. "Amazing, right?"

Kenzie takes a small bite. "Tastes like a deviled egg."

My heart sinks. Jason and I had a whole game of it, rating all the different dishes, picking our favorites. One year when we were eight or so, we ate no less than six plates of food between the two of us, then lay down in my front lawn, our stomachs distended, laughing about how ill we both felt.

I take another bite, surprised at how upset I am that she's

not the appropriate level of excited. Maybe I'm still emotion-
ally charged by this morning. Jason didn't touch me, didn't
grab my cheeks or lean in for a kiss, but there was something
so intimate about the way he asked me to believe him, something so raw and hopeful and sad at the same time.

Kenzie puts her plate down and crosses her arms. "Now
that we've successfully obtained all of Alexandria Fields' culi-
nary delights, can we talk about something other than food?"

"Shoot," I say, mouth full of potato salad.

A toothy grin lights up MacKenzie's face, and her choco-
laty eyes practically pop out of her head. "Payton wants to be
boyfriend-girlfriend." It comes out in a single high-pitched
squeal. *Paytonwantstobeboyfriendgirlfriend!!*

I swallow my potato salad, not remotely surprised. "And
I'm guessing you want the same?"

"Of course," she says. "He's a great guy, you know. He's
so cute and funny, and when you get to know him, he can be
so sweet."

Sweet. Like that supersweet time he keyed Jason's car. But
I put on a smile, even set my plate down. "I'm so happy for
you."

And I don't know why, but it suddenly feels so much like
acting.

"Thanks. It's going to be soon with Innis, too. I just know
it."

And then what? Beyond Crawford Hall and the fancy
homecomings, what would Innis and I really be like together?
The movies never tell you what comes next. The movie

version of us would have ended when Innis told me he liked me. We'd have kissed, and an indie song would have played for the credits, and all the girls would have gone home and dreamed about their own Innis.

I take another bite of potato salad, weirdly nervous. Everything I've ever wanted—scratch that, more than I've ever wanted—is about to be mine. So why is there such a weight to it? Why don't I feel like MacKenzie, heart light and totally infatuated, looking forward to nothing but rainbows and butterflies, or at least cold beer and pool parties, ahead?

Jason's words ring in my head. *You are so naive.*

"We'll see," I say. "We are going out tomorrow."

Then her face gets serious. She bites her lip.

"What is it?"

"I want to be honest with you. It's not that bad, I promise."

"Just spit it out, Kenzie."

She stares at me a sec. "All right. I may have told Payton you were hanging out with Jason."

I feel fear all through me, rushing through my blood, to the tips of my fingers, filling me up like a water balloon. Too much, and I'll just pop.

"Why in the world would you do that?"

"Calm down."

I stand up. "Seriously, why would you do that?" I ask, loudly enough that Mom looks over. I sit back down, lower my voice. "What were you thinking?"

"You made it sound like it was no big deal, like it was nothing."

"To you," I say. "To you, my best friend, who I thought I could trust to keep a secret. Innis won't think it's nothing." I look up, but Mom's back to talking to Suzanne. "My parents won't think it's nothing. *Lyla* won't think it's nothing. I trusted you."

Fear fills her eyes. "I was drunk, okay? We were hanging out last night, me and Payton, and he was going on about how Innis is so into you, and it slipped."

"What do you mean, it slipped?"

"I was trying to help you, all right, to get things going for you. I just said that he better hurry, before she gets snatched up, or something, and then he was on me about it, and then I said that you'd seen Jason a couple times, and—"

"MacKenzie." I turn away from her. "I can't believe you."

"He won't tell Innis. I made him promise."

I shake my head, because I know she's wrong. "The fact that you think you have that much control over him is funny."

IT'S JUST ME and my parents at the fireworks that night. MacKenzie made an excuse to leave not long after she dropped the bomb, likely because I sat there and stuffed my face, barely talking to her in my rage. Lyla's spending the evening with Benny's parents, who watch their fireworks at the lake, not on the hill of the town park like us.

Just after nine, the fireworks start with a raucous pop, the first of them bursting into the sky in a spattering of white. Little lights curl downward, crackling as they go, and my parents stop talking about how much fun the block party was, stop pretending like it's not totally weird for it to be just the three of us tonight. They pop one after another—in red, blue, and green bursts of color.

My phone dings after one of the fancier smiley-face ones, and I take it out, expecting it to be Innis.

Two texts, one after another.

> we're looking at the same fireworks, you and me
> i wish we could do it together

It's a ridiculous wish; he knows it as well as I do, even though I want it just the same. Even if we could be friends, we could never be those kinds of friends. We could never be us again, not the way we were.

Because too many things have changed since the last time we stared at the sky together.

Another three pop, lighting up the sky—explosive.

Things like fireworks—once they happen, they can't ever be undone.

Chapter 19

I DON'T EVEN BOTHER HEADING DOWNSTAIRS THE next night, sure that Innis is just not going to show.

He didn't text all day. I spent my entire babysitting shift checking obsessively, so much so that Mary Ryan said I was like her daddy, constantly on the phone.

But to my surprise, at six minutes past seven, I hear his car coming up the street. Luckily I did my makeup, just in case.

I jet down the stairs and call out to my parents that I'm leaving before they can try to talk to him again—I have a feeling he's going to be in an awful mood, and Innis doesn't do a good job of hiding his moods.

I'm not in his car five minutes before I know that he knows.

His face is pale and blank, and he doesn't smile once, just

dutifully asks me how the Fourth was and whether the final installment of the superhero series that should never have been made is a good movie choice. I briefly consider trying to get ahead of the problem by bringing it up myself, but I can't quite find the words.

Scantily clad ladies and musclemen run across the screen, saving a city that's supposed to be New York. Innis's hands are in his lap, nowhere near mine.

"Do you want some?" I push the Junior Mints over with a rattle, but he shakes his head.

He definitely knows.

The movie ends, and we head back to his car. The air outside is warm and muggy, swimming around us, between us, a sharp contrast from the clinical coolness of the movie theater AC. I wonder why he didn't cancel, or stand me up.

"It's crazy hot out," I say.

"It's summer in North Carolina." He raises his eyebrows at me. "Of *course* it's hot out."

Ouch.

I watch him closely as we cross the parking lot. His steps are even, quick. His lips are drawn into a thin, tight line, all: *Don't even try to talk to me about the weather right now.*

He clicks the keys, his car makes a friendly, welcoming noise, and I open the door, slipping in. He does the same.

Before either of us can pretend anymore, I turn to him. "Okay, just get on with it."

"What?" He stares at me, shocked at my boldness, but I can see he understands.

"Just go," I say. "I know you want to talk about something."

He clenches his fists, unclenches, clenches them again. "MacKenzie told me about you and Jason. Have you really been seeing that asshole?"

I don't hesitate, don't try to point out that Jason's not an asshole. "Yeah."

Innis slams his hands on the steering wheel. "Jesus Christ."

"It's not like that. He came over to his old house a couple of times, and I ran into him, and I went over there once to see his dad."

"But why?" The words are concrete, hard and cold.

"Because he used to be a big part of my life."

"His dad or *him*?"

"I don't know. Both, I guess."

Innis shakes his head in disgust. "And you don't care about what he did to my brother? You forgive him for that?"

"No. I don't."

"I really liked you."

"Don't talk like that."

"Like what?"

"Past tense."

He leans in. "Are you and Jason . . . ?"

He doesn't finish the sentence. Leaves the gaps open, for me to fill in as I choose.

"No." I rush to the words. "No, not at all."

"You're sure?"

"Yes."

"You *swear*?"

"Yes," I say, as convincing as I can, because an ill-judged kiss aside, it is true. "I swear."

He rests his hands in his lap, stares straight ahead.

When he turns to me, his face has softened. "I like you more than I've liked anyone before."

It hits me like a thud in the chest, because I wasn't expecting it. Not from him. Not tonight.

He leans in even closer, runs his hand through my hair. It feels so nice, so safe.

"You do?" My voice trembles.

A smile creeps onto his face. "I do."

He's just inches from me now, and I feel tingly all over. Vivid, alive.

You are so naive.

I put my hand on his chest, pushing him back. I can't continue this without knowing—this question is just too big—not if I want it to be real. "I have to ask you something."

Innis pulls back, looks at me warily. I start talking before I lose my nerve. "Jason made it sound like there was more to that night than I know. Like you, like you got the story wrong or something. Or went against what he said."

Innis rolls his eyes. "*He* pled guilty."

"He said that everyone pleads guilty."

"Well, that's pretty goddamn convenient."

"I'm just asking—"

"Jason hates himself, and he sure as hell knows everyone hates him. Of course he wants to change the story. Especially since he's trying to get with you."

"He's not trying to get with me."

Innis cocks his head. "Sure he's not."

I rest my hands in my lap. "You promise?"

Innis's eyes are unblinking; they don't leave mine once. "He was my friend, too. But I stopped trying to understand why he snapped. It's something that happened, that I refuse to forgive." I hold his gaze, trying to read him, trying to make everything less muddled. "The worst part is that it's messing things up with you."

He doesn't wait for me to answer. He kisses me then, presses his lips to mine, opens his mouth and takes me with him, far away from the movie theater parking lot, into our own special world, me and Innis, a world where all the other stuff doesn't exist.

He pulls back. "I wouldn't lie to you."

And of all things, I remember chem last year, sitting next to Innis while Ms. Philips explained Occam's razor to us—among competing hypotheses, the one with the fewest assumptions should be selected. In other words, the simplest answer is usually right. In the midst of all of Jason's vagueness and cryptic outbursts, there are news stories in black-and-white, testimony. Crime—and punishment. *He was charged as a minor and was sentenced to 24 months in a juvenile detention facility* . . . As much as I want to believe that it's wrong, as much I'd honestly rather believe that Skip launched himself into the fire than think my onetime best friend could so brutally and viciously hurt someone, it's a pipe dream. It's not what happened.

Everyone already knows this. Everyone but me.

There are a lot of things I wish I could believe. That Mrs. Sullivan cared about Jason too much to leave him. That Lyla got to make her own choice about the boy she loved. That I am not the kind of person who ditches a friend when popularity comes knocking. But it doesn't make them true.

"I believe you," I say.

Innis smiles.

"So we're okay?" I ask.

His voice sounds raw and honest: "Everything is going to be all right."

I lean in then, pressing my lips to his.

But he pulls back. "There's one more thing."

"What's that?" I ask, immediately nervous.

"I want you to be my girlfriend."

The *yes* spills from my lips before I can think to say anything else.

WE DRIVE TO his house, follow the circular drive around the back, park near the basement.

Three nights ago, everyone was here, in all their finery, dancing to symphony music, and now, it is just me and him, boyfriend and girlfriend, on the brink of something bigger.

He fumbles with the door, and I wonder if he's nervous, too, even though I know he's done this before.

When it finally opens, he takes my hand is his, pulls me inside, shuts the door, and kisses me long and soft.

His hands trace my outline, his fingers reaching at the sides of my shirt.

"What if your parents come down?" I ask.

"They won't," he says. "They never do."

"What about Skip?"

"Don't worry," he whispers.

He lets my shirt go, moves his hands back to my hips, and kisses me again.

"Are you nervous?" he asks.

"A little."

"Do you want to stop?"

I look into his eyes then, barely illuminated by the moon and the porch lights coming through the windows.

What am I waiting for anyway? This is what I wanted, for it to mean something, for it to be with my 100 percent certified real-deal boyfriend.

And now that's what I have. "No," I say.

"Me either."

He kisses me harder then, his lips moving to my cheeks, my chin, the top of my chest. I lose my breath in his kisses, his urgency.

His hands reach to the bottom of my T-shirt and slowly peel it off. He takes his off, too, and then he grabs my hand and leads me to the couch, and we kiss some more as he fumbles with my bra, tugging at the clasp. After a minute, I reach back and do it for him, my own fingers shaking with nerves.

It falls forward, and then his hands are on me and we lie down together.

I undo the button of my skirt before I can lose my nerve, and then he shimmies it down over my legs and my feet and I have this crazy thought that if I'd known this was going to happen I would have at least taken the time to reshave my legs.

But of course he doesn't notice, and he unzips his shorts, kicks them off, and then it is him and me in our underwear, and I feel so silly, but he kisses me again and I don't feel silly anymore.

He pulls my underwear off and tosses them to the floor, then drops his boxers, and I realize that the two of us have never been naked together like this before. But Innis doesn't act like it's weird—just like he's really, really happy—so I don't either. Then he fiddles around in the pocket of his pants, pulling out a shiny package, rips it open, and puts it on.

"Are you okay?" he asks.

I nod quick, afraid I'll lose my nerve, reach up to his shoulders, pull him close.

We kiss again as I part my legs, then he presses into me, just a little at first, his hand fiddling around so everything fits right, his kisses never stopping, and then finally he pushes all the way. "You okay?" he asks.

"Uh-huh." I wrap my hands around his neck as my breaths quicken, as my heart beats loudly, as our bodies move together, as connected as two bodies can be.

Eventually, he falls on top of me, his body beaded with sweat.

He kisses me soft and sweet, and then he pulls back and looks at me, almost bashful. "Was it okay?" he asks.

"Yeah," I say. I lean forward, kiss him on the lips again.

And just like that, I'm not a virgin anymore.

WE PUT OUR clothes back on and watch bad TV. When it's close to my curfew, Innis drives me home, smiling like he's just won the lottery.

I feel different and not different at the same time. Womanly and powerful and bashful and silly and a little relieved and kind of like maybe I should take a shower. But not dramatically different. Just a little . . . new.

Outside my house, he kisses me long and slow and then looks in my eyes like I've got the answers to a whole slew of questions he'd never even think to ask.

He tells me he'll call me in the morning. And I smile, say, "Okay, good night," and give him one last breathless kiss, because I know without a doubt that he will.

INNIS SENDS ME three texts by morning.

>good night, Liz

>you were amazing

>i'm a lucky guy

I text him back immediately.

>you weren't so bad yourself ;)

The tips of my fingers are pulsing, I feel so bold. Excited, too. It's not just about sex for him. It's so much more. And now that I've made my choice—finally, totally—everything will be easier.

I decide to go to Jason's as soon I'm done babysitting. Tell him kindly, calmly, that Innis is my boyfriend now and it's best I don't see him anymore. That this secret friendship, this secret . . . whatever it is, is over. For real this time.

Mary Ryan and Sadie seem to sense my happiness, my resolve. It's as contagious as their laughter, this in-control feeling, this power to create the life I want. The best things are out in the open, are ones you don't have to hide. My mother said it to Lyla at the bridal shower, when Lyla was going on about how comfortable she was with Benny: "Pleasant beats the hell out of star-crossed."

Jason's truck is in its usual spot in front of the apartment complex, and I park next to it. I feel nervous, sick inside, but I know I've made the right choice. I'm finally doing right by my sister, by my mother, by Innis, by me. What I thought, just a couple of days ago, that I could forgive him, could go on hanging out with him even though all the closest people in my life never can, now seems insane. Naive, just like Jason said I was. Only he didn't realize then that it was him I was being naive about, not everyone else.

My feet are lead as I walk up the stairs, like in the dreams where you can't run or scream, no matter how hard you try. But I can walk, I remind myself, and soon I'm at the door, and in a minute, it will be over. And I won't have to worry about Jason Sullivan anymore.

But my knocks get me nothing, not a shuffle of steps, not even an impatient "hang on."

I knock again to more silence. Fear pulses through me, though I don't know why. I knock louder, as my heart begins to thud fast and heavy. He's probably asleep. Or in the shower. Or a lot of other things that mean you can't come to the door. Things that are safe. Things that aren't bad things.

I should turn around, come another time, but I'm afraid if I leave, I'll never be able to say what I need to say. So I knock louder, pounding on the door urgently, trying to push away the crazy thoughts. What if he's hurt? What if he's trapped under a piece of furniture? What if he's slipped in the shower and knocked himself out and is drowning in two inches of water?

They're the sort of stupid fears Mom has about me and Lyla, the kind of paranoid thoughts I've never had about a single person before.

I try the knob, and as I suspected, it's unlocked. Mr. Sullivan grew up in a small town just an hour or so away, and he never keeps the doors locked if someone's home. I let myself in.

"Jason?" I don't see anyone. "Jason?"

I creep past the kitchen and into the small hallway that leads to his room.

"Jason?"

A groan.

My heart relaxes, and I begin to breathe again. The fact that he's okay is so important to me that I almost want to cry.

"Jason," I say again softly, as I slowly open the door to his room. It's pushy, overly intimate—I *know* this—but with Jason, it is hard to be proper.

I want to scream, but I feel tears instead.

He is lying in bed, his head propped on a pillow, one eye welded completely shut, purple and puffy, the other almost as closed and just as discolored. His lip is red, split, his face is fat and bruised—a rotten peach.

"Jason." The tears are hot now, blurring my vision. "Oh my God."

I rush over to the bed, then stop as his one open eye catches mine, cautious and wary. Almost unkind.

"What happened?" I sound sloshy, my words traveling through a vat of Jell-O.

He doesn't answer my question. "What are you doing here?"

"What happened?" I ask again. "Who did this to you?"

He coughs deep, winces.

He sighs. "I know you know."

My eyes narrow, and at first, I don't. I have deluded myself so long, I have tasted sugar kisses and I have sunned on the lake, and I have agreed to be his girlfriend, and I have slept with him on the couch in his basement, but I do not know.

And then it's so clear, so horrifyingly clear all of a sudden. MacKenzie to Payton, Payton to Innis.

Innis. Innis. *Innis.*

Everything is going to be all right.

That's what he said to me. And this is what he meant.

"When?" I ask, as the tears come harder.

"Last night."

I'm gasping, almost choking on my breath. The thought of Innis, the way he looked at me and told me it would be all right. The way he got what he wanted, but still it wasn't enough.

"Don't cry," he snaps. "Just spare me, okay?"

"I can't help it."

"Go back to your life." He sinks deeper into the bed. "Go back to Innis. That's who you want. Those are the kind of people you should really be with. Not me." He works to get the words out. "You and I are bad for each other."

I step closer. "Don't say that."

But he stares at me, and all I see is anger. "How can you not see it? I wouldn't be like this if it weren't for you!"

"No," I say. "I didn't tell him to hurt you. I would never ever want someone to hurt you."

He doesn't even look at me again as he says it. "Just *go*."

TEARS FILL MY eyes on the drive home. When I get to my house, I run up the stairs, not waiting for my mother to pester me with questions, to ask what's wrong. I slam my bedroom door, shut and lock it.

I fish under the bed for the box, but my fingers hit my underwear, stained and stiff from just last night. My body feels weighted, full of rocks and things I can't undo, but I push the feeling aside. My hands find the box, and I pull it out.

I grab an envelope full of photos and pour them on the floor. They fall around me like sad confetti. Me and Jason at the playground, me and Jason making sidewalk-chalk drawings, me and Jason with his dad's chili on our faces.

I wouldn't be like this if it weren't for you.

It's true. Innis didn't hurt Jason until he knew he was hanging out with me.

Everything is going to be all right.

Lizzie, you are so naive.

My phone dings, and I lift it up.

hey sexy

It hits the wall with a thud, the glass turning to spider-web cracks.

I look down at the newspaper clippings in the box. I don't think I've ever hated printed words so much before.

I pick them up and start to rip, and I don't stop until they're all done, broken, disjointed, hundreds of tiny pieces you can't put back together.

Chapter 20

I LOCK MYSELF IN MY ROOM, SCREENING BOTH MAC-Kenzie's and Innis's calls, rereading *The Age of Innocence* for probably the third or fourth time in a desperate attempt to distract myself.

A little after two, I hear the double *ding-dong*, MacKenzie's signature. Mom answers, and there are muffled pleasantries, then hushed voices as she tells her, most likely, that I've been in a bad mood all afternoon.

Kenzie patters up the stairs, then knocks on the door, doesn't wait for an answer, turns it. It's locked.

"I don't want to talk," I say.

"Is this about the other day?" she says through the door. "I'm sorry. Payton told me he didn't even say anything."

I drag myself off of the bed, where I've been sitting for the last hour or so, losing my place on the page. I unlock the door, whip it open.

"Payton's a liar."

"God." She steps around me and inside my room. "You look horrible." She leans over my computer, turns off the muted, weepy sounds of the most depressing band I could think of. "Nothing like feel-good music to get you out of a slump."

I shut the door behind me and turn the music back on.

She puts her hands on her hips. "What do you want me to do? I'm sorry. I really am. I can't undo it now."

Certainly not, I think. The damage is done.

I feel my lip beginning to quiver as I try to form the words. She rushes up to me, wraps me in a hug, her toned softball arms squeezing me tight. That's when the tears start—*again*—when my mascara runs all over her shirt and my breaths come in gasps. She pulls back and grabs a tissue from my nightstand. I don't refuse it.

"Sit down." She pulls me onto the bed. Her voice is low, the six-inch kind they always wanted us to use in school. "What happened?"

"Innis and I hung out last night." I briefly consider telling her everything, but the folly of my mistake, my misjudgment silences me. I take a quick sharp breath, just enough to get the last part out. "And after he drove me home, he went over to Jason's house, and he beat the crap out of him."

I wait for shock and surprise, but she doesn't flinch, just

stands up, grabs another tissue, hands it to me. She waits until I'm done crying, until my breathing steadies, to speak.

"Liz," she begins, then pauses. Her eyes are icy. "I don't want this to come off as unfeeling or anything, because you really look upset, but I just have to ask." Another pause. "Why are you so upset?"

I stare at her, incredulous. She is not moving to hug me. She is not putting a hand on my shoulder. She's just looking at me, cold and inquisitive.

"What do you mean?"

She looks down at her nails, back to me.

"As far as I can tell, Innis likes you, wants to be serious with you, *is* getting serious with you, and got a little jealous." She pauses for effect. "So I'm asking why you're so upset."

I feel fresh tears again, but I will them back, into myself, a part of myself she can't see from the outside, that is deeper than she will ever know. "He didn't just get *a little jealous*. He attacked him. You should have seen him—"

She shrugs and chuckles. A boy is badly hurt and she has the nerve to *chuckle*. "I mean he kind of had it coming, didn't he? If someone had done something to Lyla, wouldn't you be all over them? Wouldn't you want to hurt them however you could?"

The thought hits me hard. Someone did do something to Lyla—Jason. But I'm not hurting him. I'm the one sticking up for him.

"Yeah, but—"

"But what? Really. What?"

"But you should have seen him."

She raises her eyebrows. "I'm pretty sure whatever they did was still not permanently disfiguring."

The word catches me, a slap in the face. "They?"

Her body tenses up as she realizes her mistake.

"He," she says. "Innis." She won't look me in the eyes anymore.

"*Right.*" My heart pounds with anger, betrayal. "Then why aren't you surprised?"

"'Cause he had it coming. I told you."

"Stop lying," I snap. "Stop it. You come over here, all 'Payton didn't say anything,' but you know he did. Because you know he and Innis went over there together."

She starts picking at her nail polish, like an answer is underneath, just one coat down, if she just chips it away enough.

"I'm right, aren't I? Payton helped him?"

She doesn't look up.

"And you knew about it?"

Keeps on chipping.

"And you didn't think to tell me? You didn't try to stop them?"

"What do you want me to say?" she demands. "I didn't *want* to stop them. You needed a wake-up call. You needed to remember who this person is. What you're trying to give up for him." She pauses for breath. "Don't you realize what you're doing? Things are going perfectly. Things are never perfect, but they are. Next year could be the best year ever.

You and Innis and me and Payton. Have you even thought about that? And you're ruining everything. For a person who you can't even bear to be seen with in public? For someone you have to keep secret from your whole family? For someone who ruined your *sister's* life? What are you thinking?"

"I don't know." I almost feel like I can't breathe. "I don't know what I'm thinking. But I am, and I can't help it or change it."

MacKenzie shrugs. "I don't know how to help you, then."

I stare at her, longing for what we had—was it only a few weeks ago?—swim, sun, flirt, repeat. How did we become so different, so quickly?

"If you're just going to try and make me feel bad, then go. I don't need guilt—from you, of all people."

She stands, backs up, walks to the door. Before she goes, she turns to me, and I want her to say a million different things, but she doesn't. "See you later then."

She shuts the door behind her, and I feel trapped and angry and disappointed. I hear her say good-bye to my mother, then watch from my window as she walks across the street and towards her house. As soon as she's gone, I grab my keys and head downstairs.

"I'm going out." I don't wait for an answer.

I leave my phone behind, but I turn the radio as loud as it goes, roll down the windows.

There are no cars in the lot of Wellesley's Grove, so I park, hike down to the middle.

I walk beneath the trees I've known for years, and I

think about the years since Jason left, how I got rid of Lizzie, became Liz, made myself anew.

I think of how much I traded just to be popular.

It was around April that Innis actually realized I existed— we'd been in chem together all year, sitting at those high black tables in our stools with that weird eye-washer thing dividing us, but he spent most of the class bouncing around to the different lab groups, talking to Alex about cars and fishing and parties I wasn't invited to. And when it was time to pair up, I was always with Veronica.

Even after she stopped eating lunch with me and Mac-Kenzie, Veronica and I stayed lab partners. It was easier to be friends in chem, without MacKenzie around. It was our second year as lab partners: We'd trudged through biology the year before. She'd made fun of me ceaselessly when I had to get a note to skip the dissection portion, because I faint at the sight of blood, something I discovered at nine, when Jason fell off his bike right in front of me. Veronica was great at lab, deftly adjusting the microscope I could never get to work. She'd observe, and I'd take notes.

It was funny how it happened—so easy, so simple and cheesy, like a script from a movie. Innis turned to me, locked his eyes on mine, and asked me to be his lab partner for the day. Maybe it was just because Alex was out. Or maybe it was because MacKenzie and I had actually been to one of the popular crowd's parties.

But it doesn't matter why he asked. I said yes.

I caught Veronica's eyes and shrugged. She stared at me

until I shrugged again, then knit her eyebrows, whipped around, slammed her book on the desk, and scooted her stool so it made an awful screech on the dusty linoleum. Even Ms. Philips took notice, glancing from me to her with this look, like—*girls, he's not worth it.*

I suppose I knew what I was doing in that moment—that our friendship would be over.

But it was *Innis.*

I know it wasn't my proudest moment. I know I'm a horrible friend. But when Innis Taylor looks at you with those piercing eyes and asks you a question, the only possible answer is yes.

None of our lab results matched up with Ms. Philips's that day. Without Veronica, I was at a loss, and Innis wasn't one for paying attention. But we continued to be lab partners for the last couple of months of the year. And since it was last period, sometimes he'd walk out with me, follow me to my locker, then to my car. I'd lean back on the Honda, he'd lean in towards me, and we'd talk about things—I don't even remember what they were now, just things.

And then we made out at that graduation party, and even though that didn't exactly go how I'd expected, he soon learned that Kenzie and I had fakes, and that's around the time MacKenzie developed her plan for the Perfect Senior Year. She and Payton, me and Innis.

Sometimes, the stone starts rolling so fast you don't know how to stop it. "Gathers no moss," my foot. As if change is the good thing, stasis the bad. What if you move so fast, let the momentum take you, carry you, to somewhere else, some-place you never dreamed you'd be, but then you get there, and you don't even know who you are?

WHEN I GET back to my house, *Innis's* car is in front. My mind begins to race. He probably thought I was just being coy by ignoring him, that everything is fine.

I want more than anything to drive somewhere else, wait him out, but if I know my mother, she'll keep him guzzling sweet tea and chatting away for hours on end.

So I park next to his spotless car, without a hood-to-trunk keying, and flip the mirror down. I look a mess, my eyes red and puffy from crying, mascara smeared along the bottom of my eyelids. I run my hands in fists beneath them, trying to make myself presentable, comb my fingers through my hair.

Lucy rushes up to me as soon as I open the front door, and I lift her up, snuggle against her. She licks my cheek.

I hear voices, Mom, Dad, and Innis. Laughing and talk-ing loudly.

Innis is sitting at the kitchen table, as if one of the family already.

Mom looks up at me. "Where've you been? We tried call-ing you but your phone's in your room."

"Out," I say. "I forgot it."

She narrows her eyes at me, but she's too happy to ques-tion it, sitting there, basking in the glory of having Innis Taylor in *her* kitchen.

Innis shoots me a smile straight off a magazine cover.

"What are you doing here?" I ask.

"*Liz!*" Mom gasps like I've burped in front of the president.

Innis laughs, looks at Dad. "It's okay, I've grown used to her bluntness."

Dad laughs with him. *Look, the pretty little lady is being spunky. She's got a mouth on her, doesn't she? Don't tell her to get in the kitchen.*

I want to throw up.

Mom doesn't laugh, at least. "Innis dropped by to see you. We invited him in, *of course.*" She emphasizes the last two words like, without her, I'd be a social disaster. Maybe I would. Who knows, maybe I am.

I force my face into a smile. "Oh," I say. "*Cool.*" My words sound wrong, like I'm a reality-show character, trying to sound unscripted.

"Sit down," Mom says. "Have some tea."

I follow her orders. She pours me a glass, and I focus on it, like drinking sweet tea is my only goal in life. Innis smiles again, and I dutifully smile back.

He talks to Dad about NASCAR, about the renovations his parents are thinking about making to Crawford Hall—stuff he'd never talk to me about, because I'm not a guy—and Mom soaks it up like a fat, thirsty sponge. I sit there and watch this spectacle, trying to hold it together until I have a chance to talk to Innis alone.

I feel sick all over from the shame of how stupid I have been. I indulged in his so-called forgiveness, in MacKenzie's excitement, in my mother's urgings. Just twenty-four hours ago, this scene would have been my crowning achievement—and yet, even though I'm still sore from having sex with him, now everything feels wrong.

I drain my glass as quickly as I can.

"You want to go on a walk?" I ask, turning to Innis. "It's nice out. I'll show you the pond."

Innis nods. "Sure."

I push my chair back, and Innis follows suit. He says his *thank-you*s, Mom asks him to stay for dinner, but he thankfully says no, he's got a family thing tonight, he'll have to get back pretty soon. I grab the house key, and we're almost out, away from them, when Dad stops him. "Well, see you in a month, then. If not before."

I turn back. "A month?"

"Lyla's wedding," he says. "August sixth. *Duh.*" Dad thinks he's so funny, that I'm so clueless.

And I have been clueless. But not about that.

"Oh yeah." I turn up the corners of my mouth like I'm supposed to, and I force myself to walk normally to the door, not to stomp.

When we're down the street, away from the view of my house, on the wooded path that leads to the pond, Innis holds my hand. Grabs it, really, as if I have no choice.

We're surrounded by trees as if in some fairy tale, but it's not a fairy tale to me—not anymore. And I realized it too late.

I rip it away. "Don't touch me."

"What's wrong?" He looks so surprised, so confused, that

I almost feel bad for him. But then I remember what he did to Jason, and the notion disappears as quickly as it came. He steps close, putting a hand to the side of my face, running his fingers through my hair, like all he wants in the world is to take care of me. "Are you upset about last night?"

I want to throw my anger at him, to do that crazy windup that the pitchers on Kenzie's softball team are so good at, chuck it right at his head, give him a goose egg. But instead, I begin to cry.

He wraps his arms around me. "Hey," he says, as my tears come harder. "It's okay. It's not wrong or anything. We were careful. You won't get pregnant."

I wriggle out of his grasp. "It's not that," I say, but in a way, it is. I didn't want sex with Innis to be a "pro move." Just yesterday, I thought it was so much more. But now, when I look at him, all I feel is disgust.

"You beat the crap out of Jason," I say. "We slept together, and that wasn't enough. You had to go and hurt him. You couldn't let me handle it. I was going to stop seeing him. I went over there to tell him."

His arms drop to his sides, and I look up at him to see that his face has gone cold and stony. "Wait a second. *That's* what you're upset about?"

"And then you come over here and suck up to my family and invite yourself to my sister's wedding."

His voice is raised now. "I came over to ask you to have dinner with my family tonight. I thought you would *like* to be asked in person. I thought you would love that courtship crap." He pauses for breath. "And your dad asked about the wedding, and what was I supposed to say? I didn't know you were going to go crazy about a little thing."

"It's not a little thing. You should have seen him. His face was purple."

"And why the hell should I care?" Innis yells. "Have you *seen* my brother?"

I shake my head. "That was an accident."

He laughs. "So you believe Jason's lies now?"

"I don't know what to believe," I snap. "You told me it would be all right. *This* isn't all right. You can't just go around attacking whoever you want."

He scratches at his cheek. "Do you even hear what you're saying? How nuts you sound?"

"And it wasn't just about your brother," I say. "Or else you would have done it right away. It was because you don't want me seeing him. Admit it."

"So what if it was? I *don't* want you seeing him."

"You could have let me do that on my own," I yell. "Instead of being all tender towards me and texting me and saying how happy you were while you were *beating the hell out of him*."

Innis steps closer. He puts his hands on my cheeks, framing my face, so gentle and soft, but I know it's just an act. I know he has a different face for everyone in his life. I know that, given the chance, he'd do it all again. Maybe

MacKenzie was right—maybe *everyone* is right—maybe Jason had it coming. But that doesn't change the way I feel. It doesn't change the fact that when it comes right down to it, I feel more for Jason than I would for a hundred of Innis. Maybe I'm being unfair—even naive—but you can't choose who you care about, no matter how much you want to, no matter how much you tell yourself otherwise, no matter, even, if you sleep with them.

"Forget about him." Innis's voice is powerful yet calm. "Think about the good stuff. Think about last night." He leans in closer, puts his lips to my ear. "You're my girlfriend."

The words rip me apart inside. They are the words I thought I wanted, the words that MacKenzie and I schemed to get, but I don't want them anymore.

His lips meet mine, so soft and wanting, but it's wrong. I wish it weren't. I wish this were everything it should be. I wish this were the scene where the boy convinces the girl that everything's going to be okay, that all her hesitations about him are unfounded, that he's sorry and he can't wait to take her to homecoming. But it's not that scene, it's not that scene at all.

It's the scene where the girl realizes she chose the wrong guy.

I push him away, almost violently. "Stop."

Betrayal is written all over his face. I was so afraid of him using me, and in this weird way, I've used him.

"I'm sorry," I say. "I can't do this." I turn around before he can respond, walking quickly, a few paces ahead of him, not looking back. I don't say a word, just wait for his car to start, his engine to purr, before going inside.

I ignore my mother, her prodding questions.

I go straight to my room. And I cry.

For what, for who, I'm not even sure anymore. I just cry.

Chapter 21

THURSDAY IS A ROUGH DAY AT THE ELLISONS'. SADIE is cranky as hell, and Mary Ryan is full of questions I don't have the patience to answer.

When I can't take it anymore, I decide to cheat the half-hour TV limit. We huddle onto the couch, letting the colors and sounds wash over us. Sadie eventually stops crying.

After a few minutes of silence, my phone dings, and I pull it out, hoping it's Jason—or even MacKenzie.

are you just going to ignore me?

Innis.

Mary Ryan stares at my screen. "Is that your boyfriend?" she asks, hopefully.

"No." It comes out as a bit of a snap. I put the phone back in my pocket.

Sadie starts crying again, and I pull her into my lap, running my fingers over her curls, trying to calm her down. She throws her sippy cup across the room and it lands on the floor, spilling across the hardwood. The TV show ends, the commercials begin.

Mary Ryan loses interest. "Why is everyone sad?" she asks.

I flip off the television and give her a forced smile, corners up, teeth showing. "No one's sad," I say. "Your sister's just sleepy."

She just looks at me like I'm a crazy person. Fake smiles work better when they're not used on little kids. "You look sad."

"I do?" I try to sound cheerful.

"Why didn't you write your friend back?"

"Because I'm taking care of you. I'll talk to my friends later."

"That never stopped you before."

"Nothing gets past you, does it?" I ask.

"What does that mean?"

"Nothing." I hoist Sadie up onto my hip and squat down, picking up the cup. I tuck her into her high chair for a minute, because I don't know what else to do. She starts crying immediately. I grab a paper towel and tackle the spill, Mary Ryan at my heels.

"Did something happen with your boyfriend?" she asks. "Did you guys get in a fight?"

"No," I yell. "Can you stop asking me questions for one freaking second?"

I see the damage before I have a chance to fix it. Her face falls and her eyes water. Sadie cries louder. "I'm sorry," I say. "I didn't mean—"

"You're mean, Miss Liz," she yells, running out of the room. I hear her feet stomping as hard as they can up the stairs.

I toss out the soggy towels and grab Sadie. I've never been the kind of sitter who yells before, and I don't want to start now. Sadie wraps a pudgy arm around my neck, cries harder. I hand over her cup and pray for her to stop. By the time I'm up the stairs, she does.

Mary Ryan's door is closed, the puffy hot pink letters of her name and a photo of her dressed up as a princess shutting me out.

I knock twice and push the door open, poke my head in.

"Go away," she says.

"Sadie and I want to make sure you're okay." She's curled into a tight little ball, facing the wall. I sit down on her bed, plop Sadie on one knee.

"I'm sorry I snapped at you. I shouldn't have done that."

She turns slowly, her eyes wary. "I just wanted to know if it was your boyfriend," she says, her arms still crossed. "You're the coolest person I know."

I smile. "You're the coolest person *I* know."

"No, I'm not."

"Yes, you are," I say. "You and your sister. You're my favorite girls in the world."

She sits up, looks at me. "Really?" I can see the makings of a smile inching onto her face.

"You bet."

My phone buzzes again, and she stares, wide-eyed. "Are you going to answer it?"

"Naw," I say, ruffling her hair. "I'd rather talk to you."

"*Really?*"

"Really."

And I don't even have to lie to her—it's the truth.

I DON'T CHECK my phone again until Mrs. Ellison is back and I'm out the door. It's from MacKenzie, a photo of her making a goofy face. A decidedly MacKenzie version of a makeup text. I write *haha* back.

I feel relieved, but I think about what she said the last time I saw her—*I can't help you, then*—and I wonder if she'll ever be on my side again.

I amble into my house, and not even Lucy greets me. She stays on the steps, basking in the sunshine. Good for her, I think. Above it all in her puppy world.

I set down my bag in the kitchen and pour myself a glass of water.

Mom pops in from the next room, paper towels and Windex in her hands. "How was babysitting?"

"Fine."

She sets down the cleaning stuff, opens up the fridge, gets some water herself, leans against the counter, looks at me. "Just fine?"

I take long gulps of the water. When I look back, she's still waiting for an answer.

"Yeah." I finish the water. "Just *fine*."

"You know, Liz, I don't like your tone."

"Are you *trying* to start a fight?" I set my glass down on the counter. Okay, maybe I slam it.

She's annoyed with me, I can see it all over her face. Moms are good at picking up on bad moods, and they hate it when you don't share all your deep, dark secrets with them. But her face relaxes and she tries a new tactic instead. "So you finally asked Innis to the wedding. I'm glad he's coming."

I hate to break her heart, but not enough to lie to her. "I'm actually not sure if he is."

"What do you mean?" Mom asks, doing little to hide the disappointment in her voice. "He said so yesterday."

"I don't know," I say. "I'm just not sure."

"But *why*?"

I grab my glass, walk out of the kitchen, and head up the stairs. She follows behind me. I shouldn't have said anything.

"Liz," she says.

I turn around. "We had an argument, okay?"

She waves her hand. "Oh pshh, you kids find everything in the world to disagree about. You'll get over it. Trust me."

I shrug. "Whatever."

"What happened?" she asks.

"Nothing," I say.

"Come on, Liz. You can talk to me."

"It's none of your business," I snap, and I turn around, run up the stairs and into my room.

"*Don't* slam the—"

But I can't hear her finish as I slam the door behind me.

LYLA COMES OVER the next morning to pick us up for the final fitting before the wedding. She smiles big as she presents her new car, a navy blue Mercedes, an early wedding gift from Benny's parents. It shines, smells deeply of new leather. I ooh and ahh along with my mother, trying to hide how horrible I feel. Innis has called me twice and texted three more times since our conversation, and I haven't answered or responded. I'm afraid of his words, that if I let him speak he will try to change my mind.

Mrs. Barton isn't there on Fridays, and I'm glad for it. The last thing I need is that prim and proper Southern belle poking at us with her bony fingers. Better yet, Erica has to work, meaning one less person to judge me.

As I take my turn trying on the altered dress, I catch a hint of tattoo through Amy's sleeve. I bet she has to cover it, that Mrs. Barton would never approve, and I feel a surge of camaraderie for her—she has secrets, too. My dress fits perfectly, and then it's on to Lyla, who stands there, rigid yet delicate, like a dress form. Mom watches closely, making sure everything is done just so, taking pictures on her phone.

When Amy's done, we follow her and Lyla to the dressing

room, sit ourselves down in the plush chairs as Amy care-fully unfastens each beaded button, lifts the dress over Lyla's head.

Mom leans to me once Lyla is back in the fitting room. "Isn't this fun?" she asks, somewhat desperately.

"A real riot," I say.

"What is going on with you, Liz?"

"Nothing. I'm here, aren't I? Doing everything you guys want me to."

"Is this about Innis?"

"No," I lie, but she's my mom, and it's so hard not to tell her. "I don't know."

"You said you had a fight. Did you work it out?"

"No, we didn't."

Her face falls, and in this weird way, it's like I'm breaking up with her.

"And I don't think we're going to," I add.

Mom knows me well enough not to ask anything more.

LYLA IS QUIET on the way home, while Mom rambles on about this detail and the next. She parks in the driveway and follows us in. Lucy runs to Mom, begging for treats, and I head up to my room. I hear Lyla behind me on the stairs. "I have to get something from my closet," she calls.

But she doesn't go to her room. She follows me into mine, shuts the door behind her.

It's an ambush. I lie down on the bed, knees up, relaxed.

I refuse to be pulled into her drama right now.

"What was that about?" she asks.

"What?"

"Back at the shop. While I was changing?"

I sit up, wait for it.

"About you and Innis having a fight?"

I shrug. "Why do you care?"

"Because I'm your sister."

"Ha," and it comes out sharp and bitter as the gingersnaps our grandmother always tried to make us eat. "Yeah, I'm sure that's it."

"So it has nothing to do with Jason?" she asks.

"No." I don't meet her eyes. "Nothing at all."

But Lyla steps closer, totally not buying it. Sisters are hard ones to fool. She knew I was lying when I was a kid, when I stole an extra scoop of ice cream when no one was looking. She knows I'm lying now.

Lyla steels herself, lowers her voice. "Are you still hanging out with him?"

There is so much I want to ask her. If Skip was the first person she slept with, or if she made a mistake like I did. If she's ever found herself so caught up in someone who, by every account, by all opinions, is the opposite of right. I want her to stop being the bride, to stop being Skip's ex-girlfriend, to stop being one of the many people who got hurt by what-ever happened that night. I want her to just be my older sister, here for support and advice.

But I'm afraid. "Why are you even asking me this?"

Her voice rises a pitch higher. "Because you promised me!"

And with those words I know: she cannot be my sister above all else right now.

I don't tell her that it was inappropriate for her to demand that promise. That one night doesn't undo a lifetime of friendship. Instead, I look at her, tell her the only thing I think she can stomach. "I'm not. Chill."

There's more to the story, of course. There's the fact that I would be seeing him if he'd only let me. But some secrets are just too heavy to share, even with your sister.

"I'm glad," she says cautiously, even though she doesn't sound very glad—or very convinced.

She turns back, heads for the door, but then she stops, returns, sits back down on the bed. Her engagement ring catches the sunlight, and she looks particularly perfect right now, every hair in place, her makeup set. "I have to say this, Liz, and I don't want to, but I have to."

"What?" My heart beats faster at the harsh tone of her voice.

"If you are seeing him—" She takes a breath, then spits the words out fast. "I'm sorry, but if you are, I can't have you in the wedding. You can come and all, but you can't stand up there next to me. I can't take it."

The first thing I feel is fear. That she'll find out I have spent time with him, that she'll keep her word. But the anger comes quickly enough. How *could* she?

"But I'm your sister." I raise my voice.

"You said you weren't seeing him."

"I'm not," I say. "But geez, Lyla, is that necessary? You're supposed to love me no matter what."

"I do love you." Her eyes fill with tears. "So very much. But this is *my* day. I can't have you standing there beside me if you're doing this."

She doesn't wait for a response. Just folds her hands together, stands up, carries herself out the door, as pretty and perfect as if she were walking down the aisle.

I wait for her to come back and poke her head in—*Psych! Boy, you really are on edge. What's wrong with you?*—to laugh about how bad she just got me. To hug me and tell me she supports me no matter what. To tell me she's my sister, and that a boy will never come between us. Isn't that one of the cardinal rules of sisterhood?

But I hear her talking to Mom, then the open and shut of the front door, and the rev of the brand-new engine as she pulls away, and I know that she won't.

I LOCK MYSELF in my room for the rest of the afternoon. Listen to angry music. Try not to think about the two new missed calls I have from Innis.

I text Jason.

how are you?

I can see him typing—maybe he didn't mean what he said—but then he stops, and I'm left by myself, staring at my phone. Suddenly, a thought shocks me, shames me even more. Am I a Ladder Girl, as Veronica used to call them, one of those annoying serial daters who won't let go of one boy until she's got the next one in her grasp? I know deep inside that Innis and I are not right for each other, but am I only so sure because I think that Jason is on the sidelines, waiting for me?

That is not who I am. That is not me. And I have to prove it.

I bound down the stairs, grab Lucy's leash. She pants at me eagerly, and we head outside.

It's gray today and windy. Looks like it's going to rain. Lucy loves it because it means she can scamper about without overheating. I turn her away from the neighborhood, towards the path that leads to the pond. I don't have the energy to parade her around, in front of all the people, all the neighbors who expect me to be this person that, more and more, I know I'm not.

Lucy shuffles around and squats in front of the tree where Innis Taylor held my cheeks in his hands, tried to make it work with us only two days ago.

Lucy and I wind around the pond, and when we get to a bench, I sit down. She curls up next to my feet, plops down.

I pull out my phone, afraid to lose my resolve.

Innis answers on the first ring.

"Liz," he says. "Hey."

"Hi." My voice sounds weak, because I feel the fear all around me, the recoil deep inside. What I'm about to do is not only undoable, it's not what you're supposed to do. It isn't the natural order of things. It doesn't follow script.

"I knew you would call." He sounds kind and confident, like he's got our whole future mapped out, like I only need to hop on the bandwagon and enjoy.

"It's not that kind of a call—"

"I'm sorry I hurt Jason," he interrupts me. "But it has nothing to do with us. I meant what I said. We're good together."

I swallow, speak softly. "I know."

"So maybe tonight? I have to be home for dinner, but then I'm free. We could go to a movie or something. Oh, and my mom told me to ask you what the exact date of the wedding is—your dad said early August, right?—because my other suit needs to be fitted or something."

His confidence snaps me into action, gives me back my voice. Because here he is, knowing I've been upset with him, ignoring him, and he just assumes he's still my date to the wedding. It's like he's never not gotten something he wants. It's like he feels . . . *entitled* . . . to me. As if he's earned me, with fancy French dinners and family galas and awkward first-time sex and the ultimate honor, the grand title of "girl-friend."

"Innis, I only called to tell you that I can't really see you anymore."

The line is silent a minute. Lucy nuzzles my feet, but I shoo her away.

Finally, "What do you mean, you can't *see* me?"

I force myself to soften my voice. "I'm sorry, but it's over."

"But what about the other night?" he asks. "Correct me if

I'm wrong but you usually lose your virginity to someone you want to be with."

"It was a mistake," I say.

"A mistake? Did it mean nothing to you? Because it sure as hell meant something to me."

And that's the thing. For months, I have been telling myself that Innis is what I want, that all I have to do is find a way for him to like me. I've been so focused on the grand plan, the Perfect Senior Year, landing the most popular guy in school, even though I'd always been just a regular girl before, that I forgot to ask myself if it's what *I* really wanted.

And it is so clear now that it's not.

"You've slept with lots of girls." I force the shakiness out of my voice. "Don't act like this was any different."

"It was different." His voice is strained, pleading. "What have you been doing all summer? Pretending to like me just for fun?"

"No," I say, a note of pleading in my voice now, too. "I thought it would be different."

"You mean you didn't expect dear sweet Jason to come home."

"No, I—"

"What, like you're not thinking about him? That lying dick."

"Innis, stop."

"Tell me it's not about him, then. Tell me everything didn't change because I gave him what he deserved."

The line hangs, waiting.

"Tell me!" He's yelling now, and even Lucy seems to sense the tension, she paws at my legs, scratching.

"I don't know what to say to you."

"Screw you, Liz." He hangs up without another word.

Chapter 22

I DON'T GET THE GUTS TO GO OVER TO JASON'S UNTIL early evening. I pull a pack of peas out of the freezer and neglect to tell Mom where I'm going, practically asking to be punished at this point.

Mr. Sullivan answers the door. "Lizzie," he says. "I didn't know you were coming over."

"It's a bit of a surprise. I hope I'm not interrupting. I brought peas for Jason."

"So you heard." He shakes his head. "I knew working at a gas station was a bad idea. I told him he should wait until he finishes his last year of school and gets on his feet. But he was adamant, wanted to keep busy, help out."

"The gas station?"

"He didn't tell you where it happened?" Mr. Sullivan heads to the kitchen and pours me a glass of sweet tea. "Two guys attacked him as he was leaving work. I told him to quit. Too many shady people hanging around there." His eyes get a bit watery. "I can't risk something like that happening again."

He hands the glass of tea to me, and all I can think of is Jason's kindness towards me. He could have told his dad that it was my fault, but he didn't. "Thanks."

Mr. Sullivan brushes his hands over his eyes and composes his face. "I was actually about to head out. I hope you don't mind. Jason's in his room."

"No problem. Sorry to show up unannounced."

"You're welcome anytime," Mr. Sullivan says. He grabs a leather messenger bag and tosses it over his shoulder. "He'll be happy to see you."

He walks to Jason's door and cracks it open. "Lizzie's here."

On the way out, he gives me a kiss on the cheek.

I walk slowly down the hall and peek my head into the room.

"Hey," he says. His face is a mishmash of black and blue and yellow, his right eye particularly puffy, his lips still full and fat.

"I brought peas for your face." I don't wait for him to reply, because a real friend wouldn't. I sit down on the bed and slowly lower the package to his cheek. "You didn't answer my text. So I thought I'd just show up."

He winces before relaxing into the cold. "I don't want to

get in the way of you and Innis."

"I'm not going to see him anymore. I told him it's over."

His eyes look up to mine. "I didn't ask you to do that."

"I know." The pack of peas slips, and I readjust it, hold it steady. "You didn't have to. I promise I didn't know he was going to do that."

He pauses, his eyes on the ceiling. But then he says: "I know you didn't."

"Then why did you say that I belonged with him?"

His shoulders crunch up as he winces, but then he relaxes them again. "Maybe I thought it was true, that you'd changed. You have."

I shrug. "So have you. But we still grew up together. We still know each other better than anyone."

He twists a corner of the sheet. "It was a long time ago," he says finally.

"So what? It was a time that matters."

His voice is almost a whisper. "It's not where you start that matters. It's where you end up."

I stare at him a minute, and I want to ask him about what happened that night, for all of the truth, not just little snippets, but maybe for the first time, I trust him that there's a reason he hasn't told me everything. I need to be his friend right now, and that's all I'm going to do.

"I don't want to be your secret," he says. "It's not fair to me, or to you."

"I don't want you to be my secret, either. Maybe you don't have to be."

He looks at me, his face calm, and he looks like the Jason I've always known. I brush my fingers across his forehead, where the skin is smooth, where it's safe.

"Will you sit with me?" he asks. "For a while?"

And I nod, smile. "I'll stay for as long as you want."

I REMEMBER THIS one time when we were around nine. A girl in my class was making fun of me on the playground because my sweatshirt had a cat on it. Jason tried to get her to stop at recess, but she was ruthless. When we got home from school that day, he had a brilliant idea. He took two huge fabric shears from his dad's office, and we proceeded to cut up every piece of my clothing that had an animal on it, at least ten or twelve items by the time we were done. We thought it was hilarious. Mom was horrified. She called Mr. Sullivan, and we were both grounded for a week.

And it's funny, but that's the first thing I think about as I slip my key in the lock at my house that night, just past ten thirty. Me and Jason, at it again.

I'm no sooner inside than I hear Mom stomping down the hall. Her eyes, on fire, catch mine. "Where the *hell* have you been?"

"Nice to see you, too." I squeeze past her, head for the stairs.

"It's almost eleven. You don't answer your phone. You miss dinner. Don't even think about going up to your room. I'm not done with you."

"Fine." I turn around on the stairs. "What do you want?"

She puts her hands on her hips, takes a deep *humph* of a breath. "Where were you?"

In seconds Dad is behind her. "Why don't you tell your mother where you've been, Liz?"

"Out."

She stomps her foot. "I am tired of this *out*. You have no right to just come and go as you please in the car that your father and I generously let you drive. Now, try this again, you little brat. Where were you?"

"Please don't yell, Genevieve." Dad puts a hand on Mom's shoulder.

"I'm only yelling, *Greg*, because *your daughter* thought it fit to just skip out on dinner and is now refusing to give us a hint of where she's been. *Remember?*"

"Yes," he says. "But let's everyone just calm down."

"Calm down?" Mom snaps. "Why do you *always* make me the bad guy?"

"I'm not making you the bad guy, Genevieve. I'm just trying to—"

"Useless," she says. "You're completely useless."

That sets him off. He crosses his arms, as if only now realizing that all of this is my fault. "Well?" He stares at me. "Where were you?"

There's something weirdly comforting about seeing your parents band together, just missing the turnoff for the big fight, even when their joint enemy is you.

"I went to Jason's, okay? Is that what you want to hear?"

Mom shakes her head, and I swear this little piece of her

looks delighted. "I knew it. I just knew it."

Dad clears his throat. "You told your mom and sister you were not going to spend time with him anymore."

"Well, I guess I changed my mind." I sit down on the staircase. Let them chew on that.

"What happened to Innis?" Mom asks.

"It's over with Innis," I say.

The disappointment on her face is only there for a moment, turns quickly to anger. "Fine," she says. "Do what you want with him. But I forbid you to see Jason. I absolutely forbid it."

"Why?"

That throws her for a loop. "Because I said so."

"Way to pull a line out of the mom handbook."

"I don't have to explain myself to you."

I stand back up, steady myself on the rail. "You don't *have* to explain yourself. But don't you think that if you're going to forbid me from seeing my best friend who I grew up with, you should at least give me a reason?"

I stare at her, daring her to say it. *Because he lives in West Bonneville. Because he hurt the precious Taylors. Because, dear baby Jesus, what would the neighbors think?* But she won't tell me how she really feels; she's been bred well enough not to say such things out loud.

"He's dangerous," she says finally. And by the smug look on her face, I can see that she's at least succeeded in fooling herself.

"How do you know it wasn't an accident?" I ask.

"Because he pled guilty. Why in the world do you believe it was?"

"Everyone pleads guilty," I say. "It's called a plea bargain."

She shakes her head at me like I'm talking gibberish, but I see a hint of understanding on Dad's face.

"I'm right, aren't I? You said so the other night . . ."

Dad leans against the railing. "The justice system is very flawed, yes, and it is standard to take a plea—"

"*Greg!*" Mom shrieks. "Have you lost your mind?"

He shrugs. "I'm not saying he's not guilty, but she is kind of correct about that."

"I don't care how many people take plea bargains. He is a dangerous person who wants to spend time with our daughter!"

"You know who's dangerous?" I change the subject, afraid of pitting them against each other again. "Innis."

"What do you mean?" Dad stands up straighter, all thoughts of the flawed justice system gone. "If he laid a hand on you, I—"

"No." I glance to my mom, and even she looks thrown. "No. But he beat the crap out of Jason. He and Payton Daughtry went over to his house and jumped him. You should see him. He's all messed up."

"Well, don't you think he kind of had it coming?" Mom asks.

"Oh my God," I say. "Why does everyone act like he's got the right to just attack people?"

Mom doesn't lose steam. "I'm just saying that out of your

two little love interests, one is a convicted felon, and one isn't."

"He's not my love interest. He's my friend."

"And your *friend* is tall and dark and handsome and dangerous and the poor little underdog who Miss Elizabeth Grant is just waiting to save."

I stand to face her. "You don't know what you're talking about." Before she can say another word, I bolt up the stairs.

But I can't help it—a tiny part of me wonders if she's right.

My parents take away my car for a week.

Mad as I am, I'm almost impressed. Mom always says she's going to take away car privileges but never does. She's serious this time. She wants to stop me from seeing Jason, and she's going to any lengths she has to to do it.

On my first day of punishment, Innis texts me repeatedly, asks to have a conversation "face-to-face." The thought of seeing him now seems unbearable—I've already said what I needed to say—so I lie and tell him I'm fully grounded—it's partially true at least. He seems to understand that, if nothing else.

Needing a distraction, I go to MacKenzie's. She's been on me to come over, and she's pretty much my only social outlet without the car, not that I have a whole host of social outlets *with* the car. She leads me up into her room and barely gets the door closed before she starts pressing me for intel.

"Did you and Innis have sex?"

I sit down on her bed. "Payton told you?"

She clasps her hands together, so pleased that I can see she doesn't know the whole story. "Liz Grant, I swear I wasn't sure if you had it in you."

I raise my eyebrows. "Apparently I did."

"What? You're not feeling guilty, are you? It doesn't make you a slut, no matter what Veronica says."

I ignore her jab about Veronica. "Did Payton also tell you that Innis asked me to be his girlfriend?"

"No! Oh my God!"

"And that I broke up with him?"

She sucks in a breath. "Are you crazy?"

"Why are you surprised? You saw how upset I was."

She shakes her head, like she can't wrap her mind around what I'm telling her. "I know. But when Payton told me, I thought you guys must have made up and you just hadn't told me because you were mad at me."

"MacKenzie, I slept with him before we talked. The night he beat up Jason."

"What?" She sounds hurt. "And you didn't tell me? I was at your house and everything."

"I didn't want you to judge me."

She pouts. "I wouldn't judge you."

"You are judging me."

"Not for that. I'm *proud of you* for that."

I roll my eyes. "You shouldn't be. It was a mistake."

Her eyes brighten. "And what does Innis think?"

"What do you mean?"

"Because from the way he was talking to Payton, he sure

didn't make it sound like you guys were broken up."

I shrug. "He wants to talk in person."

"That's good. Very good."

"You aren't listening to me. That's not what I want."

"You want Jason, right? To take *him* to homecoming."

"I don't know."

"Well, you're going to have to think about it."

"I have thought about it! The whole world does not revolve around homecoming! It's a dance!"

"Maybe not," MacKenzie says. "But the world does revolve around your sister and your friends and what people think of you—I don't care if you think that's shallow—it's true. Innis is crazy for you. He'll take you back."

"I have to go," I say.

"Trust me," she says.

But I leave without saying any more. What she doesn't understand, and what she may never understand, is that I'm finally at the point where I have to start trusting myself.

Chapter 23

I CONTINUE TO SEE MACKENZIE THAT WEEK—I REGularly visit after I'm done babysitting—and she tries a range of tactics. Pros and cons lists. Persistent urging followed by a puppy-dog pout. At a certain point, she always lets it go, tells me about Payton, about how things are going with them. In these precious moments between us, Innis and Jason fade to the background, and I remember what it was like to be friends without the drama of them.

Innis continues to text, to say he's sorry, that he can't wait to talk. He even calls a few times, but I don't know what else I can say. So I ignore him.

Mom spends the week glaring at me through dinner, like I'm an enemy, while Dad tries to keep the peace, talking about the latest Fantasy NASCAR goings-on, asking me about babysitting.

But through the carless week, the carless and, more importantly, Jasonless week, it's the nighttime that keeps me going.

After Mom and Dad have gone to bed, after the TV turns from late-night hosts to infomercials, right around when the honeysuckle reaches the height of its dewy perfume, we talk. About the little things, the daily things, more than anything else. How often he ices his jaw. The games I play with Sadie and Mary Ryan. The oppressive heat, the way Dad skimps on the AC to be cheap, how his dad does the same.

Some nights, we talk about being kids. He doesn't remember things like our silly games half as well as I do, so I have to outline them for him in great detail: the way we played detectives, used flour to dust for fingerprints, ripped almost every scenario out of a TV show; how we proclaimed the tile in my kitchen lava, took turns climbing from chairs to countertops to make it through without getting burned.

The minutes tick by, and two o'clock in the morning turns to three, and everything from our words to the sound of our voices is safe. We talk as if we are just a girl and a boy. Childhood friends who just realized they liked each other right around the time that it matters. His voice over the phone is deep and thick and delicious, like hot fudge, melting through all the ice cream it touches, turning it milky and soft. I giggle, perhaps more than I should. As a laugh catches me in a higher octave, I think of how I sound like Lyla used to when she used to curl up in her room on her cell and waste our family minutes talking to Skip. But I don't dwell on that thought, because Lyla and Skip—that's not safe.

Occasionally, we hit the thorns, the subjects that divide us, that remind us even roses can make you bleed. I am sitting in the kitchen, eating a late-night orange and flipping through all the junk mail, and I see yet another college pamphlet. I mention it, and Jason's quiet for a moment, and then I wonder—can a convict even go to college? Is it even legal? And I make a note to look it up later, and the next day I do, and it turns out you can, but not the sort of school I'm probably going to go to, and who knows if his dad has the money or if he can get in, and did he even take classes in juvie or is he way behind? A million questions accost me, but I don't ask them the next time I talk to him, because I want it to be just the way it is between us. I don't want it to change.

LYLA AND SUZANNE come over on Saturday, the first day I get the car back. My sister gives me a terse hello and a forced smile before she heads to the kitchen, her big binder in tow. I can tell my mother has told her everything. Maybe because she's got a tightness on her face, like she's just gotten out of an awkward trip to the doctor. Maybe because I've known Mom and Lyla all my life, and that's how the two of them work.

I want to leave right then. I want to get in the car and go over to Jason's before Lyla has a chance to cast me another judgy look, but by the way Mom asks if I'm going to stay and help, I know I've got to be a good sport. If she sees the slightest hint of Jason written across my face, the car will be taken away just as soon as it was given back.

The four of us spend the morning tinkering with the final shot list for the photographer, the final song list for the band. Suzanne and I manage to get at least get some Pink Floyd and Stevie Wonder on there, instead of the long list of wedding-only disco hits that Mom pushes for. Lyla may be a lot of things, but she's not a brick house.

At one point, in a fleeting moment of Lyla-ness, while my mother and Suzanne are upstairs deciding on which pearls Lyla should wear for the wedding, my sister looks at me, gives me a quick, fast hug. When she pulls back, she smiles softly. "Thanks for helping with everything. It's all going to be okay."

I want to believe she's saying that, no matter what I do, things will be all right between us. I want to believe that she feels bad about what she said before, that nothing in the world would tempt her to throw me out of the wedding. Because we are sisters. We are stronger than this.

That's what I want to believe, but as she composes her face and goes back to her binder, I doubt it's actually true.

IT'S AFTER ONE before Lyla leaves, before the lunch dishes are cleared away, before Dad abandons the yard work and comes in to watch the Braves, before Mom runs out of excuses to keep me in the house. I force myself to wait a bit longer, just for show. I sit in my room, lie back in my bed, and dillydally just long enough to prove I'm not going to run off to Jason's the first chance I get.

Innis texts while I wait.

you ungrounded yet?

I think about what to write, start typing, *yes, but* . . . but then I delete it, keep it simple: *i don't want to see you*. And it's true.

At two, I head downstairs. Mom's dusting knickknacks in the formal living room and rearranging the antique frames that hold shots of me and Lyla.

"I'm going to the mall," I say.

"Which one?"

"The one in Greendale."

She looks at me askance. "By yourself?"

"Marisa is meeting me." I've gotten so good at lying, I almost fool myself, my voice is so steady and calm. "The girl who came over when Innis's dad picked me up."

"Okay." I can see that she doesn't trust me, not quite. But she seems to make a decision then, maybe based on my week of good behavior, maybe because she wants to believe that her baby girl wouldn't continue to associate with people like Jason, maybe because I've never been the impulsive type, the passionate type, and definitely not the rebellious type, not until now, when I have a reason to. "Have fun."

I paste on the most innocent smile I've got. "I will."

The drive to his house is agonizing. Every traffic light, every crossing pedestrian, every slow granny in front of me an object between us, one I can't wait to get past.

Eventually I do. I park next to his truck, take the stairs two at a time, knock three times, wait.

Milliseconds feel like seconds feel like minutes and hours and lifetimes, and then he opens the door, the drumming of my heart a percussive soundtrack. His face looks so much better already. The cut on his lip has healed, and many of his bruises have begun to fade. His left eye is still more closed than it should be, but he manages to give me a signature Jason look, a slightly lifted eyebrow, the makings of a crooked smile, a delectable blend of desire and understanding.

"Hey." He leans down, moving to kiss either my lips or my cheek. I don't figure it out soon enough, and his lips land on the edge of my mouth.

He laughs. "Well, that was awkward."

I feel achingly clumsy, but I manage a small smile.

"Come in. My dad's at work."

His words give me chills, a not-so-subtle reminder we have the apartment to ourselves. Seeing him now, after not seeing him for a week, after speaking with him for hours each night, there is want in every bone in my body, in the jillion hairs on my head, in the tips of my fingers and the pit of my stomach.

He makes a show of offering me sweet tea, but I decline.

We hover, strangely, in the living room, because what is happening is so new. And it's amazing how you can know someone forever and then find this secret place, like a password-protected clubhouse, where only the two of you are allowed in.

"You want to show me your old photos?" I ask. "I saw a box on your dresser."

"Sure." He's obviously grateful for the suggestion. Can this boy who has spent the last two years locked away with so many different kinds of people, struggling against more than I ever have and more than I likely ever will, be just as nervous as I am?

We walk into his bedroom, and he grabs the box, pulls out a photo with a slightly shaking hand—in it, I have ketchup all over my face.

"You sure were a cute kid." He sits on the bed, and I sit next to him. "I don't even remember this being taken. Do you?" He turns to me as he says it. I shake my head.

His hand is trembling harder now, and I pull the photo away, put it back in the box, rest my hand on his, and trace the outline of his thumb and forefinger.

"Have you thought about us before?" I ask.

"Yes." He says it without hesitation. "Many times."

"Me too."

We stare at each other, waiting to see who goes first. Sitting here next to Jason, I feel all of the things I never felt with Innis, as much as I tried to tell myself I did. With Innis, the butterflies were the challenge, the conquest, the wondering if someone so popular could possibly like me, the sheer appreciation of Innis's looks, of his power in our town. But with Jason, there is no wonder. I know he likes me, it's not that. With Jason, it's just that if he kisses me, I feel like I'm going to explode. And if he doesn't kiss me, I'm going to explode, too. His breath is hot between us, and I am hyperaware of my thumb tracing the lines of his rough hands. Of all of the different parts of him that I could touch.

"This is kind of weird, isn't it?" I ask.

He looks at me, his eyes so penetrating, so steady, I think mine might burn up if he doesn't stop.

"You think too much," he says. And that's when he leans in.

His kiss is relief. Soft and smooth, his mouth on mine; our hands laced together.

I kiss back, and slowly, our mouths open. We find each other, and it is so sweet and delicious that I forget to breathe until he pulls away, and I suck in air.

"Remember when you said it's not where you start, it's where you end up?" I ask.

He nods.

"What if I end up with you?"

We dive back in, our tongues exploring, our lips forming soft, perfect shapes.

There was fire and there was burning and there was a night that should never have been. A night that changed everything.

But now, there are fireworks.

After a minute, he pulls back, and his smile is wide and true.

"What if you do end up with me?" he asks. "Wouldn't that be wild?"

Chapter 24

On the way back to my house, I do go to the mall. Not the one in Greendale, the one I went to a lifetime ago, with a troupe of girls to help me choose a dress, but the small one in Bonneville, just a few minutes away. I head straight to the cheapest store and back to the clearance rack, just so I have something to show for my so-called trip that's taken now close to three hours.

I'm fingering a shiny black necklace with plastic beads, when a girl says, "Excuse me," as she reaches for a pair of faux-pearl earrings.

Her voice is unmistakable. Sharp, direct, and free of the overdone Southern drawl that Mom calls charming and I call fake. I turn to see Veronica standing beside me.

"Liz." She looks startled, then immediately regretful. Apparently a cheap pair of earrings wasn't worth the cost of running into me.

"Hey." Veronica's hair is thick and straight, hanging past her shoulders, longer than I remember it. She's wearing a touch of eye makeup and a sundress we picked out together. Behind her, Alice, her twelve-year-old sister, gives a quick wave before turning to a bin of neon-colored socks. "How've you been?"

"Fine." Her lips form a thin line, and she doesn't return the question.

The worst thing that happened between me and Veronica was what didn't happen. The big blowout was actually between her and MacKenzie, not her and me. We didn't scream about how we didn't want to be friends anymore. We didn't rip up the notes we'd written each other, or block each other online. We barely even traded harsh words.

The end of me and Veronica was a slow burn, so slow that I didn't know it had started until it was well on its way. And it started way before that stupid party. It started before MacKenzie, even.

Veronica and I were always a ticking time bomb, because she never understood why I'd want to be popular in the first place. It's not like she was too cool or artsy or whatever, it's just that she never saw the point. The first time we hung out outside of class, early freshman year, I told her about Jason, how much I hated him for ditching me for the "popular crowd." I really think I used those words. She just looked at me with curiosity and said, "Are those the people you really want to be around, anyway? They always have so much *drama*."

Looking at her now, I ache to tell her everything that's happened, to get her practical Veronica opinion on it all.

"We should hang out sometime," I say.

She waits a second before answering. "Maybe."

I grasp at anything to fill the space. "My sister's about to get married."

"I know," she snaps. "You told me when she got engaged."

And it stings, because when Lyla got engaged, Veronica and I were still friends. She looks back at her sister. "I should probably be going."

"I was serious. We really should hang out. Maybe this week?"

She almost seems to open up, let me in. But then she glares at me, her eyes almost black. "I think you're probably too busy."

And like that, she turns around, grabs her sister by the elbow, and walks out of the store as quickly as she can.

My phone rings at seven the next morning, way too early for a Sunday. I force myself out of sleep, picking it up groggily. The number on the screen makes me smile, though I still haven't programmed it, out of fear that Mom or Lyla or anyone else would see it.

"Hey," I say. How is it that my fingers are tingling from nothing more than a phone call?

His voice is happy and open. "Come outside."

"Now?"

"If you can."

I tiptoe down the hall to see if my parents are up. I can hear the shower running through their bedroom door. Dad gets up early, even on Sundays, but Mom must still be asleep. "Be there in a second."

I head down the stairs and look out the front window. There's Jason's truck, idling in front of his house, pumping gray clouds of exhaust into the morning light. The coast looks fairly clear, so I slip out the front door in my sleep shorts and a tank top, flip-flops on my feet. I'm so excited to see Jason that I don't even care that my hair is messy, that I've got no makeup on.

I open the door to the truck, and the smell hits me immediately, sugar, flour, and pure nostalgic warmth. The polka-dot box sits on the dash.

"You didn't."

"I was driving to work, and I saw the light on," he says. "I figured my boss wouldn't kill me if I was a few minutes late, given that I'm recovering and all."

He opens the lid, and the sweet smell is even stronger.

"Still your favorite?" he asks.

"Are you kidding?"

Your first time having a real Krispy Kreme doughnut is a rite of passage in North Carolina. It has to be the real deal, fresh from the shop when they have the HOT light flicked on.

Jason and I had ours together when we were five or six. I'd

stayed over the night before, and Mrs. Sullivan slipped into his room superearly, got us out of our bunk beds, and told us we were going to have the best doughnuts of our lives. She always said that fresh Krispy Kreme doughnuts were the only thing North Carolina had on New York, food-wise. When she handed them to us, they were still hot, and they melted in our mouths, just like she'd said they would.

"You first," he says, and he picks it up and places it in my mouth. I bite down, the layers and pockets of pastry turning to warm sugar-air in my mouth. I take it from him, and he grabs his own, and we chew and smile and laugh at the crumbs of glaze on the corners of our mouths, just like we did when we were kids.

"I can't stay," he says. "I just wanted you to have that."

"You are amazing," I say. "Do you know that?"

He flicks a crumb of sugar off of my lips. "You deserve amazing, Lizzie Grant."

WE MAKE PLANS to hang out after his shift is over, around five. I go back to bed and sleep in late. When I finally get up, I spend the afternoon helping my parents around the house. I figure any brownie points I earn now might help down the road. When the upstairs toilets are cleaned and the laundry in the machine, I walk up to my room, flop back on the bed, thinking about Jason, how there are only a few hours until I see him, touch him again.

As five o'clock gets closer, I find myself thinking of one of the last times we hung out before things changed. We were at the community center pool, doing our lap competitions, Jason beating me as usual. The water beaded against his skin, brown in the deep of summer. I was just starting to feel self-conscious about my body; we were only just beginning to look at each other differently.

He swam to the edge, easily five seconds ahead of me, leaned his head back on the concrete, lay there, smiling in his victory. When I swam to meet him, he didn't make fun of me like he usually did, didn't shout, "Oh, snap!," do his stupid Marlon Brando impression (*I coulda been a contenduh*), any of that. Instead, he grabbed my hand and pulled me close to him. I leaned my head on the concrete, too, and we floated like that, shoulders touching, staring up at an impeccable June sky. And I wondered, for those few moments, if Jason was about to be mine.

And here I am, so many years later, so much changed, a rough, windy road bringing us to the point where we are—*finally*—us again.

I'm about to leave when I see a missed call on my phone from Mrs. Ellison. I'm instantly scared, that I shouldn't have been so stupid to go out in the truck with Jason, kiss him where anyone can see. I call her back, and she doesn't answer.

There's a nagging, though, a dark blurry shape in the corner of my mind. What we have now is a reprieve—he still hasn't told me exactly what happened, and I haven't told him that I slept with Innis. I tell myself it will be okay, that whatever Jason has to tell me about that night can't possibly be that bad, that what happened with Innis won't have anything to do with the way he feels about me.

I inform Mom that I won't be here for dinner, that I'm going to dinner and a movie with Marisa. She looks at me a little questioningly, but I'm out the door before she has much of a chance to protest.

I get to his place at five thirty. He answers the door with a smile, with a look that says we're alone again, and I walk in, kiss him right on the mouth. "How was your first day back?"

He shrugs. "It was work. How was your Sunday?"

"Uneventful." I think about the missed phone call, whether I should tell him about my irrational fears.

He hovers at the door, with a smile on his face that says he has a plan. "You hungry?"

And I decide right then not to tell him anything, that these are our moments, and I shouldn't ruin them. "Definitely. Where do you want to go?"

"Do you still like Best Burgers?"

I raise my eyebrows. "Of course I do. But I haven't been there in years." It's a hole-in-the-wall spot on the more industrial side of town. Dad loves it, but Mom says there's no ambiance, which is kind of the point.

"Great," he says. "Let's go."

The place is just as good as I remember it. We order cheeseburgers and take a table by the window. After a few minutes, a girl with great big hoops stuck through her ears comes out with two greasy, sloppy burgers, a bucket of fries, and two Cokes.

I think about what MacKenzie used to say—*the bigger the*

hoop, the bigger the ho—and as the girl smiles at me, I realize that sometimes MacKenzie is an idiot.

Jason digs into his burger, while I pinch the straw and tear the bottom off, then lift it to my mouth and blow. The wrapper shoots at him, hitting him square in the nose.

"Oh, you've got it coming." He grabs his straw, rips off the wrapper, sucks up a bit of Coke, and spits it right at me. It hits my cheek, then splatters on the table, and an older lady turns to us and gives us her meanest behave-yourself look. We just laugh.

I eat my burger, and I get mustard all over my face, and he smiles, licks his thumb, wipes it away.

When we're done, Jason pays for the meal, a grand total of $10.50, and I'm riding our high, thinking that cheap burgers beat French roasted chicken any day, when I turn around and see, of all people, Erica and her husband, Dan.

"Erica!" Her name slips out like a curse word.

"Hey, Liz." Her voice is venomous as she flits her eyes to Jason. "You remember Dan."

"Hey, Dan." It's the part where I should say, "And you remember Jason? My old next-door neighbor?" But I just can't.

"We should probably get going. Enjoy your dinner." I head for the door, only looking back to make sure Jason's behind me.

In the car, I realize that my breathing is heavy, panicky. Erica's probably texting Lyla right now.

"Are you okay?" Jason asks.

I don't answer his question. "Are you mad at me for not introducing you?"

Jason pauses a second, thinking it over, but then he shakes his head. "It's going to be a little awkward. No way to avoid that."

"Do you remember Erica?" I ask.

He nods.

"She's Lyla's best friend."

"I know," he says.

"I don't want you and me to be a secret. But when push comes to shove, I guess I just don't know what to do."

Jason lifts his hand to my face, then tucks a stray hair behind my ear. "It's okay," he says. "We'll figure it out together."

Chapter 25

His apartment is empty when we get back.

"Where's your dad?"

"He goes out with friends sometimes." He grabs my hand, pulls me towards his room. I push Erica, Lyla, all the rules I'm breaking out of my mind, because right now I don't care about anything but this moment.

We fall into his bed, kiss until my lips are numb. We hold each other, our hands moving swiftly, exploring.

I feel this deep confidence inside myself, this comfort, this familiarity with Jason that I cannot deny. Soon, my hands are lifting his shirt over his head, and I'm pulling my soft cotton sundress over mine, and when he reaches inside my navy bra, my breaths quicken, my heart rocks my chest. I shake all over, and so many parts of me come to life at once, and it feels so good, so right.

It feels so different than it did with Innis.

His hands wander down to my underwear, reaching, but I stop them. I can't handle it again—the hurt and betrayal, the surprise. I don't want him to feel surprised, either.

I breathe in deeply. "There are things I want to know before we do this. And there are things you should know about me."

He leans his head on his elbow, relaxed, and for the first time, I think he trusts me enough to tell me. I think he's willing to answer the questions I've had for so long.

He takes a deep breath. "Do you believe in me? That I'm a good person?"

I nod. "I do. But I still have to know." I take his hand in mine. "I know it's hard to tell things. Don't you think I'm lying here, afraid of telling you what I have to say?"

"It can't be half as bad as what I have to say."

"It doesn't matter," I say. "The past is the past. But I still have to know."

He cups my face in one hand and gives me the softest and sweetest of kisses. "Okay. But you go first."

"Okay." I brace myself. I have to tell him before I lose my nerve. I take a quick breath, ignore the shame I know I shouldn't feel, but that I feel nonetheless. "This won't be my first time."

His eyes narrow, and I can tell, in an instant, that it's not what he thought I was going to say. He sits up. "It won't?"

"Don't look so shocked." I sit up, too.

"It would be mine," he says.

"Seriously?" I am so used to being the inexperienced one that I didn't even stop to think that Jason might not have had sex. Virgin, I think. The very word sounds girly. It's just not something you think about with guys.

His eyebrows knit together. "Who was it?"

I bite my lip.

He looks at me long and hard. "It was Innis. God, I didn't think you were like that."

I feel tears well in the back of my eyes. "*Like* that? I was about to be 'like that' with you."

Jason rehooks his belt. "That's different."

I scramble to pull my bra on, my sundress back over my head.

"It was only even once. And I regret it. There. Are you happy?"

He shakes his head. "When?"

"A couple of weeks ago."

Jason lets out a held breath. "Maybe you should go."

"Are you serious?"

"You told me you weren't seeing him anymore."

"And I haven't!"

"Yeah, after he was all over you. I'm sorry, but the thought, of him, of you . . ."

"You know, I could have lied. I could have been vague and evasive, just like you've been to me. But I didn't. I wasn't. I care about you. Enough to be honest."

"Apples and oranges." His face is stony.

"Yeah," I snap, getting up now and putting on my flip-flops. "I slept with someone I was dating and was honest about it, and you *attacked* someone and won't tell me the whole story. And I'm in the wrong?"

"I told you to trust me. I thought you did."

"And I have. And you still have the nerve to judge me over this?"

But he shrugs, looks at his feet. "What do you want me to say? If it were anyone but him . . ."

And I don't think I can quite believe it. He's actually going to sit there and slut-shame me. "Maybe if you could tell me why exactly you hate him, in a way that's not totally and completely cryptic, this would make a lot more sense."

He opens his mouth to speak, but then he shuts it again, looks down at his hands.

"You've got some nerve, you know," I say.

And I grab my bag, rush out the door, before he can see how badly he's hurt me.

When I get home, my mother is practically waiting for me at the door.

"Movie get out early?" she asks.

"It was sold out," I say, absolutely straight-faced.

"What was the name of it again?"

I rattle it off without missing a beat.

"You've been seeing this Marisa person a lot lately."

I shrug. "Do you want me to have only one friend?"

"No." She stares at me, and I stare back, challenging her

to just come out and say it, to ask me directly. I feel so upset about what happened that I almost crave the fight.

But she doesn't. Maybe it's because the wedding is in less than three weeks, and she's got so many other things on her mind, maybe she wants me to own up and tell her myself, or maybe, and I have to stop myself from laughing at this because it's so funny, she actually believes me.

Innis calls me three times that night. I answer on the third.

His speech is slurred. He sounds drunk. "I miss you."

"How many beers have you had?"

"Five or six. I don't know."

"Have some water. Go to bed."

"You're so good to me," he says.

"I'm not."

"Can I call you tomorrow? Can we talk?"

"No. You should stop calling. I told you it's over."

I hang up before he has a chance to protest.

I SLEEP THROUGH the alarm the next morning, and I'm hot and sweating and fifteen minutes late by the time I get to the Ellisons' house.

Mrs. Ellison opens the door, bag on her shoulder, obviously ready to go.

"Sorry," I say. "I overslept."

"Liz." She stops, one hand still halfway on the door, keys in the other.

"I can stay later if that helps," I offer. "I hope I haven't made you miss something."

She just looks at me, and her lips turn to the slightest frown.

Behind her, a girl walks up. "Everything okay?" She's got bright red hair, and I recognize her from my sophomore biology class, though I can't remember her name. Sadie is latched on her hip.

Mary Ryan comes up behind her. "Miss Liz!" she says, clapping her hands together. "You came to play. My mommy said you weren't coming to play anymore!"

I realize all in a rush that my missed-call paranoia wasn't paranoia at all. It was very real. "Seriously?"

"I'm sorry," she says, but she doesn't look sorry at all, standing there, her body rigid. "My husband said he was going to call you last night. He must have forgotten."

I stare at her, hardly able to believe it. I don't know how she found out, whether she really did see me with Jason in the truck, or if someone chatted up the ladies in the Home-owners' Association, or if it just spread through one of the myriad cogs of Bonneville's rumor mill, but it doesn't matter, this sucks.

"Jane, can you take the girls up to their rooms, please?"

Jane grabs Mary Ryan's hand, but Mary Ryan rips it away. "I want to play with Miss Liz," she says, her voice rising to a piercing scream.

"Mary Ryan Ellison." Mrs. Ellison raises her voice. "Obey Jane this minute. Go up to your room."

"No," she says, and she stares right at me, waiting for an answer. I look up at her mother, who I want to slap across the face, then back down at Mary Ryan. "I'm sorry, but I can't play with you anymore. But you're going to have a lot of fun with Jane."

"But why?" she asks.

Mrs. Ellison looks at me, like—*Are you going to tell her?*—when she is the only one who can possibly give the real answer. I pull myself together. "I've got to help out my mommy, okay? She needs my help. You'll have a great time with Jane."

Mary Ryan looks at me funny, then pouts. "Okay."

And just like that, she lets Jane drag her away.

Mrs. Ellison closes the door behind her, and it almost looks like she's ready to thank me for smoothing things over, for letting her completely off the hook with her own daughters. But I don't wait for her to say a word. I turn and stomp away down the street.

I can't bear the thought of going home right away, so I head to MacKenzie's instead. Mrs. Weston says she's still in her room, but she lets me up anyway. I knock twice and hear her groggy groan, then open the door. The shades are drawn tight and her sheets are in a mess at her ankles.

"Sorry," I say. "I can go."

"No, no." She pats the space next to her on the bed. "Come on. Sit down." She narrows her eyes at me. "I thought you had to babysit this morning."

I will not cry, I will not cry, I will not cry. I will be the indignant, angry working woman I deserve to be. I was fired without due cause.

MacKenzie just stares at me.

"She replaced me."

Her eyes open wide for a split second, and in that second, I see a genuine morsel of surprise. But as quickly as it comes, it's gone.

"What?" I ask.

She shrugs. "What do you want me to say? She probably heard about you and Jason from someone."

"Who," I ask. "You?"

"I don't even know Mrs. Ellison," she says, matter-of-factly. "God, you're paranoid."

"So just because she finds out I'm hanging out with him she has the right to fire me?"

"Relax. Of course not." MacKenzie props her pillow behind her and folds her hands in her lap like a condescending talk-show host. "But what did you think was going to happen? Everything would just go on like it was?"

"Can you try to look a little less gloating?" I snap. "Like you actually care what happens to me?"

She whips her face back like I've slapped her. "I care more than *anyone* what happens to you. That's why I say the things I do. Jason doesn't care what happens. His life is already screwed up. I don't want you to get dragged down, too. Sue me."

"You're just jealous because I actually found someone I

care about. I didn't pick someone from the lacrosse lineup so I'd have some arm candy for homecoming."

The words are out of my mouth before I can even process what they really mean. She gasps, and her eyes start to tear up. It's not true, and deep down, I know it. Payton's never been my cup of tea, but MacKenzie is over the moon about him. She has been since the moment she first saw him in the cafeteria.

I'm happy for her. I'm happy that she's found someone who likes her back. Someone who is easy to be with, who won't piss off her family and the whole freaking town. But that's not what I just said.

"I didn't mean it like that. Really, I didn't—"

"Go to hell, Liz," she says.

"Come on," I say.

"Just leave me alone."

And she punches down her pillow, turns to her side, and refuses to give me another look.

Chapter 26

Innis calls again that day, but I don't answer.

Jason doesn't.

I feed my mother more lies, tell her Mrs. Ellison cancelled last minute, not that she replaced me, that those girls probably think I grew tired of them.

I go to bed with all the wrong thoughts on my mind, wondering when exactly life went from this fantasy, this game I thought would surely sway in my favor, to a great unknown, a puzzle that hurts my brain every time I try to figure it out.

Because it wasn't losing my virginity on the couch in Innis's basement that turned me from child to adult, it wasn't the first time I used my fake or went to a party I knew I wasn't supposed to go to, or the first time I lied to my parents. It's right here, right now, learning without a doubt that life isn't fair, that if you're bold enough to go after what you want, you will get burned.

I haven't heard from Jason, I've ended it with Innis, Veronica will probably never forgive me, and MacKenzie and I will hardly ever see eye to eye again. I'm waiting for the inevitable explosion from my sister, because I know Erica will tell her. I know that the next time I see her, there will be so much anger waiting for me.

I have given up everything for him. And I may not even have him. Maybe that's the lesson of adulthood. In the end, you've only got you.

THE PHONE WAKES me on Tuesday morning, the first Tuesday of the entire summer that I don't have to babysit. It's ringing and persistent. Begging, almost.

Jason.

I answer in an early morning haze. "Hello?"

"Are you up?"

"I am now."

"Can you come outside?"

I look at the clock on my nightstand. "Geez, it's not even six."

"I have to go to work, but I don't want to go without talking to you. Please?"

I drag myself out of bed, and glance out the window. Sure enough, there's his truck.

"Fine," I say. "I'll be down in a minute."

I brush my teeth and splash water on my face, change into shorts and a tank top. My parents are both asleep—they don't get up for another half hour at least—so I slip out the front door unnoticed.

I open the door of his truck. "What, I don't even get some apology Krispy Kreme?"

"I'm sorry it's so early," he says. "I needed to talk."

"Drive somewhere, then. We shouldn't just sit here."

"All right." He presses the gas, the truck jolting forward. At the edge of my neighborhood, he makes a left, away from town, out towards the country.

He's silent, his hands gripping the steering wheel, and I don't ask where we're going, as long as we're going.

When the houses are gone, when open, grassy stretches surround us, when the low sun stares at us over a road that definitely needs paving, he pulls over.

"Are we far away enough?" he asks. "Can we talk?"

I nod.

Jason takes a deep, sharp breath. "I shouldn't have said those things to you," he says. "I know you didn't have to tell me, that you only wanted to be honest."

"I'm not a slut." Already I can feel myself getting upset. "Sex was a big deal to me. I wanted it not to be, but it was. And even if it wasn't, I still wouldn't be a slut. It's really sexist to think that way."

"I know," Jason says. He pauses. "Do you still care about him?"

"No," I say. "And now I wonder if I ever really did. It never felt like it does with you."

He turns to me. "It's all right," he says. "It was just hard to hear about you guys."

"It was hard to tell."

"I know," he says. "It was my fault. You didn't do anything wrong."

"Thank you," I say. "Now can you be honest with me, too?"

His hand cups my chin, and I feel like life is in some way complete, that the feather touch of his fingers is enough to make everything okay. "Don't leave me," he says.

"I won't."

He looks away, locks his eyes on the empty, open road.

"That year was so stupid," he says. "I know it, now. I thought I was so cool because Innis Taylor wanted to be friends. I had all this anger I'd never dealt with towards my mother, and I was starting to understand things about my dad that I hadn't before."

"Okay."

"We were in the same homeroom, and he'd tell me about his weekend fishing trips, and I'd complain that my dad never did stuff like that. Then one day they brought me, and his dad let us drink beers on the boat, and I thought, this is what I've been waiting for. I'm going to do whatever I want. I'm going to have fun and take risks, and screw anyone who tries to stop me.

"I don't think you knew how stupid we were then. Skip drove us around drunk. We took shots and raced on the Jet Skis. We smoked pot all the time. I got arrested for having drug paraphernalia on the swing set of the elementary school near their house. Skip and Innis got off scot-free, because I was holding all of it." He scoffs. "Things might have turned out a lot different if I hadn't been wearing those god-awful cargo pants."

"I didn't even know that happened," I say.

He shakes his head. "I guess I didn't talk to you much by that point, did I?"

"No, you didn't."

"It's amazing that the three of us are still alive." He stops, looks at me.

"It's okay. Keep going."

"Innis's parents were out of town, and Skip was going to throw a party, but your sister wasn't around for some reason, and so Skip didn't want to have any other girls over. He loved your sister so much, I'm not sure if you even realize how crazy he was about her."

My heart pounds faster. I'm scared of what he's going to say.

"We were drinking and eating pizza. We'd all had a bunch of beers, and Innis and I only drank when Skip was around, so it still hit us pretty hard. We wanted to make a fire in the pit in the backyard."

He stares out the front window, closes his eyes, opens them again. "Only thing is, we were terrible at it. We had a bunch of wood but no kindling. And it had rained the day before, so none of the wood would catch."

He pauses, but I nod, urge him on.

"It was my idea, one of my best"—he laughs, but it is dry and empty—"to get the lighter fluid and a bunch of newspapers. When we went to the lake, they brought one of those tiny Weber grills, and there was charcoal and lighter fluid in the garage. We put way too much of it on. Then I stood back and lit a match, and the whole thing caught so good, and we all cheered and then laughed because it must have singed some of my arm hair or something—we could smell burnt hair.

"The rest of the night went by so fast, and I don't even remember what we were talking about, we were just getting drunk. Every once in a while, the fire would die down, and we'd throw some more lighter fluid and newspaper on it. We thought the burst of flames was hilarious."

Jason rests his hands on his thighs, defeated.

I nod, and it seems to reassure him.

"If it had been any other night, at any other place, if things had worked out even a little differently, it would have been just another stupid fight. You do stupid shit when you're fifteen."

He glances to me, but I just stare at him. I am afraid of what he is about to say, but I am afraid of not knowing even more.

"I pushed him, ran at him, probably harder than I've charged at anyone before or since. And I punched him two or three times, and then he lost his balance, and he fell, and he"—Jason gasps, as if he's in an airtight chamber, only so much oxygen left—"he was on his side, right on the flames, and then," his eyes water, the first tears spilling over, "there was an explosion, this burst of flames, like I was watching a movie, and then I heard screams, and I don't know how long it took, but then Skip was back up and he was running at us, screaming, and his face. His face. One whole side of his face was on fire.

"Innis tackled him and held him down until the burning stopped, and then Skip was wailing, and it smelled, Christ, it smelled like a barbecue, and Innis looked at me and he said, 'What the hell were you doing? What have you *done?*' And that's when I saw the tipped-over can of lighter fluid. He must have fallen right on it. We'd left it right there like idiots. I freaked out. I ran. I ran all the way home, and I didn't stop until I was there. They arrested me the next morning."

"Why did you run?" I ask. "Why didn't you call 9-1-1?"

More tears come then, his face a wet web. "I don't know, I was scared. I knew Innis would. I don't know, I thought— I *didn't* think."

"So it was an accident?"

"God," he says. "I didn't mean to burn him. I meant to hurt him, yeah, give him a black eye. But I never thought, I mean, I never would have done anything if I'd have known how it would all turn out."

"But why didn't Innis say it was?" I ask. "Why blame you? You guys were friends."

Jason shakes his head. "I've thought about that, too, believe me. And I think—I think that—I don't have a sibling, so I don't know—but what if something awful happened to Lyla? Wouldn't you want someone to blame? It was so easy to put it on me. If it's just a freak thing and it's the lighter fluid's fault, then Innis is culpable, too, you know?"

It's so unfair, because Skip didn't deserve to be hurt so badly, but Jason didn't deserve all the blame either. "Why couldn't you just explain? Why even take the plea?"

Jason sighs. "Because I was guilty, in a way. I did attack him. And I ran. No one ever found the can of lighter fluid. My lawyer tried but the Taylors threatened a restraining order if she kept bugging them. Even if they'd found it, I still would have been guilty of something. Punching someone near a fire with lighter fluid hanging around isn't model-citizen behavior. We agreed to 'assault inflicting serious bodily injury'"—he mimes air quotes—"which means, basically, that I meant to do what I did. She was worried that if I didn't take it, they'd try me as an adult and it would be on my record forever. And what was a jury going to do? I had the prior, Innis was ready to testify, everyone in town loved the Taylors, and Skip's face—God, it was so *bad*.

"The funny thing is, well, the not funny thing is, the prosecutor agreed to eighteen months, with parole at twelve. But nothing says the judge has to follow it, he can do whatever he wants. He added six months to my sentence, for kicks. He was in the same frat at Duke as Mr. Taylor, not that that had *anything* to do with it." He pauses, starts to say something else, stops. "And that's pretty much it."

The tiniest bit of relief pulses through me. It's not what they said, at least. It's not what my mother or my sister or a hundred other people in Bonneville think. It is better, if only through technicalities. It is better than I imagined.

But there's one thing that still bothers me. "Why did you attack him in the first place?"

"It was stupid," he says. "It doesn't matter. Even though it was an accident, I should never have done what I did."

I take a risk, put my hand lightly on his arm as his tears come harder. He doesn't pull back. "It does matter." I know, deep down, that Jason is not a violent person. "It matters to me."

He says it softly, almost as if, after all this time, he's still ashamed. "He called my dad a fag."

"What?" I draw my hand back, stare out the window. It's so not what I expected. I'd figured it was over a girl, maybe that he'd even had a thing for my sister.

"He said that's why my mom left."

I look back at him, thinking of how to say what I need to, but he keeps going.

"That's why I didn't want to tell you. Because it wasn't just my secret. It was his, too."

"But Jason—"

"Back then, I had only barely figured it out myself, and my dad wasn't comfortable talking to me about it—he still isn't—and I couldn't stand to hear it from Skip . . ."

"Wait," I say. "Do you really think no one knows?"

He shrugs. "I did then. My dad is still so weird about it. He's had a boyfriend for like a year, and he still tells me, of all people, that he's going to a friend's house. Skip was the first person to ever say it out loud. And I guess I . . . I lost it."

I feel this deep, aching pain, because I remember walking into Mom's bedroom one afternoon and her sitting there, back to me, on the phone with Suzanne, saying in a low voice, "And Danny, with his *lifestyle*, it's no wonder his wife left." When she heard me behind her, she turned, startled, but then just plastered on a fake smile like she'd been talking about nothing more exciting than who was making what for the Fourth of July block party. Maybe she didn't think I'd catch the innuendo. Maybe she didn't care if I did. It was right at the end of middle school, and it definitely didn't surprise me, but I didn't like the way she said it—"lifestyle," like he'd decided to go vegan.

Jason blew me off right around that time, so I never told him, but I wonder if I had, maybe it wouldn't have been such a shock to hear it from Skip. Maybe he wouldn't have reacted the way he did. Maybe Skip would have two perfect sides to his face, maybe Jason never would have gotten locked up, maybe Lyla wouldn't be marrying Benny, maybe I would never have gone after Innis.

"I kind of knew," I say.

"About my dad?" he asks.

"People were talking. I should have told you."

He shakes his head. "This isn't your fault. It's mine. It's always been my fault."

His body begins to rock, and I scoot closer, the stick shift awkwardly poking at my thighs, but I don't care. I lift my hand to his shoulder, rub back and forth, let him know that I'm here. Finally, he looks up. "Can you forgive me?"

"Jason," I say. "It was years ago. It was an accident. It was a stupid moment that got bigger and more horrible than it ever should have. There is nothing for me to forgive."

When his eyes finally lift back to mine, I lean in and press my lips hard on his.

Because for the first time in years, the only thing keeping me from loving Jason Sullivan is gone.

Chapter 27

MOM GRILLS ME ABOUT WHY I'M NOT BABYSITTING, but I lie and say that the girls are sick. I'm not ready to tell her yet that I got fired. Even if she took pity and spared me the argument, there'd be that classic Mom *I told you so* all over her face.

Innis called three more times today. I thought about answering, about confronting him on his lies, but I stopped myself. I feel awful about what happened to Skip, but it doesn't change what Innis did, that he put Jason away based on a lie. And now that I know that, I can't bear to hear his voice.

Lyla and Benny come over for dinner that night.

All day I've been bracing myself for a blowout, but Lyla

spends the whole meal shooting questioning glances at me instead. After I ask her to pass the salt and receive an especially angry sigh, Benny wraps his arm around her, gives her shoulder a squeeze. "Everything okay?"

Her eyes catch his, and in the second they do, her scowl fades, and she is the Lyla we all adore again, and I love Benny for that, the way he has of calming her, grounding her. I wonder if she'd ever believe me if I said that Jason had the same effect on me.

After dinner, Dad pours himself and Benny glasses of Scotch, and they head to the living room. I'm weirdly jealous of the bromance they've got, even though I never have been before. There is no way my dad will ever smile at Jason the way he does with Benny, will ever pat him on the back and ask what he wants to drink.

Lyla and I share dish duty while my mother wipes down the table. With Benny out of the room, she's back to being caustic. "Could you go any slower?" Lyla snaps at me. "I'd like to go sit down and relax."

"So go. I'll finish these."

Lyla drops her dish in the sink, and it clatters and splashes. "What, so you can hold it against me later?"

"What are you talking about? I'm trying to help."

"Girls," Mom says. "Please."

"Well, you're doing *anything* but helping," Lyla says.

I whip the towel down and shake the water off my hands. "Fine. Dry your own dishes."

I stomp out of the kitchen, past the front room, where

Benny gives me a worried look, and Dad obliviously sips his drink, then up the stairs, where I slam the door—hard.

Lyla opens the door and reslams it in a matter of seconds. "Don't walk away from me."

"Geez, Lyla, you're not Mom."

"So you're just going to force me to confront you?" she asks.

I sit down on the bed. "I'm certainly not going to confront myself."

"You just go out to dinner with him now, like it's nothing? You know that I know, and you're not even going to bring it up, you're not even going to try and apologize to me?"

I shrug, staring at her, defeated. "What do you want me to say, Lyla? Apologizing would imply I'm doing something wrong. I'm not."

"How could you?" Her voice dips into desperation, sadness. "After what he did to Skip." She's full-on crying now.

"It's not like what they said. It was an accident. He told me that the whole thing was a mistake. There was a can of lighter fluid on the ground and an explosion, and he never meant to burn him."

"And you *believe* him?" She crosses her arms and looks at me like I'm the biggest idiot on the planet.

"Yes," I snap. "Of course I believe him. I *love* him."

The words are out before I realize I was thinking them, but once they are, it's so obvious that they're true.

She gasps, backs away from me, like I'm contagious and should be quarantined. Her hand reaches for the door, and she starts to walk out, but at the last second, she turns back. "Don't even think for one second I'm going to let you stand up there with me at my wedding."

"Good." I'm yelling now, too. "I wouldn't want to anyway."

Lyla slams the door behind her, and in a few seconds I hear her tell Benny that they're leaving and the rumble of her new car. Before anyone can stop me, I pull on shoes, grab my car keys, and run down the stairs as fast as I can.

"Where do you think you're going?" Dad asks, but I ignore him as I slip out the front door.

Mom follows me. "Damn it, Liz, you cannot just walk away like this."

"Leave me alone."

And they stand there, dumbfounded, as I pull back, speed out of the cul-de-sac. I know they're not stupid. They know where I'm going.

But I don't care what they think anymore.

Mr. Sullivan is "out with a friend" again, and this time, Jason and I don't bother with words. We run through the living room, back into his bedroom, past his desk littered with papers and the case full of books, thoughtful ones, good ones, ones that make me love him even more.

We fall back onto the bed with a thump. Things move faster, and in a matter of minutes, my dress is off, and I wrap my arms around him and pull him on top of me.

"Are you sure?" he whispers in my ear. And they're the

nicest words I've ever heard, because I know right then that he actually means them. I know that Jason would wait for me, would never pressure me, would move on my time frame alone.

And that's what makes me so sure I don't need to wait.

I lock his eyes, nod, kiss his scruffy cheek. "I'm sure."

"Just a sec." He pushes himself up and steps out of the room, and I am alone, the blades of the fan whirring above, making goose pimples on my bare skin. I hear him opening drawers quickly, one after the other, and then the sound stops, and he's back. I hear the crunch of foil, see him toss the wrapper away, and then he hovers over me, leans down, grasps my cheeks in his hands, kisses me again, soft this time.

"You're sure?"

I nod again. "Are you?"

He kisses me. "Surer than anything."

His hands do what they need to, but his eyes don't let mine go. He is clumsier than Innis was—it is his first time and all—but the clumsiness is nice. It's like he and I are on some new adventure together, just us. And a whole other world is ours to discover.

In a few moments, we are one.

It is wonderful and awkward and sweet. It is a feeling in my heart, an understanding I've never had with anyone before. It is a wholeness, within me and around me. It is me and Jason. And it has never been better.

When it's over, he cuddles next to me, traces the curve of my shoulder with one hand. "How did I get so lucky?"

Before I know it, my eyes are filling with tears.

"What?" he asks. "What's wrong?"

And it spills out of me, because I am more open to him than I ever have been before. I don't have it in me to hide anything from him anymore. I tell him about Lyla and about Mrs. Ellison, about MacKenzie's pros and cons list. I tell him I'll be okay, that none of this matters, that I want to be with him no matter what. It's their problem, I say, as if saying it means they can't hurt me, can't tear me down.

Jason listens, wipes my tears, kisses me softly, but he doesn't say a word. He doesn't have the answers, either.

I don't go home that night. I know I'd have more of a leg to stand on with my parents if I did, but it doesn't seem worth it. I can't taint this night with an argument.

We wake up early, around five, leaving just enough time for me to slip out before Mr. Sullivan gets back from his boyfriend's house. Jason walks me to the car, and I kiss him good-bye, promise to come over again tonight, my parents' rules be damned.

THEY'RE WAITING FOR me in the front room when I get there, keeled over on the couches, half asleep. Lucy runs to greet me, her barks waking them both. Mom is up and ready to go in an instant. "Where were you? What do you think you're doing? How dare you walk away from us like that. You're grounded, you hear me?"

I scratch the top of Lucy's head, then stare at Mom. Dad

is up now, too, and stands behind her, arms crossed, trying to look scarier than he is.

"Go ahead and ground me. Throw me out of the wedding. Do it all. It's not going to change anything."

Her jaw drops. Before she can think of the appropriate response, I amble up the stairs, slip into my room, close the door softly, and hop into bed.

Mom follows me in, and I tell her I'm going to sleep.

"This conversation is not over, Liz," she says.

"I know."

But she must not know what to do next, because she turns, walks away, and shuts the door behind her.

I close my eyes, pull the covers tight, and think about Jason until I fall asleep.

"LIZ." MOM IS above me, her voice too loud and angry for so early in the morning. She shakes my shoulder. "Liz."

"What time is it?" I pull the covers up higher.

"It's nine," she snaps. "And if you hadn't been out all night, it wouldn't feel so early."

"Go away," I say.

She sits down on my bed, shakes my shoulders. "Liz! Aren't you supposed to be babysitting?"

I flip the covers down, look at her. "Actually no. Mrs. Ellison replaced me on Monday."

"Oh, great," she says. "Well, I can't say I'm surprised."

"Thanks, Mom. Real supportive."

She shakes her head. "Why are you doing this?"

"What do you want me to say? Seriously? What explanation will make it better?"

"How could you do this to your own *sister*?"

I sit up in bed. "I'm not trying to do *anything* to Lyla. This isn't my fault."

Her anger melts into a frown, and she looks down at her hands, then back up at me. "How could you do this to me? After all I've done for you."

I pull the covers back up again. "How does this have anything to do with you?"

She shakes her head so fast and vicious I think she's going to give herself whiplash. Then she stares at me, and she looks almost like a kid. Like I did, when Jason left me. Her eyes glisten.

"Everyone knows," she says, her voice shaking. "The whole neighborhood is talking about it. At the Homeowners' Association meeting this week, they all got quiet as soon as I came in the room! If Suzanne hadn't been there, patting the chair next to her and inviting me to sit down, I would have walked away immediately. How could you put me through this?"

It's like I barely know her. "Why do you care about what some nosy gossips think more than your own daughter's happiness? They'll be talking about something else next week!"

"No, they won't." There's only desperation left in her voice. "They don't forget things like this!"

I lie back down, shaking my head. "This is insane, you

know. You're not in middle school."

She tries another tactic. "I forbid you, Liz. I absolutely forbid you from doing this."

"Whatever."

She stands up and begins to violently pick up every single bag I own, tipping each one over, napkins and pens and loose change and old Starbursts falling to the floor.

"What are you looking for?" I ask.

"Your phone and keys," she says.

I point to the bag hanging on the door.

She whips it away with anger, fishes around, finds what she wants. Her eyes lock on the phone's cracks but she doesn't say anything; maybe she doesn't have the energy for that battle right now. "Don't even think about going anywhere." She storms out the door.

"You can't stop me!" I yell, and I flip over, pull the covers up, shutting out everything else. What sucks the most is that I don't want to fight with Mom and Lyla and MacKenzie. I want to blush when they ask me about Jason, tell them all the nice things he says. I want Lyla to narrow her eyes at me and ask me what base I've gotten to, remind me to use protection with a conspiratorial smile. But it won't ever be that way—not with them.

Even so, I am sure, in the deepest part of myself, that Jason and I are right for each other.

And that's what keeps me together, as everything else comes undone.

~

MOM COMES IN once an hour the rest of the afternoon, and we riff on a version of this same fight, without getting anywhere.

It's almost two, and I'm getting ready for her to come up and yell again, while counting down the hours until I can see Jason, when I hear a knock on the front door and Mom's muffled voice. I sit up straight when I hear steps on the stairs. I can't imagine her sending MacKenzie up to talk to me, not when I'm supposed to be grounded for life. And I know it's not Lyla; these steps aren't hers. Maybe it's Mrs. Ellison, I hope, coming to apologize for the family's rash decision, coming to let me know that the girls can't possibly go the rest of the summer without me watching them. That I'm a good babysitter no matter who I date.

There's a hard and fast knock.

I open the door, and instantly my throat feels like it's closing in on itself.

Innis is holding an obscenely large cluster of flowers—roses in bright, cliché red. The smell of them fills the room immediately, choking out every last bit of breathable air. He is wearing a button-down shirt and his nicest pair of khakis, but his feet are absurdly bare, because my mother doesn't let anyone come upstairs with their shoes on, not even her daughter's scorned-but-hoped-for suitor. He's got an audacious smile on his face, and he looks absolutely absurd.

"What are you doing here?"

His mouth falls to a frown and his hand holding the

flowers droops, the long stems pointing at me like a bouquet of swords.

"You said we could talk in person," he says.

"I said to stop calling."

He pushes his way in and closes the door behind him, and I feel suddenly trapped by his near-perfect body, the over-the-top flowers, the conversation I don't want to have.

"As soon as your mom saw me, she said she hoped I could talk some sense into you." He smiles, as if it's as simple as that: *If you weigh out all your options, it's easy to see that I'm the better choice.* He sets the flowers gingerly on my bed.

"This isn't going to change anything. I meant what I said. You shouldn't have brought the flowers."

"A beautiful girl deserves beautiful flowers."

"Stop with your crap," I say.

"It's not crap. Okay, so I haven't been very understanding. I should have known you were going to want to see him. But it doesn't matter. When we're together, it feels right. Maybe I don't show it like I should, but I'm not perfect."

I shake my head, because no good can come of this speech. The grand gesture, the one girls dream of, that's pulled from script upon script of teenage dramas, quotes taped up on lockers, the one that doesn't *really* exist in real life, is here. And I don't want it. It makes me sick.

"We can't end everything," he says, "because you're con-fused."

That's what makes me lose it. "I'm not confused," I snap.

"I know exactly what I'm doing, and I know that I care about Jason in a way I never cared about you. I'm sorry to have to say it, but you just can't get it through your head. It's over."

He shakes his head. "But you slept with me. You lost your virginity to me."

I won't let him do this. I won't let him bully me.

"Well, I slept with him, too," I say. "How do you like that?"

His jaw drops, and his face goes red. "You slept with that asshole?"

"I did."

Innis stares at me. He's a boy who's been indulged all his life. Been spoken to sweetly by practically every girl he's run across. He still thinks that if he brings me flowers and calls enough times, he can turn this whole thing around.

His hands form fists, and he closes his mouth and continues to stare, then parts his lips, finally able to make words. They come out as a whisper, but they're sharp as a knife just the same. "You're a slut."

He turns around without saying another word, stomps out of the room, slams the door behind him. It's not a minute before I hear the rush of footsteps, and then Mom is at my door.

"Is everything okay?"

"No."

"Did something happen? I heard the door slam."

"You need to give up on this," I say. "This dream you have."

Her mouth opens, shuts.

"He isn't who you think he is."

She steps closer, and her eyebrows knit together. "What did he say to you?" she asks.

"Nothing, Mom. Just leave me alone."

"You can tell me," she says.

"Just leave me alone," I beg. "Please."

I REFUSE TO eat dinner. I don't want to be down there, sitting with the both of them, pretending things are okay.

The phone rings around eight. The house phone, not my cell, likely still sitting in my mother's purse. Mom must feel bad about what happened earlier, because she walks up the stairs and hands it to me. "It's MacKenzie," she says. I take it.

"Hey."

Mom stands there staring at me, but I shut my bedroom door so I won't have to see her.

"You *slept* with Jason Sullivan?"

I wait for the patter of steps down the stairs before answering.

"I don't have the strength for your judgment right now."

She gasps. "So it's true."

"And what if it is?"

She laughs, and she almost sounds like the MacKenzie I know and love. "Two guys in—what?—two weeks? That's bold."

"Are you going to call me a slut now, too?"

"Is that what Innis said?"

"What do you think?"

"Well, you're not, okay? And he's one to talk. He's slept with a ton of girls."

"It's different with girls."

MacKenzie sighs. "It shouldn't be. But I guess it is. Damn, I can't believe you're more experienced than me now. Two guys. You woman of the world!"

"What are you, proud of me?" I ask. I sit back on my bed, stretch my legs out. If MacKenzie can put it all behind her, if she can give up her senior year plans, then maybe there is hope for everyone else.

"So where did this happen?" she asks.

"Where did what happen?" I ask.

"Where did you . . . you know."

"Oh," I say. "In his room."

"Hey, hey. An upgrade from the basement!" She giggles. "Jason's not ugly, at least. Even if he is a social pariah."

"So you're not mad?"

A pause. "I was," she says finally. "But when I thought about it, I knew you wouldn't sleep with him unless you were crazy about him, and while I seriously doubt the wisdom of your choices, and know that my mere association with you is going to knock me down several notches in terms of popularity, and that all my double-date plans are pretty much screwed, I guess I can get over that if you feel *this* strongly."

My heart swells. "I love you, Kenzie."

"I love you, too," she says. "You going to see him tonight?"

"I think so."

"I'll try and talk some sense into Innis. Get him to hook up with a freshman, get his mind off you. Payton's having a party tonight. I'd ask you to come, but . . ."

"Yeah, I know," I say. "Social pariah. It's okay."

"But next time you have some wild sexual development, make sure I don't hear about it from my boyfriend, of all people."

"Okay," I say. "I promise."

Chapter 28

At eleven on the dot, I leave the house. Before I go, I creep past my parents' room to check that they're sleeping. Dad's crackling snoring and Mom's heavy breathing are both intact.

Mom doesn't know I keep a spare car key in my dresser, and I slip downstairs with it in my hand. As I imagined, my phone is tucked away in her purse. There are four missed calls. Two from MacKenzie, two from Jason.

Coming over, I text him, and as quietly as I can, I walk out the front door, towards the car. They might hear it start, hear me peal away, but it doesn't matter now. I've got to see him.

The radio station is playing late-night club music. The

bass thumps through me, and for the first time in a long time, I feel like dancing. I imagine me and Jason, in another town—New York City, maybe—shaking it in a club surrounded by strangers, jumping up and down and sweating and drinking and laughing, no one even knowing what he did or didn't do, what it is I gave up.

There is so much more than this little world. Jason and I can find it together.

He's sitting on the apartment steps as I pull up, and I park and hop out quick, eager to see him.

"I was getting worried about you," he says. "When I didn't hear from you at all."

I plant a kiss on his lips, hold him. Marvel at the fact that I *can* hold him, that he is finally mine. "My parents took away my phone and my car," I say. He nods behind me. "I hid the extra key after last time they did it."

"Smart girl." He kisses me quick, and I feel so light I could float. "You're almost as bad as me."

He tells me his dad's gone again, and we walk up to the apartment, go into his room, sit on the bed and talk. I don't tell him what happened with Innis—that chapter is finally over, and I don't want Jason to have to think about him at all—but I do tell him about MacKenzie, how she's forgiven me, how if she can, anyone can. I tell him about what I thought about on the drive over, about the two of us in a big city, where no one knows our past, where no one can judge us.

He just leans in and kisses me so soft.

THE SEX LASTS longer this time—I'm starting to see why people rave about this. There is a sense of living, this feeling that I've never had before. This possibility, tucked away deep within me, just waiting to be unlocked.

When we're done, I take his face in my hands, and I don't even hesitate, because there's nothing holding me back.

"I love you," I say.

He doesn't miss a beat. "I love you, too."

I PULL ON my underwear and one of his T-shirts and sneak into the kitchen, feeling scandalous, even though I know Mr. Sullivan isn't home. I pour myself a glass of water and drink it down in a few gulps, pour another.

I head back to Jason's room, and he's got his hands behind his head, the sheets up to his hips, and he's leaning back and smiling at me like he's the king of the world.

"Hey, beautiful," he says.

"Hey."

He motions me back to bed, but before I get in, I see the blink of my phone. Two new texts.

They're both from MacKenzie.

One just after midnight.

> you okay? innis left here an hour ago.

And another around twelve thirty.

> i'm sure it's no big deal, he just seemed really mad

I look at the clock on my phone. It's already one thirty.

"Who's that?" Jason asks.

"Kenzie."

He smiles. "I'm glad you guys made up."

"Me too."

I quickly type a text.

   i'm fine, hope you had a good night xoxo

And then Jason reaches for my arm, and I give it to him, and he gives a little jerk, and I fall back against him, and he snuggles me against him, and we are one again.

I WAKE TO the sound of an opening door.

At first I think it must be Mr. Sullivan, and I freak out, pulling the sheets up around me, but when I look at the clock, it is only after two, too early.

I curse Mr. Sullivan for growing up in a small town—why in the world don't they lock their doors?—and listen in terror to the *thunk, thunk, thunk* of heavy footsteps coming towards us, the sound of doors opening and shutting, the flicker of lights coming on.

"Jason." My heart is beating wildly now, the blood rushing through my head so loud it sounds like the whoosh of the ocean. "Jason," I say again, shaking his shoulder. My voice cracks, and I am so scared and so sad, because we have found each other, finally, and now some psycho killer is here, some armed robber, some *someone* who is totally not supposed to be here right now is going to take it all away. "Jason, someone is inside the house."

"What?" he asks, groggy and dazed, and in the streetlight streaming in through the window, I see the whites around his eyes. If I die now, if the killer gets us, then I will never see him clear and sharp again.

Jason's door whips open, slamming against the wall, and then there's a rush of steps, and it's only after it's too late, after the guy has launched himself on top of Jason, that I realize what's going on.

"Innis?" I say, my voice shaking. "Oh my God, what are you doing?"

For an instant, I feel relief. We are not going to die at the hands of a psycho killer. We are going to be okay.

"What the hell, man?" Jason yells. "Get the hell off of me." Jason tries to lift his arms but they're pinned on either side by Innis's thick, lacrosse-player legs and his sudden proximity, his altogether hugeness.

"Liz?" he asks. His voice is slurred, and the whole room now smells of whiskey, but he is with it enough to know what he's doing, to take whatever plan he has into action. He turns to me, his arms now holding Jason down, too. "A little sleepover, huh?"

"Get off." Jason squirms beneath him, but Innis slaps him, hard across the face.

"Shut up," he says.

"Why are you here?" I ask, my voice pleading. "What are you doing here?"

But Innis ignores me. He looks down at Jason. "You hurt my brother," he says, his words melding together in a boozy haze. "You tried to kill my brother."

"You know I didn't, man," Jason says. "You know I didn't."

"You're not even sorry," Innis says. "You never were. You *ran!*"

Jason shakes his head. "It was an accident," he says. "I shouldn't have run, but it was an accident."

Innis's voice is like a dying animal's, gasping for air. "I don't give a shit if it was an accident! You still did it! And now you did your time and just get to move on with everything. You even get to fuck my girlfriend." He nods to me. "And you think I'm just going to let you get away with it?"

Jason squirms again, but it's no use. My mind races in a hundred directions, trying to figure out Innis's next move.

Innis pushes one hand against Jason's throat, pressing him back, not enough to choke him, but just enough to make him stop moving. And then with the other hand, he reaches into his pocket and pulls out the knife I've seen before, *the best*, as he told Alex that day in Walmart. He flicks it open with one fell swoop. A glint of engraved initials.

"Get off the bed, Lizzie," Jason snaps, as soon as the knife is out. "Get off the bed *now.*"

I'm still half-naked, and I feel as if Jason and I are unprotected, vulnerable, raw. I have no idea what Innis is doing, but I can't just stand in the corner and watch this madness happen. I sit up, slowly, eyes never leaving the knife in Innis's hand. He waves it in the air in front of Jason's face.

"You don't want to do this." I try to force calmness into my voice. "Whatever you're thinking about, you don't want to do it."

"Lizzie," Jason is yelling now. "Get away from me."

But I can't help it, I scoot closer. "Please," I say. "Don't hurt him. You'll regret it."

Innis glances to me, his hand still at Jason's throat. He brings the knife just inches from Jason's cheek. "Will you still want him if his face is all messed up?" he asks. "Or will you be like your slut of a sister? On to the next one!"

He brings the knife closer.

"You'll get in trouble," I say. "You'll miss your whole senior year."

"Will I?" Innis presses his hand closer to Jason's throat, until his breath becomes labored. "I'm not gonna kill him, Liz. Jesus Christ, have a little faith in me! I'm just going to show him what it's like to have a scar that won't go away."

"They'll lock you up for that," I say. "It'll still ruin everything. And for what?"

He moves the knife even closer. "Who's to say it's not just some guy from juvie, scuffed him up a little? Who'll even know it was me?"

"I will," I say. "I'll tell everyone."

Innis laughs, loud and harsh and scary. "Who the hell is gonna believe *you* over me? Whoever believes you guys over me?"

The knife is so close now, I can hear it scratch against Jason's stubble, and I think he's actually going to do it, I swear he's about to do it.

"Get away, Lizzie," Jason yells.

But I can't. I reach for Innis, touch his shoulder, but he doesn't look away from the knife in his hand. I squeeze.

"Please," I say. "Please don't do this."

"Lizzie," Jason yells again.

And I'm yelling now, pleading, my voice swimming through hot tears. "Stop it," I scream. "Just stop it."

"Lizzie, get off the bed!" Jason yells.

Innis's eyes catch mine for just a second. "Yeah, Liz, get out of my way!"

His arm comes at me, and I feel a blow to my cheek, hard and heavy and solid, with a sharpness at the end, a searing snake of pain. I land on the floor.

Both of them keep yelling, and I can't make out the words, but I pull myself up, head already aching.

There's a creaking of bedsprings, movement, but I can only stare, straight ahead, at the mirror in front of me, at the girl in the reflection, so terrifying and strange that I almost doubt it's me, a line across my cheek, and I scream as the blood trickles, slow and thick and drippy, like red honey, and then I'm out.

Chapter 29

WHEN I OPEN MY EYES, THERE IS A WOMAN IN A PALE blue uniform hovering over me and asking my name.

My head aches like nothing I've ever felt before, a hot white pain that reaches from the back around to my temples. And my cheek—instantly, I remember the blood, my banshee of a reflection—I lift my hand to feel it, but the lady shoos it away. "Don't touch."

My heart begins to race, and she glances to a monitor. "Relax." Her drawl is thick but her voice is kind, calmer than the *whir-whir-whir* of the siren, the bump and shake of the ambulance. "You're going to be okay. You've lost some blood through the cut on your cheek, and you hit your head pretty bad when you fell, but you're going to be okay. Can you tell me your name?"

"Liz Grant."

"Very good. Your birthday?"

I start to say it, but then it hits me. Jason. I have no idea what happened to Jason.

"Miss?"

"My friend," I say, stammering, tears welling up in my eyes. My voice cracks. "Did you see my friend?"

"I'm sure your friend is fine," she says. "Now, can you tell me your birthday?"

My head spins. He has to be fine. Someone had to have called the ambulance. Someone had to get me here. But what if he's not?

"Miss, I need you to tell me your birthday."

I rattle it off to get her to stop. "But did you see my friend?"

She's not listening. She's shining a flashlight in my eyes and taking my pulse and doing things that seem so inconsequential now.

The tears pour down my face then and my breathing quickens.

"Miss," she says. "You have to please try and stay calm. Like I said, I'm sure your friend is fine. *Miss.*"

But it's no use, the tears won't stop.

IT'S STILL DARK out when we get to the hospital. I continue to gasp and cry, and the EMT lady isn't calm like before. I'm scaring her, I know I am, but I can't help it.

The door of the ambulance opens and the warm night air hits me, they roll me over the concrete and through the double doors, and it's like a movie, but it's a horrible movie, because I'm not watching it happen, I don't get to cut to the cute guy speeding down the highway, eager to see his girlfriend, make sure she's okay.

The nurses inside are even less helpful than the EMT. They ignore my questions about Jason, they hook me up to an IV and do the same tests the EMT did, and they say the words *possible concussion* and *stitches* a lot, between plying me with questions about what medications I take and whether I have any allergies.

I'm fine! I want to scream. *I am not important right now! Just tell me that* he's *fine!*

Eventually, a lady in a white coat comes in, sticks her hand out.

"I'm Dr. Puri," she says to me. Her voice is warm, her words are soft. I take her hand. "You've had quite a night. You're doing wonderfully."

The tears come faster, because I'm not wonderful. I'm the opposite. "I need to know that my friend is okay," I say.

"What is your friend's name?" she asks as she shines the light in my eyes again, as she looks at the chart.

"Jason," I say.

"And your friend was with you?" she asks. "During the attack?"

I nod weakly.

"Can you tell me what happened tonight?" she asks.

And I open my mouth to speak, to tell her, but where do I even start? When did this all start? Tonight, when MacKenzie texted to say Innis was mad? Or yesterday, when I taunted him? Or before that, when I slept with him? Or when Jason came back? Or when Jason left? Or when he hurt Skip? Or when Skip called Mr. Sullivan a fag? Or one of the hundreds of dominos that led me here tonight, bleeding and broken and wanting only one answer, but there are so many questions, infinite questions, before I can get what I want.

"Just go slowly," she says, seeing the confusion, the chaos, all over my face. "Start with how you got hurt."

"My . . . a boy . . . someone I used to be friends with, he came over . . . he, he had . . ." But it's no use, because the tears start again. "I need to know about my friend," I say. "I can't say anything until I know about him."

It's UNCLEAR HOW much time passes. Seconds or minutes or hours. Dr. Puri repeats some of the same questions as the nurses before cleaning my wound, numbing my cheek, and giving me stitches—twelve, she says, which I guess is kind of a lot—while I stare at the wall and try to calm down.

When she's done, I'm alone again. It's bright and fluorescent in the hospital, and I don't know if the sun is up yet, if a new day has come, if it is a day that won't have Jason in it. With every passing moment, I hate the sound of gurneys even more, the flip of doors and the cacophony of hospital sounds that I must sit through.

Is it possible that this is it, that life is, in the end, just a collection of effed-up circumstances, just a stupid silly game where you find love, find the greatest love, the greatest of all loves, find more than you'd ever thought possible with another person, find a way that it finally all makes sense, and then you lose it? And I know that nothing ever will heal that loss.

And I am about ready to scream at all of it, at the pointlessness of it, when I see Mom's face through the window.

She rushes in, her cheeks wet with steady tears.

"Mom," I say, and the tears are coming hard on mine, too. "Mom."

She reaches through the equipment somehow, gives me a hug, and over her shoulder, I see him, standing there behind Dad, standing there next to, of all people, my sister.

"Oh my God, Liz, I'm so, so sorry. I can't believe I encouraged you to be with him. I'm such a horrible mother."

Dad and Lyla are in now, too, hugging me. Jason hangs back, looking in through the window, giving us our space. My bones ache at how much I want to see him.

"It's okay, Mom."

"Are you in pain?" she asks. "The doctor says it's probably not a concussion, but oh God, your face . . ." The tears start up again. "Your face. I just, I can't believe it."

"She's going to be okay," Dad says. "You're going to be just fine, Liz."

My sister stares at the right side of my face, and I realize I can lift my hand. I do, and it meets a swath of gauze. "Don't, Liz." Her lip quivers. "Don't."

I look at her. "It's going to be bad, isn't it?"

"I don't know." Her voice betrays her, and she leans into Mom for support.

"Did the hospital call you?" I ask.

They look at each other then, all three of them, like they've got some kind of terrible secret. At the window, I see that Jason has stepped away.

Dad finally talks. "Jason drove to our house," he says. "Scared the hell out of us, standing there, sweating and out of breath on our front porch, in the middle of the night. He told us everything, that he'd made sure you were breathing, taken your pulse as he waited for the ambulance. He wanted to get in the ambulance with you, but they wouldn't let him. We rode over here together." Dad looks back to the empty window. Then he looks back to me. "We told them he was family, Liz. He wanted to see you so badly."

My sister looks down at her feet—Ashamed? Forgiving? More confused than ever? Mom, she just stares at me. In fact, she won't take her eyes off me.

"He got you to safety," Dad says. "We owe him for that."

I see Jason's face at the door again and I smile, open my eyes wide, begging him to come in. Dad takes Mom's arm, leads her reluctantly away, Lyla following.

Jason crosses the room in two quick steps, and then he's at my bed, right here in front of me. And he is okay.

"I was so worried about you," I say, my breath already coming in gasps. "I was all alone and no one would tell me about you, and I thought—I don't know—I thought he did something to you, and what if, what if—"

"I'm here." He leans in. "And I'm fine."

I reach my hand to his, and I hold it, and all I can think is that I don't want to live a single day on earth where I don't have the chance to hold his hand.

He leans down and kisses me, right there with my whole family watching through the window. "I love you so much," he says.

"I love you, too."

He pulls back, brushes the tears from underneath my eyes with his thumb.

When my breathing calms, when I feel my heart beat normally again—or almost normally—I ask him: "What happened?"

"I don't want to upset you," he says.

"Too late."

Jason cocks his head to the side. "What do you remember?"

I shake my head. "I remember seeing my face with blood on it. Then nothing."

He nods. "Innis let me go as soon as he saw what he'd done. He freaked out, and then he was just gone—out the door—and I wanted to go after him. I wanted to kill him, Lizzie."

"But you didn't go after him?" I ask, because if I know one thing, I know this. The violence has to stop. It will just snowball and snowball, getting bigger and bigger each time, until there's no turning back, until every last one of us is broken.

Jason hesitates. "God, I wanted to."

"But you didn't."

He shakes his head. "Turns out I love you more than I hate him."

Chapter 30

MY THERAPIST IS A COOL, TATTOOED LESBIAN WHOSE practice is located twenty minutes away.

Angie adjusts herself in her chair, fingers her thick glasses. "How's your cheek feel?"

Mom, who has never believed in therapy, didn't put up a fight when Dad insisted they get me in to see someone *right away*. Dad explained that I'd been through a supertraumatic experience, and that the lines of communication weren't exactly the most open between all of us right now.

"It's not that bad," I say. "I still have the strong painkillers, and it's more gross than anything, so many stitches and Neosporin and bandages and all that."

"Have you looked at it yet?"

Mom sees it every day—she's my official bandage changer—and my sister has taken a look, but not me. "I don't really see the need."

"Uh-huh." Angie ticks something off on her notepad.

"What?" I ask.

"Nothing," she says. "I like to check in about it."

"You think I'm in denial?"

"Do you think you're in denial?" she asks.

Here we go. I like Angie. It's been exactly a week since the night Innis attacked me and Jason, and this is our third session. So far, I've done a lot of crying, and she's done a lot of passing of tissues, and it's been good. She's not uptight or old or traditional, and I don't worry that she's going to judge me for anything, so I've told her all of it, the whole sordid tale. For the most part, she's been cool, but then every once in a while, she does her therapist talk—"Oh, do *you* think you're in denial?" kind of a thing—and it's almost like she's *trying* to be annoying.

"The way my mom sucks in her breath every time she sees it, it's obviously a big deal, and I'm going to look different," I say. "That doesn't mean I want to see it myself before I have to."

Angie nods. "Let's backtrack a bit. Last session, we talked a little bit about how you think this is, at least partially, your fault."

"That's because it is my fault."

"Why is that?"

"I already told you."

"Can you tell me again?"

My face gets hot, but I swallow, push the tears back down. "It wasn't just the stuff that had happened before that made him snap. It was all of it put together. If I hadn't led Innis on all summer, if I hadn't toyed with him like I did, then he would have been able to let it go. Both times he tried to hurt Jason, it was because of me."

Angie purses her lips and stares at me. When I don't say anything else, she adjusts again before speaking.

"Even if that is true, which I'm not sure that it is, it would still not be *your fault*. It would still be his fault. He is the one who broke into a home. He is the one who brought a weapon."

"That's what you have to say," I stammer.

Angie makes *such a huge deal* about the fact that I feel guilty about this. I've told her that it doesn't matter. I've already agreed to testify for the prosecution when Innis's hearing comes up in a couple of months, and I'm not going to be all—"it was my fault, really"—up on the stand. The lawyers have made it clear that with his past, Jason will not be a reliable witness; it's all on me. But that doesn't mean I don't still, in the back of my head, know that there are things I could have done differently, ways I could have circumnavigated all of this.

She stares at me. "What would you say to Innis if you saw him today?"

"I'm sorry," I say.

She makes another note.

ANGIE WAITS UNTIL the next session to tell me that she thinks it would do me good to confront Innis. She has told me that though my guilt might be natural, it is not warranted, and that calling Innis out on what he did could be a good way to move through it.

When I get home, I tell Mom. It's the Monday before Lyla's wedding, and she has enough on her mind, but it doesn't stop her from picking up the phone.

"What in the world are you suggesting?" she asks as soon as she gets ahold of Angie. "Why would you urge a *minor* to put herself in danger like this?"

Mom vigorously shakes her head as she listens to Angie's responses, and they have two more phone calls to talk about it. Mom and Dad even have a long conversation in their bedroom, the door closed and their voices soft, but eventually, she's okay with the idea.

Jason doesn't like it either. I meet him at his house, after his shift at the gas station, and he paces in fury.

"What kind of idiot would put you through that?" he asks.

"She thinks it will be therapeutic."

"It's insane," he says, his lips turning down, his breathing quickening like he's scared for my life.

"She said you could call her to talk about it," I say. And he does. And eventually he comes around, too.

MacKenzie also thinks it's a horrible waste of my energy and resources. "Why give that asshole even another ounce of your time?" she asks, when we talk the next morning on the phone. She's already explained to Payton that she will have absolutely nothing to do with him if he so much as thinks about Innis ever again. He's acquiesced, for now, but I wonder whether everything that happened will break them up, eventually.

Even the lawyers are wary. They remind me that I shouldn't talk about the case or my planned testimony. Innis was picked up the night he attacked us for a DWI, and apparently there's a pretty strong case against him. I think they're worried I'll go over there and come out of it deciding I won't help out after all.

Surprisingly, it's only Lyla who seems to be on board. Lyla, who has her own history with the family, who feels she failed me as a sister this summer, who is willing to listen to any idea if there's a chance it might help. Lyla, who is getting married this Saturday, who should be thinking about other things, not me, not Innis, not everything that happened that led us to this moment. My parents hemmed and hawed about postponing the wedding, but I absolutely refused, and Suzanne agreed, reminded my dad that he would not be getting his deposits back if he changed the date this late.

JASON COMES OVER on Wednesday morning, the day I'm set to go to Innis's. I'm sitting on the wicker love seat on the porch, legs in the sun and *Heart of Darkness* in my hands.

"Hey." He rushes up, leans down, and gives me a kiss.

"Hi." I put the book down, lace my hands through his.

I'm not worried about people seeing us anymore—everyone

knows everything by this point, anyway. I've seen Jason every day since that night, and I plan on seeing him every day indefinitely.

Mom comes out then, a smile on her face. "Y'all want tea?" she asks.

"Sure, Mom," I say.

"Yes, ma'am," Jason says.

She brings out two ice-cold glasses and we say our *thank-yous*, Jason being extra polite and Mom being polite right back. I'd be naive to think that a guy with a juvenile record is her first choice for her daughter's boyfriend, but even so, she seems to have accepted us, in her way. Maybe it's because Jason took care of me that night. Maybe it's because she sees him like I do now, the same Jason we all knew and loved for all those years. Or maybe, finally, she trusts me.

Mom goes back inside and I take a sip of sweet tea. "You sure you don't want to go to school with me next year?" I ask. Jason's set to go to another high school, given the location of his condo, but since the house next door is technically still Mr. Sullivan's, he actually could go to East Bonneville.

Jason tilts his head towards mine. "You know I *want* to be at school with you. But there's no way I can go back there. I need a fresh start."

"I know. But it doesn't hurt to ask, does it?" I'm terrified of facing a whole school year, every rumor, every superficial friendship—possibly even Innis, if they only give him probation—alone.

Jason squeezes my hand. "Speaking of 'doesn't hurt to

ask,' can I just double-check whether it's a good idea to go to Innis's? Maybe you could wait a little bit?"

I scoot closer, nuzzle into his shoulder. "Angie thinks it will help me. Move on and everything. Otherwise, I'll be stressing about it until the hearing. That's at least two months away, without any postponements."

Jason runs his fingers through my hair. "It's just so soon," he says.

"She thinks I'm ready. And it's all arranged."

Mom called Mrs. Taylor and set everything up for today. Like it's some twisted playdate in another universe.

"It could be unarranged."

"Stop worrying." I look up, catch his eyes. "Think of the pygmy goats." In the days right after that night, it seemed that all we could manage when we were together was to watch cute baby animals on the internet—even funny movies seemed like they required too much energy.

Jason laughs.

"See? It's hard to feel crappy when you think about tiny goats."

LYLA AND I arrive at Crawford Hall at noon, as planned. We pull around the back, park in front of the detached garage.

"Weird to be back?" I ask, as she turns off the car.

"Pretty strange," she says. And then her lips pull to a frown. "Are you okay to do this?" she asks.

I nod. "Are you?"

She nods back.

I flip down the mirror. My bandage is smaller now, no gauze, no extra tape. My stitches came out yesterday, but I still haven't looked at the cut properly, leaving all the after-care to Mom. I've been trying to make up for my appearance with extra eyeliner and lip gloss, but I still look so strange, like an alien spaceship has landed on my face. I flip the mirror back up. "Come on," I say. "Let's go."

I glance to the basement as we walk from the driveway across the back lawn: a hundred lifetimes ago I thought I was the luckiest girl in the world just to have an invite down to Innis's den of iniquity. We pass the pool, still and shimmering and perfectly maintained, where MacKenzie and Payton used to hook up. We walk up the stairs of the huge back porch, where I sat with the Taylor family and listened to Innis regale us with stories of Sally the cat. From the porch, I look back, across the lawn, and try to guess where the infamous fire pit used to be, where everything was put into motion. I can't tell, and maybe it's better that way.

I wonder what Lyla is remembering, if it's good or bad or all jumbled up.

Mrs. Taylor, herself, meets us at the door. No house-keeper or anything, just her. She's dressed in slim black pants and a muted silk blouse that hangs perfectly on her, minimal makeup, a simple black headband. Nothing fancy, as there is nothing to celebrate, but nothing too casual or irreverent, either. Good breeding, especially in moments like this.

"Liz." Her eyes flicker, for a millisecond, to my cheek. "Lyla. Come in, girls."

We don't exchange any pleasantries, even though it's been years since she's seen Lyla, even though there is so much to be said. *It's been too long! How've you been? Did the library fund-raiser make as much as you'd hoped? You all set for the wedding, Lyla? How's your cheek doing? Healing well from the night my son attacked you? I hear tea tree oil works wonders, saw it in a magazine.*

"Innis is in the living room," she says. Then she looks over to Lyla. "Did you . . ."

Lyla's eyes dart quickly to mine, but I nod at her; the plan stands.

"I'll just hang out right here," Lyla says, taking a seat on a tufted ottoman in the hallway.

"Would you like water or something else to drink?" Mrs. Taylor asks. Lyla shakes her head.

Mrs. Taylor takes a deep breath, clasps her hands together. "All right then, this way, Liz."

I follow her down a side hallway into a room that's not half as fancy as all the others. A room without gilded mirrors and antique seating. The kind of room where it looks like regular people live. Windows look out on the backyard and the room spills into an equally normal-looking, if not a little large, kitchen.

And in the corner is Innis. He's sitting on a beige sofa, looking down at his hands. He's in a navy polo and khakis, boat shoes on his feet, and there's a bulky black bracelet on his left ankle. His parents were able to post bail, of course, but due to the violent nature of the crime, the close proximity of the victim—that would be me—home monitoring was a must.

"Are you all right?" Mrs. Taylor asks me.

I nod. "I'm fine."

"All right, then," she says. "I'll just be in the other room."

Innis looks up at me then, follows me with his eyes as I take a seat on the couch across from him.

He doesn't speak until his mom is out of the room.

"Hey," he says.

"Hey."

He looks like Innis with the brightness turned down, like you just erased a layer of color from his face, left a shell of a person, someone with all the life and vitality sucked out. Someone who has no experience with the high road, who, when push comes to shove, takes and takes and takes some more. There's a darkness in every single one of us, tiny, crazy thoughts, they flit out as quickly as they come in. But when he gets them, he embraces them, acts on them. He's like an angry child working at a jigsaw puzzle, pressing the pieces as hard as he can, banging his fist upon them until there's a semblance of a fit, slicing them and tearing them until he gets the satisfying *thunk* he craves—until he has a picture before him that, to him, looks the way he wants it to.

His eyes lock on the bandage on my face, and he looks back down.

My therapist was right. There was nothing I could have done.

I am allowed to break up with someone. I am allowed to be with the person I want—no matter what happened in the past—without it coming to this.

I'm not sure how much time passes—if it is seconds or minutes—before I breathe deeply, ready to talk.

"I don't want to stay long," I say. "But I just want to say this. Jason and I didn't deserve any part of what you did. It was horrible and scary and something that never should have happened, no matter what you think or thought we did to you. And if you don't let go of your anger, you're going to have a miserable life."

Innis's hands squeeze together, release. He looks up, and his eyes are dripping. I've never seen him cry. "I never wanted to hurt *you*."

"But you did." I hear my voice rise, feel my heart beat faster. I take a deep breath, force myself to calm down, push back the tears threatening to break through their weak levee. "You knew I cared about him, and you wanted to hurt him. You knew that would hurt me, too."

He shakes his head, looks up at my bandage, back down as quickly as he can. "But your face. I never meant to—I only thought I'd scare him. I wasn't even going to really hurt him."

"Maybe you were and maybe you weren't. It doesn't matter," I snap. "You came at us, drunk and with a knife. What did you think was going to happen? Did you really think you could control a situation like that?"

"But if he hadn't—"

"Let it go." My voice is fully raised now, shutting him down. "Let the past go. Your brother has. We all have. It was an accident, you know it, and you put him away for a year and a half with your lies. And now you've hurt me in a way you can never, ever take back."

He looks up at me, pleading for forgiveness that's not fully mine to give. "I never wanted any of this," he says.

"None of us did."

And I stand up, walk out of the room as fast as I can.

Because I have used up all the words I have stored away for Innis Taylor. And from now on, my words will be saved for others.

IN THE HALLWAY, I see Skip and Lyla, sitting on the ottoman together, as close as they used to be when they sat on our porch, when they kissed in Skip's car in the minutes before curfew, when they hung out on the couch in our living room, watching reality TV. Skip is turned towards her, their knees almost touching, the good side of his face to me. If I took a picture now, showed it to a stranger, they'd see a couple, young and in love. It shocks me, but in this weird way it seems okay. Like in another universe, it's just your average everyday moment.

Lyla looks up. "You ready?" she asks.

I nod.

"'Bye, Skip," she says.

"'Bye, Lyla," he says.

BOTH OF US are quiet as we pull out of the circular driveway, away from Crawford Hall. I wait until we're back in our own driveway to grill her.

"What was that about?" I ask.

Lyla turns off the car and faces me. "You first. How did it go? How do you feel?"

"Good," I say, and surprisingly, it's true. It's like a weight has been lifted, a tiny one, but one just the same.

"Really?" she asks.

"Really."

Lyla nods.

"So what happened?" I ask.

She picks at the skin around her nails, the same thing I do when I'm nervous. "He came in and asked if he could sit down next to me. I said yes. He said that he was sorry about what Innis did to you, that he thought it was somehow his fault—I told him it wasn't, of course—but then he changed the subject, started talking about us."

"And?"

"He said that he was sorry he broke up with me like that. He said that it must have been really hard for me. He said that he was glad I was getting married."

"Seriously?" I ask.

"Yes," she says. "And he meant it. Skip has always been a good guy. He had his flaws like anyone, I guess, but he was always good to me."

"It looked like something was going on with you two, the way you were sitting there together."

I bat at Lyla's hands and she stops picking. She tugs at the ends of her hair instead.

"What happened?" I ask.

"He said that he never stopped loving me. And—" she stares straight ahead. "And I guess I said that I never really did, either."

"What about Benny?" I ask.

She whips her head back towards me. "I love Benny with all my heart."

"But you love Skip, too?"

She nods solemnly. "And Skip, too. In a different way. Like in a memory kind of way. An old postcard of a favorite place kind of way." She hesitates. "Now, do you promise not to tell anyone ever what I'm about to tell you?"

"Yes," I say. "Of course."

"I mean, no one ever. Not Mom. Not Dad. Not Jason. Not your diary."

"Lyla, I don't have a diary."

"Well, if you start one, don't tell it. Okay?"

I nod.

"Skip kissed me."

"Oh my God, Lyla! You're getting married on Saturday."

"I know," she says guiltily, her eyes starting to well. She brushes the tears away. "I know."

"Did you kiss him back?"

"No," she says quickly. "I don't know. Maybe for a second. It was a good-bye kiss, I guess. It was wrong."

"You're not going to do anything crazy, are you, like leave Benny at the altar or something?"

"No," she says. "I love him, and this doesn't change that. This doesn't change it at all."

I put my hand on her shoulder. "Don't kill yourself over it," I say. "No one's perfect."

"I know," she says.

"Are you going to tell Benny?" I ask.

Lyla pauses a moment, then shakes her head. "Skip and I are over. It was a crazy road getting there, but we are finally, totally over."

Chapter 31

SATURDAY IS GORGEOUS, WHICH IS GREAT, BECAUSE Lyla would accept nothing less on her wedding day.

Mom, Suzanne, Lyla, Erica, the three other bridesmaids, and I are in an upper room of this rustic barn where she and Benny will be saying *I do* in mere hours. We're wrapped in satiny robes, and a couple of girls from one of the salons downtown are doing the makeup for all of us.

Mom removed my bandage for makeup application, but I insisted on sitting in a corner as far from the mirrors as possible. I may have taken Angie's advice about confronting Innis, but I still haven't been able to look at my face.

Mom and Suzanne have been obsessively looking up antiscar gel on the internet, and they finally decided on one from Europe last week, which Mom is convinced will beat the doctor's prognosis. The dermatologist said that there would always be a scar, about three inches long, from just in front of my ear to the middle of my cheek. Hopefully, it will be no more than a white, slightly raised line, something thin, something that can be (almost) covered with makeup. I will always have a reminder of Innis and Jason and this summer, of the most awful night of my life. Right on the side of my face for me to run my finger along. Remember.

Now, the makeup girl, Sophia, is painting my cheek with some kind of allergen- and infection-free primer that Mom also found on the internet.

She works way longer than she does with the other girls, applying layer after layer of cakey concealer, so when she holds the mirror in front of me, I smile at the lack of bandage, at the way I look like just a normal girl, no scars here, even though when I turn my face, really look closely, my skin is weirdly opaque. Plastic-like. But hey, it won't show in the pictures—a small victory, at least.

STANDING ONLY ABOUT a foot from Lyla up at the altar, I tear up through the entire ceremony, careful to dab each one before it swims down my cheek, reveals the real me.

I'm not sure if it's just the wedding I'm crying for, or for what I know my sister gave up with Skip, or for the fact that I'm up here, standing with her, after all, and me and Lyla are me and Lyla again—and in a weird way, closer than we've ever been before—but it doesn't matter, the tears keep coming.

Lyla doesn't shed any, even though Benny is a blubbering mess. Instead she stares into his eyes, promises to love him forever, kisses him in front of everyone she knows, and smiles like she's the happiest girl in the whole wide world— and today, I really think she is.

The reception is a blur. Aunts and uncles and grandparents and everyone fluttering around, drinking too much, dancing badly. Everyone must have gotten the memo from my mother, because no one asks me a thing about what happened, or even makes any kind of eye contact with my face—and I'm thankful for that, because I don't want to think about any of it on what's supposed to be a happy day.

Kenzie's the perfect date. She and I drink too much champagne and do the twist so low, we fall right over. We dance through the slow songs, arms around each other like awkward middle schoolers, while the real couples look deeply and profoundly into each other's eyes, and we get three fat slices of cake between the two of us.

At one point, Lyla pulls me aside, and she tells me "thank you" for being her sister, and I say "thank you for being mine."

And maybe it's when I see so many people I love gathered around, singing "Shout" in unison, or maybe it's when my mom hugs me and it feels like it's me and her again, without any of the drama of this summer, or maybe it's when Kenzie pulls me into a corner and demands we swap some seriously intimate details of our sex lives, it's so clear to me all of a sudden: It's not about friends and enemies, my side or yours. We're all just trying to be the best version of us, the only way we know how. When Mom was judging Jason, she was being the only kind of mom she knew how to be. When Kenzie was yelling at me about throwing everything away, it was only because to her, that's what a good friend would do. I spent a summer trying to figure out what was right, weighing the words of everyone else, cursing myself for my inability to be what others expected of me, when there was only one answer, really.

Lizzie or Liz, it doesn't matter—I can only ever be me. I can only ever follow my own heart.

But it is so achingly wonderful to know that when I do, the people who really matter, they'll be right there beside me, even if I make a mistake or two in the process.

AFTER LYLA AND Benny have been carted off in their limo, after MacKenzie's mom picks her up and the band packs up their instruments and there's more than enough champagne in all of us, when my parents are about to head home, Jason arrives to pick me up.

I hug my parents good-bye and tell them it was the best wedding ever, which it was, and climb into the truck.

"You look gorgeous," he says.

"Like the new, bandage-free me?" I ask.

He leans in to kiss me. "I like it a lot."

Jason drives back to his house, and Mr. Sullivan meets us at the door.

"Liz," he says. "Aren't you just all dolled up? You look like a proper young woman. God, you kids grow up way too fast."

He hugs me tight, like he has every time he's seen me since that night. Now that he knows all, that Innis and Payton were the ones who beat Jason up, that Innis came into his home when he was gone, he's been very protective. His eyes look from Jason to me and back to Jason again like if he looks away too long, one of us might disappear.

"All right. I'll leave you alone. I'll be in my room if you need anything." He heads back, and it's just the two of us.

I walk straight to the bathroom, change out of my dress and into the more casual clothes I packed in a bag, carefully take the hundreds of bobby pins out of my hair, let down my hairspray-crusted curls.

"You want to watch a movie or something?" Jason asks when I walk out of the bathroom.

I hesitate, staring at him, not completely ready for what I'm about to do.

"What is it?" he asks.

I touch my face, softly. "I should probably take this makeup off," I say.

He nods. "You want me to put the bandage on?"

I shake my head. "Not really."

"Okay."

I go back into the bathroom, turn off the lights and close the door, work a pump of face wash into a lather, and gently rub it in circles onto my face. Forehead, nose, one cheek, two cheeks. I keep on rubbing, feeling the layers of makeup wash away, and then the unmistakable raised ridge, my battle scar. When I've rinsed it all off, carefully patted it dry, I look up at the mirror, see whether my eyes have adjusted to the dark, but they haven't. I shut them, cup my fingers over my eyes.

"All right," I call through the door. "Come in now."

The door opens with a creak, and I feel Jason standing behind me.

"Turn on the lights," I say.

He does.

"I'm afraid to look. Is it horrible?"

"You're beautiful," he says.

"You have to say that. It's like in the boyfriend handbook or something."

Jason laughs. "Might be." I feel him wrap his arms around me from behind. "But that doesn't change the fact that it's true."

I pull my hands back before I can stop myself, whip my eyes open.

At first all I see is me. My hair and my eyes and my nose, but then there it is, a white ridge, tinged with red, reaching across one side of my face, turning me into someone else altogether.

I catch Jason's eyes in the mirror. "It's all you see, isn't it?"

Jason shakes his head. "All I see is you. This is just a new part of you, that's all."

"I look awful," I say.

"No. You look powerful and wonderful and all of the things that make you you."

And I want to call bullshit, I want to point at my face and say, *But look, look at this right here!*, but I don't. Because I see his face, his reflection, instead, and there is no horror, there is no cringing, there is only love, so pure, so easy to recognize.

I turn around to face him.

"You promise I don't look like a monster?"

He laughs. "You are the furthest thing from a monster that has ever walked the earth."

I smile, lean up, and kiss him, his lips a perfect answer to mine.

We are not five years old and running through the sprinklers while Mr. Sullivan makes us peanut butter and jelly. We are not eight years old, playing detectives, building our own private worlds. We are not ten, sneaking away on our bikes and gorging ourselves on funnel cake. We are not fourteen, navigating the changes in us, the pubescent divisions, and the coldness of those eighth-grade lockers. We are not even sixteen, missing and loving and judging each other from two different worlds altogether.

We are here. And we are now. And after everything that happened, all the good and the bad, the beautiful and the awkward, the sexy and the innocent, the loving and the angry, the scarred and the unscarred, we are still Lizzie and Jason. We will always be Lizzie and Jason.

I pull back, my arms still linked around his neck.

"Thank you," I say.

"For what?" he asks.

"For everything."

acknowledgments

A huge thanks to the many people who made writing this book possible.

To my agent, Danielle Chiotti, I cannot express how grateful I am that you a) have never given up on my writing and b) don't mind dealing with the occasional writer freak-out. To my editors, Laurel Symonds and Kelsey Horton, as well as the entire Katherine Tegen team, thank you so much for believing in this book and offering your amazing and insightful notes to help make the story better.

The North Carolina juvenile system is a tad too complex for my layman understanding, so immense thanks to Grace Salzer, whose legal knowledge prevented me from relying on Google searches alone. Also, thanks to Sweta Patel and

Daniel Whitesides for doctors' perspectives on the hospital scenes.

I am so grateful to all of the friends and family who have enthusiastically supported and encouraged me over the years, especially my parents and my sister. Finally, to Thomas and my nutty dog, Farley: Thanks for always knowing how to make me laugh. It's a crucial step in the writing process.

JOIN THE

Epic Reads

COMMUNITY

THE ULTIMATE YA DESTINATION

◀ **DISCOVER** ▶
your next favorite read

◀ **MEET** ▶
new authors to love

◀ **WIN** ▶
free books

◀ **SHARE** ▶
infographics, playlists, quizzes, and more

◀ **WATCH** ▶
the latest videos

◀ **TUNE IN** ▶
to Tea Time with Team Epic Reads